No Clue at the Inn

Kate Kingsbury

WHEELER

CHIVERS

This Large Print edition is published by Wheeler Publishing, Waterville, Maine USA and by BBC Audiobooks Ltd, Bath, England.

Published in 2006 in the U.S. by arrangement with The Berkley Publishing Group, a division of Penguin Group (USA) Inc.

Published in 2006 in the U.K. by arrangement with the author.

U.S. Softcover 1-59722-196-1 (Cozy Mystery)
U.K. Hardcover 1-4056-3721-8 (Chivers Large Print)
U.K. Softcover 1-4056-3722-6 (Camden Large Print)

The text of this Large Print edition is unabridged.
Other aspects of the book may vary from the original edition.

Set in 16 pt. Plantin by Carleen Stearns.

Printed in the United States on permanent paper.

British Library Cataloguing-in-Publication Data available

Library of Congress Cataloging-in-Publication Data

Kingsbury, Kate.
    No clue at the inn / By Kate Kingsbury.
        p. cm. — (Wheeler Publishing large print cozy mystery)
    ISBN 1-59722-196-1 (lg. print : sc : alk. paper)
        1. Pennyfoot Hotel (England : Imaginary place) — Fiction.
    2. Women detectives — Fiction. 3. Female friendship — Fiction.
    4. England — Fiction. 5. Large type books. I. Title. II. Wheeler large print cozy mystery.
    PR9199.3.K44228N6 2006
        813′.6—dc22
                                                        2005033695

No Clue at the Inn

Acknowledgments

My grateful thanks to my wonderful, dedicated editor, Cindy Hwang, for all the times you've come through for me. Bless you.

To my husband, Bill, for your unfailing support and understanding. You are, indeed, the wind beneath my wings.

To Anne Wraight, in Canterbury, England, for all the incredible books, magazines, and brochures that give me so much pleasure and so much information. I'm truly grateful.

Chapter 1

"I simply cannot believe we are almost at the end of 1912. How time does fly." Cecily Sinclair Baxter waited for a response from her husband, who sat at the opposite end of the breakfast table, hidden behind the pages of the *London Times.*

When he didn't answer, she picked up the envelope from the embossed silver platter and carefully slit it open with a slim ivory letter opener. The letter was addressed to both Mr. and Mrs. Hugh Baxter, and normally she allowed her husband to take care of such matters. Since Baxter was engrossed in his newspaper, however, she felt justified in taking matters into her own hands.

In any case, she was most curious to know why the cousin of her previous husband had gone to the trouble of penning a letter to her, instead of ringing her on the telephone.

She was rather proud of the fact that her house, situated just yards from the common in the fashionable London suburb of Wimbledon, was one of the few to boast a telephone. It had taken weeks of arguing with the telephone company, but finally, thanks to Baxter having set up his business as a personal financial advisor right there in their home, the coveted line had been set up.

The problem now was that none of her personal friends had a telephone with which to ring her. Unless they used the public system, of course, which was terribly inconvenient and somewhat demeaning. Edward Sandringham, on the other hand, had access to a telephone right there at the Pennyfoot Hotel. With a sigh, she corrected herself. It wasn't a hotel now. Edward had turned it into some kind of motoring club. Thank heavens he'd at least kept the name of Pennyfoot.

She unfolded the single sheet of paper, noticing at once the crest embedded at the top of the page. A large scrolled *P* entwined with double *C*. Pennyfoot Country Club. She had to admit, the name did hold rather a ring to it.

Quickly she scanned the first few lines, then uttered an audible gasp that prompted Baxter to lower the pages of his precious newspaper.

"Is something wrong?"

"No . . . well, yes . . . that is . . ."

The pages rattled as Baxter laid them down on the table. "What *is* it, my dear? Not Michael, I hope? Andrew?"

Cecily stared at him, her heart beginning to thump with alarming irregularity. "No, no, not the boys. As far as I know, that is. I haven't heard from either one of them in absolutely ages. You'd think they'd have the time to jot down a few words to their mother now and then, wouldn't you?"

Baxter narrowed his light gray eyes. "The letter?"

"So sorry, darling. You know how distracted I get when it comes to my two sons." Cecily smiled fondly at her husband. They had been married less than two years, yet at times it seemed to her as if they had been married forever. On the other hand, every detail of their wedding, so soon after the death of Edward VII, was still as vivid in her mind as if it had all happened mere days ago.

Baxter's eyes crinkled at the edges. "Yes, I do know how easily you are distracted, my love. But I am on pins and needles with apprehension, wondering what startling news could possibly be contained in that letter that is causing it to tremble in your hands."

9

Cecily took a steadying breath. "Perhaps I should read it to you."

"I think that is an excellent idea."

"I'll get straight to the important part."

"Please do."

She wrinkled her nose at him, then began reading. " 'I have been called away on urgent business to South Africa, where I shall be spending several weeks. Unfortunately this means I shall be absent from the club during the Christmas Season. I recently lost my manager, and I haven't been able to find another one as yet. I hesitate to ask, but I was wondering if you both would consent to manage things at the Pennyfoot for me while I'm away.' " She looked up, studying her husband's face in an effort to gauge his thoughts.

He said nothing at first, but raised his hand and smoothed it over his dark hair.

She absently noted that the gray wings at his temples had widened somewhat since they'd left Badgers End. Her heart skipped with excitement. They had not returned to the Pennyfoot since then. It would be so marvelous to go back there for a short while, and relive all the wonderful memories.

Baxter, however, seemed less enthusiastic about the news. "Spend Christmas at the Pennyfoot . . . *working?*"

"Oh, come now. It will be fun!" Cecily leaned forward, determined now to take Edward up on his offer. "We can have a reunion! We'll invite Mrs. Chubb and Gertie down from Scotland. It's been so long since we saw our godchildren. Goodness, the twins must be so big now. How I'd love to see James and Lilly again!" She clasped her hands and gazed appealingly into her husband's handsome face.

"But, my dear, think of the work involved. You must remember how tiring it was when you owned the Pennyfoot. You worked such dreadfully long hours for weeks . . . no, months on end."

"So did you. I really don't think I could have kept up with it all if you hadn't been my manager." Cecily breathed a sigh. "Those were wonderful days."

"Viewed from a distance, I suppose they do seem that way. I'm not so sure, however, that I would enjoy being at the beck and call of everyone again. In any case, managing a country club, I imagine, must be quite different from managing a hotel. We don't have the experience —"

"Piffle!" Cecily straightened her back. "What can be so different? People stay there, they eat there, they are entertained

11

there, and they go home. We can hire Madeline to help with the Christmas decorations, and we can put on a pantomime. I'm quite sure Phoebe would love to help with that. I wonder if the members of her dance team are still living in Badgers End. It will be so good to see them all again. I've missed everyone so much. Oh, there's so much to think about! I shall start making notes this very minute."

It was Baxter's turn to utter a deep sigh. "I can see you've made up your mind about this. Does Edward say exactly when he would want us down there?"

Cecily quickly read through the rest of the letter. "No, he doesn't. I shall have to ring him. He says he wrote the letter rather than using the telephone because he wanted to give us time to think it over." She looked up again. "But it will be Christmas in another month. We simply have to decide right away."

Baxter picked up his teaspoon and stirred his tea, even though Cecily knew quite well he had stirred it earlier. She watched him anxiously, prepared to argue against every one of his objections.

"Why don't I give the chap a ring," Baxter said at last. "I'll find out exactly what the duties would entail. Then we can make a final decision."

Cecily let out her breath. "Then you'll ring him today? He's very likely anxious to hear our answer."

The spoon chinked against the bone china as he laid it in the saucer. "I promise I'll ring him just as soon as I get into my office." He glanced at the pendulum clock ticking away on the wall. "Which I must do right now if I'm to get any work done this morning." He rose, bringing Cecily to her feet as well. "I will see your later, then?"

Cecily swept around the table and raised her chin for his kiss. "Please don't bury yourself in there for too long. You know how involved you become in your work."

"I won't." He dropped a light kiss on her mouth. "I'll join you for the midday meal."

"You won't forget to ring Edward?"

"First thing, I swear."

"Thank you, darling." She watched him leave the room, then wandered to the window that overlooked the street. The light clip-clop of horses' hooves echoed across the pavement as a carriage swept by, while two ladies wearing warm coats and decorative hats hovered on the curb.

A thick, damp fog hung dismally in the air, almost obliterating the row of elegant houses opposite her. The clammy London

13

fog was so different from the light sea mists of Badgers End.

Sometimes days would pass by before she saw the sun, whereas the ocean mists of Southeast England would dissipate as soon as the sun had warmed the sky, no matter the time of year.

How she missed the sweeping bay with its bobbing fishing boats — the white cliffs rising high above, topped by the cool green grass of Putney Downs.

When she closed her eyes, she could see so clearly the sparkling white walls of the Pennyfoot Hotel, with its roof garden nestled among the chimney pots, dominating the majestic Esplanade with its grandeur.

She missed the rose garden and the bowling greens. She missed the picturesque church and the vicarage. But most of all she missed her good friends — Phoebe Carter-Holmes, with her fussy little ways and her determination to keep up appearances at all costs, and the gentle, sometimes mysterious, Madeline Pengrath, with her strange healing powers and her uncanny ability to see beyond the boundaries confining mere mortals.

The ache in her throat was almost unbearable, and she turned away from the window in an effort to dismiss the bittersweet memories from her mind. At that moment the door across the room was flung open, and Baxter charged in, his face reddened by his obvious agitation.

"I'm sorry, Cecily, but we will *not* be working at the Pennyfoot Country Club during the Christmas Season."

Dismay held her rigid. "Why ever not? I don't understand. It can't be that difficult? Surely Edward can —"

"Forgive me for interrupting, my dear, but I'm quite sure you will agree with me when I tell you what Sandringham has just told me."

A feeling of foreboding, such as she hadn't felt since her adventurous days at the Pennyfoot, chilled her. "What is it? What's happened?"

"Sandringham said in his letter that he'd recently lost his manager?"

"Yes, I believe he did. But what —"

"He didn't say *where* he'd lost him, I presume?"

"No, just that he hadn't had time to find anyone else, but —"

"Well, I can tell you where he lost him." Baxter sank down heavily on his chair then, apparently realizing that his wife was still standing, shot up again. "The poor blighter drowned in an abandoned well."

15

"A well?" Cecily frowned. "What well?"

"According to Sandringham, it was on vacant farmland that was waiting to be sold. The chap was wandering around there and *supposedly* fell in."

Something in Baxter's tone of voice worried Cecily. She sat down, thus allowing her husband to do likewise. "Supposedly? Are you suggesting it wasn't an accident?"

Baxter dismissed the question with a jerk of his hand. "I don't know what to think. Sandringham seemed to think there was something odd about it. He said the chap was known to have one too many down the pub at times, but he wasn't a habitual drunkard. No one seems to know why the poor blighter was wandering around a deserted farm in the first place. It wasn't as if he had money to buy the place. All very suspicious if you ask me."

"What do the constables have to say about it?"

"Well, you know what Northcott is like. Ignoring the whole thing, as usual. Sandringham wanted him to notify the inspector, but Northcott told him there wasn't any evidence of foul play. Didn't satisfy Sandringham, though. He said he knew the chap rather well. Said he didn't think he was the sort to poke around a

16

place like that on his own, much less careless enough to fall into a well."

Cecily felt a familiar tingling in her ears.
It had been a long time, but she remembered well the tantalizing urge to delve
into a mysterious situation and search for
answers. That urge had landed her in more
trouble than she cared to admit, but oh,
how she missed the excitement of the hunt
and the tremendous satisfaction of cor-
nering the prey.

"You can wipe that bemused expression
from your face," Baxter said, somewhat
shortly. "I know what you're thinking and
the answer is an irrevocable no. We are not
going down to Badgers End this Christmas. I won't have you risking your life, not
to mention mine, in yet another reckless
escapade. If this manager chap has met
with a violent end by someone else's hand,
then the constabulary can take care of it.
And that's the end of it."

Cecily stiffened her spine. "I think not,
my dear husband. This is as much my decision as yours, and at the very least, we
can discuss it."

Baxter's face, when he so desired, could
be as cold and as impervious as an iceberg.
"May I remind you that you are my wife,
and as such, I have a responsibility for your

health and well-being."

"You may remind me all you like," Cecily said evenly. "Nevertheless, you are very well aware of the contempt with which I hold such old-fashioned notions. I am your wife, undoubtedly, but I am also your partner. My wishes are every bit as important as yours. I was under the impression we had agreed upon that before our wedding."

"You agreed. I simply neglected to raise an objection."

"Because you knew very well I would not have married you had you done so."

Baxter's features relaxed just a little bit. "Perhaps so. Very well then, I shall rephrase my words. I'm far too fond of you to allow you to risk bodily harm in the pursuit of what could possibly turn out to be another of your pesky investigations. Not to mention the risk of inciting the wrath of Police Inspector Cranshaw, who no doubt is under the blissful, if sadly mistaken, assumption that you had left your nefarious past behind you forever."

Cecily allowed him to finish, then folded her hands and regarded him with her brows drawn together. "You know, Bax, sometimes I think I liked you better when you were a man of few words."

18

After a long moment, Baxter's mouth twitched into a reluctant smile. "Indubitably, my dear madam."

"The fact remains, Edward is in dire need of someone to take care of the Pennyfoot while he is away. You and I share a vast amount of experience and knowledge that is simply going to waste right now. It would be criminal to refuse Edward the benefit of our administration, particularly since he hasn't been able to find anyone to replace his manager. You know, as well as I do, how crucial the Christmas Season is to a hotel in a place like Badgers End. He cannot simply close the place down. It would likely ruin him."

"It's not a hotel. It's a country club."

"I'd prefer it, dearest, if you didn't split hairs."

"It's not exactly splitting hairs. One has to be a member to stay at a country club, and members are bound by certain rules and regulations. We shall have to learn those rules and see that our patrons abide by them."

"You always did enjoy flaunting your authority. You'll be in your element."

Conflicting expressions flitted across his face, and taking advantage of his indecision, Cecily pressed her argument home.

"Besides," she added quietly, "you know very well that James would never forgive us."

It was a low blow, and one that she knew would strike home. Baxter owed his life to her dead husband, and vice versa. As he lay dying, James had thought enough of his friend to extract a promise from Baxter to take care of his wife in the event of his death.

Baxter had fulfilled that promise with loyalty, integrity, and commitment. The sole uncertainty he had confessed to on the eve of their wedding was that James might not approve of their marriage.

Cecily had settled his doubts on that score. Now she waited, holding her breath, wondering if the memory of James could still influence the decisions of this resolute and beloved man who had taken her as his wife.

It seemed a long time before Baxter answered her. The clock ticked loudly in the otherwise silent room, while outside a dog barked at a passing horse and carriage, and the faint roar of a motor car — a sound Cecily would never get used to — signaled yet another roadhog about to invade the fashionable street.

Finally, Baxter heaved a sigh, rose from

his chair, and moved to her side. He reached for her hand and brought it to his lips, before murmuring, "You make it difficult for me to refuse. If I agree to this, however, I must ask two things."

She eyed him warily. "And they are?"

"First, since I am well aware it is futile to forbid you to poke your nose into what doesn't concern you, I must insist that you swear you will not take a step in any direction without informing me of your intentions."

She nodded in relief. "Done. And the second?"

"That at all times, while in public, you call me by my given name, Hugh. I refuse to answer to Baxter. It gives one the impression I'm still your underling."

She could feel her grin stretching her mouth. "I have a confession to make. Even while I was the owner of the Pennyfoot, and you were my manager, never once did I ever think of you as my underling. I was always in awe of you."

Baxter grunted, though she could tell he was pleased. "Then, my dear madam, you had a remarkable way of concealing your reverence." He bent down and brushed her lips with his. "You will call me Hugh?"

"I will call you anything you want, as

long as we are together again at the Penny-foot Hotel."

"The Pennyfoot Country Club."

Cecily sighed. "Very well, but it will always be a hotel to me, no matter what changes Edward may have wrought." She caught his hand and clung to it. "Oh, Bax, think of it. Badgers End at Christmastime. It always was my favorite time of the year there."

His eyes mirrored his concern. "You have missed it that much?"

She pressed his hand to her cheek. "I can be happy anywhere with you, you must know that. But Badgers End is special. It's where we fell in love. It will always be my favorite place to be with you."

He squeezed her hand, then let it go. "I can only hope, my love, that we are not making a mistake. It will be difficult enough after all this time to fall back into the managing duties of a large establishment. But if there is a potential crime complicating matters, I dread to think what might happen."

"You always did worry too much." Cecily rose from her chair. "There could be nothing more to this man's death than a simple accident."

"And if it's not an accident?"

She smiled blithely at him. "Then, dear Hugh, I imagine we will be reliving more than our managerial duties."

"And that," Baxter said heavily, "is exactly what worries me."

Chapter 2

Ten days later, Cecily alighted from the carriage, her heart too full to speak as she gazed at the impressive facade of the Pennyfoot Country Club. She noticed at once that the front entrance had been refurbished, the new double doors making the approach to the hotel even grander.

Memories crowded her mind — faces, voices, laughter, and tears. Visions of elegant women in magnificent gowns floating across the sprung floor of the vast ballroom while musicians filled the air with stirring melodies. Memories of nimble waiters weaving between tables bearing trays loaded with sumptuous meals.

In its heyday the Pennyfoot had been the most renowned hotel on the southeast coast. His Majesty Edward VII had stayed there many times, and the celebrated composer, Jerome Kern, had paid them a visit from America, though no one had known who he was until much later. Aristocrats, gamblers . . . even smugglers . . . had been signed into the guest books, and more than one philanderer had whiled away a weekend in pleasurable pursuit of a comely maiden.

Cecily's eyes misted as she remembered Gertie, her chief housemaid, enormous in her pregnancy, heaving huge pots of water to the stove, while frail little Doris stoked the coals. She could picture Mrs. Chubb, the belligerent housekeeper, arms folded across her bountiful bosom, face smudged with flour, glaring at Michel, the French chef, whose accent disappeared with a full glass of excellent brandy. How she missed them all.

"Hope you had a pleasant journey on the way down from the Smoke, m'm."

Cecily tucked her hands inside her muff, and smiled at the eager young man who had met them at the railway station and driven them with such gusto down her beloved Esplanade. "Yes, thank you. Raymond? Is that your name?"

The young man nodded, his dark eyes narrowed against the stiff, salty breeze from the sea. "Yes, m'm. I'm the stable manager, though now it's horses *and* motor cars. Raymond Stebbings at your service." He touched the brim of his cap. "Welcome

25

back to Badgers End, Mrs. Baxter."

"Thank you, Raymond. It's very good to be back." She took a deep, cleansing breath of the fresh sea air and let it out on a sigh. Although thick clouds had turned the water a dark gray, the ocean seemed fairly calm, with only a few white flecks of foam here and there.

How clearly she remembered the sharp smell of salty brine, the fierce chill of the wind on her cheeks, the mournful cries of hungry seagulls wheeling above the gentle waves. Caught up in nostalgia, she was speechless again.

Baxter moved to her side. "I, for one, Raymond, will feel a good deal more welcome once we are enclosed inside the warm walls of this establishment instead of freezing out here on the oceanfront."

Raymond gave him a smart salute. "Sorry, sir. If you'll come this way, I'll take you into the club. I'll see to your luggage later."

Baxter nodded and, grasping Cecily's arm, followed the lithe young man up the sparkling steps of the Pennyfoot to the enormous double doors, upon which hung a pair of lush holly wreaths, trimmed with red and gold velvet ribbon.

Raymond opened the door with a

sweeping gesture that narrowly missed knocking Cecily off her feet. Baxter clicked his tongue in annoyance, but Cecily hurried into the foyer, anxious to see what changes Edward had made to the interior.

To her immense satisfaction, everything looked much the same, though the blue Axminster had been replaced by plush gold and green carpeting that just about covered the entire floor of the foyer and swept grandly up the curving staircase.

The grandfather clock still stood in the corner, partially obscured by a small Christmas tree. The long desk where the guests were registered seemed to have been unaltered by Edward's renovations.

In front of the desk, a tall, boney-faced woman in a black afternoon dress and frilly white apron stood between two nervous-looking housemaids.

Raymond stood back, allowing Cecily and Baxter to approach, and the woman bustled forward, dipping a slight curtsey as she reached them.

"Mr. and Mrs. Baxter, in the absence of Mr. Sandringham, who regrets he was unable to wait for your arrival, it is my extreme pleasure to welcome you to the Pennyfoot Country Club. My name is Miss Bunkle, I'm the Pennyfoot's housekeeper, and I'd like to introduce two of our house-maids, Jeanette and Moira." She beckoned with a sharp movement of her hand. "Come forward, girls."

In their navy blue ankle-length dresses and white aprons, the two maids looked somewhat alike. Both of them seemed impossibly thin, with dark hair scraped back from their scrubbed faces. The difference was in the eyes. Jeanette's confident brown eyes sparkled with mischief, while those of the younger girl, Moira, were lighter gold in appearance and clouded with anxiety, as if she were terrified she would make a mistake.

Both maids darted forward and dropped a curtsey, muttering, "Good morning, madam. Good morning, sir."

"Should you require a personal maid," Miss Bunkle said, "Jeanette will be most happy to oblige."

"Thank you, Miss Bunkle, but I doubt that will be necessary." Cecily gave the maid an encouraging smile.

Jeanette seemed disappointed, while Miss Bunkle appeared a trifle put out. "Very well, madam," she said, her expression suggesting that Cecily had made a grave error in declining a personal maid.

Cecily turned her attention to the housekeeper, noting with some surprise the knitting needle securing the tight bun on top of her head. Apparently Miss Bunkle was not one to observe traditional costume. "My husband and I are happy to be back in the Pennyfoot Hot . . . Country Club. As soon as we are settled, we'll schedule a meeting and familiarize ourselves with our duties."

"Very well, madam." Miss Bunkle flicked her fingers at Jeanette. "Take Mr. and Mrs. Baxter to their suite and see that they have everything they need. Then I'll see you in the kitchen. Raymond, fetch the luggage and bring it up to the suite right away."

"Right ho!" Raymond winked at Moira, earning a frown from Miss Bunkle, before disappearing through the front doors.

Jeanette headed for the stairs and Cecily followed, conscious of Miss Bunkle's sharp gaze on their backs as she and Baxter ascended to the first floor.

"You'll be in Mr. Sandringham's suite," Jeanette explained as she led them down the hallway to what used to be Cecily's rooms. "He's done it up a bit since you was here, m'm. Got it all posh, he has."

She paused at the door, unlocked it, and pushed it open. Cecily walked in, her eyes widening at the sight that met her eyes.

The wall between the sitting room and the room next door had been removed, doubling the space. Sleek settees and armchairs replaced her Queen Anne furniture, and the chaise lounge had been relegated to the bedroom, where, much to her astonishment, a private and quite modern water closet had been installed.

"Oh, my." She clutched her throat at the sight of gleaming brass fixtures above a marble basin, and a footed tub that looked big enough to hold two people. "I've never seen anything quite like this."

Baxter, staring over her shoulder, seemed dumbfounded.

"Only one like it on this part of the coast, m'm," Jeanette informed her. "Even the hotels in Wellercombe don't have private WCs like this."

"I say," Baxter murmured, "Sandringham certainly does well for himself."

Cecily dropped her muff on the bed. "This is all very nice. Tell me, Jeanette. How do you like working at the Pennyfoot Country Club?"

Jeanette seemed surprised at the question. "I like it very well, m'm. Miss Bunkle can be a bit of an old biddy at times, and Frenchie gets on my nerves with his banging and shouting, but —"

30

Baxter frowned. "Frenchie?"

"Yes, sir. Frenchie. The chef."

Cecily hid a smile. "She's referring to Michel," she said solemnly.

"Oh, good Lord. I'd forgotten he was still here."

"Well, he's still in the kitchen," Jeanette said with a smirk, "but I wouldn't say he's all there, if you get my meaning. Especially when he's been at the brandy."

Cecily saw Baxter's frown of disapproval and hurriedly asked, "What about the manager, Mr. Wrotham? Was he a good man to work for?"

Jeanette shook her head, while Cecily did her best to ignore Baxter's raised eyebrows. "No one liked him, m'm. Least, no one as I know. Had a big opinion of himself, he did. Talked to everyone like dirt. Like he was better'n anybody else. You'd have thought he owned the place the way he carried on sometimes. I'm not surprised someone done him in."

Baxter cleared his throat. "Quite, quite. Well, run along now, girl. Mrs. Baxter will let you know if she needs you later on."

"Yes, sir." Jeanette bobbed an untidy curtsey and hurried out, pulling the door closed behind her.

Baxter muttered an oath under his

breath. "That girl is entirely too familiar. Miss Bunkle will have to keep her in her place."

Cecily sank onto the bed and began easing off her elbow-length gloves. "I rather think we'll have to get used to some relaxation of customs. Things are changing so rapidly it's difficult to keep up with them."

"The world may be changing," Baxter said firmly, "but manners are not. As long as we are in charge of this establishment, I insist that the staff treat everyone with the proper decorum. Just as they did when we were here. It hasn't been that long since we left, and I refuse to allow the integrity and the reputation of the Pennyfoot Hotel to be besmirched by impertinent staff. I don't care who they are."

Cecily smiled as she watched him pace back and forth, his hands behind his back. "Bax, darling, as you yourself pointed out so adamantly, this is no longer our Pennyfoot Hotel. It's Edward's country club. Whether we like it or not, things have changed."

"That doesn't mean we have to put up with insubordinate staff. I certainly don't intend to, and I sincerely hope that you will not stand for it, either. Not only is the Pennyfoot's reputation at stake, but ours, as well. If Edward has allowed the standards to deteriorate, then it will be in everyone's best interests to restore some sense of decorum." He paused in front of her, a scowl marring his handsome features. "And you promised you wouldn't call me Bax."

She rose. "Only when we are not alone. Calm down, dearest, it's not like you to become so agitated over something so trivial."

He started to say something, but she laid her fingers on his mouth. "Jeanette reminds me of Gertie when she first started at the Pennyfoot. You must remember how sullen and rebellious she was? Always cursing and complaining?"

To her relief a smile tugged at his lips. "I remember only too well. I despaired of her ever losing that stubborn insolence."

Cecily laughed. "To be perfectly honest with you, I don't think she ever did. She just tempered it somewhat when she was in our presence."

Baxter folded his arms around her. "No doubt you are right. I wonder if life is treating her well. And Mrs. Chubb, for that matter."

Cecily pulled back to look up at his face. "Well, we shall very soon find out. I've invited them all as guests for the Christmas Season and they have accepted. Gertie, Ross and the twins, and Mrs. Chubb. They should arrive tomorrow."

Baxter did his best to look unaffected by the news, but his eyes gleamed with pleasure. "Why didn't you tell me?"

"I did mention it, actually. You weren't listening to me. It will make our duties here much more pleasant when we're surrounded by old friends."

"I'm sure they will be ecstatic to find themselves guests in the very establishment where they once waited on people. A refreshing turnabout of events, I would say."

Cecily hugged him. "Then you are pleased?"

He dropped a kiss on her nose. "I am pleased, my love. This was a good idea."

"Then you'll be even more happy to know that Samuel, Doris, and Daisy will also be here, though Doris might be a little late in arriving since she has theater engagements."

"Well, you have been busy." He moved away from her, and wandered over to the windows that overlooked the grounds. "Our former staff — all back as guests. It will be good to see everyone again. Though

I hope they arrive soon. It looks as if it might snow."

She went to stand beside him. "Everything appears to be much the same out there."

"Yes, though the lawns seem a little ragged, and the topiaries need trimming."

Cecily sighed. "They never did do as well after poor John Thimble died. I wonder if the roof garden is still there. We need to take a tour of the place as soon as we've talked to Miss Bunkle."

Baxter sniffed. "Odd sort of woman, didn't you think? Looks like a good meal would do her good, and did you see that knitting needle stuck in her hair?"

"Yes, I did wonder about that myself." Cecily went back to the dressing table and sat down in front of the huge mirror. "I'll have to ask her what she thought of the late manager, Barry Wrotham."

"I was hoping you'd wait a day or two before concerning yourself about him."

"I'd intended to wait until tomorrow, at least." Cecily began pulling the long pins from her hat. "But that was before Jeanette uttered that interesting comment about someone having done him in, to use her quaint expression."

Baxter groaned. "I might have known

you'd pounce on that. I shouldn't have to warn you about taking the word of a housemaid as fact."

"Quite right, darling. But since Edward, also, was under the impression that Barry Wrotham's death was not an accident, it does raise some questions, don't you think?"

"Questions which, no doubt, you will do your utmost to have answered," Baxter said dryly.

Cecily smiled. "As you would say, indubitably."

He came and stood behind her, looking gravely at her reflection in the mirror. "You promised me you would not do anything impulsive without consulting me."

She gazed at his image, marveling yet again at the circumstances that had granted her a second fulfilling love in her life. "I promised, my love, and I shall do my best to keep that promise."

"I wonder why that doesn't ease my mind."

"Because you are such a worrier." She removed her hat, then rose and moved into his arms again. "I am not about to do anything that would jeopardize my life right now. I'm far too happy. Besides, I would imagine that in a day or two we shall learn quite a bit about the Pennyfoot's previous manager without any real effort on my part."

"I am happy to hear that."

"Besides, it's Christmas. Church bells, Christmas carolers, sleigh rides, candles on the Christmas trees . . . how can one be preoccupied with dark thoughts at such a joyous season of festivities?" She moved away from him. "I had messages sent to Phoebe and Madeline, informing them that we would be arriving today. I'm anxious to meet them again. I want to ask them if they'll assist me with the decorations and the pantomime."

"You plan to present a pantomime?" Baxter shook his head in wry amusement. "You have a little over two weeks left before Christmas Day."

"All the more reason to begin preparations right away. I have decided to try our hand at Aladdin. I heard that Doris performed in the pantomime last year, so she can play Aladdin and she will be a tremendous help. If she gets here on time, that is."

"I trust you're not asking Phoebe to use that infernal dance troupe in your pantomime."

"It wouldn't be a Pennyfoot presentation without them."

"Of course. The tradition must go on.

Even if it spells disaster."

She laughed. "I have to admit, poor Phoebe had her share of disasters. Fortune tended to work against her at every turn. I can only hope —" She broke off as a sharp tap sounded on the door.

"It's about time," Baxter muttered as he strode through the door into the sitting room. "I was wondering what that dratted lad had done with our luggage."

There was a pause while Baxter opened the door then, from the sitting room, Cecily heard Jeanette's clear voice announce, "I've brought some tea and scones, Mr. Baxter. Miss Bunkle says Mrs. Baxter must be dying for a cuppa."

Cecily hurried into the room as Jeanette carried the heavy tray over to a low table in front of a settee. "How thoughtful of Miss Bunkle," she murmured, seating herself on the green sateen couch. "Thank you, Jeanette."

"Yes, m'm." The young girl turned to Baxter. "Raymond said to tell you that your luggage will be up in a short while. We've just had eight toffs arrive and he had to take care of them.. He said to say he's sorry for the delay."

Baxter nodded, his expression clearly stating his displeasure.

Jeanette reached for the teapot, but Cecily raised her hand. "Thank you, but I can manage. I'm sure you have quite enough to do with guests arriving."

"Yes, m'm, that we do. All eight of them arrived at once, they did. Toffs from London with their wives. Raymond says the men are belchers from Lincoln's Inn, whatever that means."

"Not belchers," Baxter said shortly. "Benchers. They are barristers, the governing body of the Inns of Court."

Jeanette appeared unimpressed. "Oh, well, anyway, the ladies are all dressed up really fancy —"

"Since everyone is far too busy to attend to our luggage," Baxter said, sounding pompous now, "perhaps your presence downstairs might be helpful."

Jeanette gave him a cheerful grin. "Yes, sir. I'm on my way." She scurried over to the door, then apparently remembering she'd omitted a curtsey, turned and dipped her knees. "Oh, I nearly forgot, m'm. Miss Bunkle said you had a visitor. Since you'd only just arrived and everything, she asked the lady to come back tomorrow."

Cecily uttered a small gasp of disappointment at the thought of missing one of her friends. "Oh, who was it, do you know?

Mrs. Carter-Holmes? No, she's Fortescue now, of course. Or was it Miss Pengrath, perhaps?"

Jeanette shook her head. "Neither, m'm. It were Mr. Wrotham's widow. Said it was urgent she speak to you. Miss Bunkle said to tell you she'd be back tomorrow afternoon."

"Thank you, Jeanette." Cecily waited until the girl had closed the door behind her before turning to Baxter. "Well, what do you suppose the widow of Edward's manager would want to talk to me about?"

"I hesitate to speculate." Baxter raised his chin and closed his eyes. "I can guarantee, however, that she's not coming to welcome us to her dead husband's position."

"My thoughts exactly," Cecily answered with a great deal of satisfaction. "It seems as if we shall learn more about the late Barry Wrotham than I anticipated. I can hardly wait."

Chapter 3

The meeting with Miss Bunkle and her staff went very well. Cecily was relieved to discover she hadn't forgotten any of the intricacies of managing a hotel, and according to Miss Bunkle's reports, there didn't seem that much difference in the general day-to-day procedures involved. A country club, as she had already pointed out to Baxter, really wasn't that much different from a hotel after all.

Baxter visibly relaxed as the meeting progressed. He seemed to approve of Miss Bunkle, in spite of her odd hair ornament. When he complimented the housekeeper on her firm control of the staff, the woman actually blushed, much to Cecily's amusement. It would seem that marriage had not robbed Baxter of any of his suave charm.

She said as much to him later, as they stood at the wall of the roof garden looking down on the cove below. With his hair ruffled by the blustery wind blowing directly off the ocean, he seemed younger and more carefree than she'd seen him in many months.

This little interlude would be so good for both of them, she thought as Baxter turned to face her with a quizzical expression.

"Charm? I wasn't attempting to charm the lady. I was simply trying to establish a working relationship. I have the impression that Miss Bunkle can be a bit of an old battleship when it comes to rules and regulations."

"A trait which I'm quite sure has earned your utmost admiration."

He tilted his head. "You're not just the tiniest bit jealous, by any chance?"

She laughed out loud. "Of course I am, darling. You happen to be an uncommonly handsome man."

"Who happens to be married to a very beautiful lady."

"You see? You can't help being charming. Even to your wife."

For answer he placed an arm about her shoulders and pulled her close. "So what do you think about the new rules? Not too confining, on the whole?"

"I thought most of them unnecessary. Particularly that ridiculous one about women being barred from the lounge bar and the card rooms."

"Ah, yes." Baxter heaved a heavy sigh. "I had a feeling you would raise some objections to that one. At least we can be thankful that since we are now a country club, the card rooms are no longer illegal. We do have to remember, however, that the new rules are tradition and have to be observed."

"They should be done away with, if you ask me. Positively Victorian. This will set the Women's Movement back five years. I find it utterly appalling that a man cannot take his wife into certain rooms of an establishment where they are both residing. Rooms into which, I might add, two years ago women were at least tolerated. It simply doesn't make sense."

"I do hope you are not going to make an issue of this, my love." Baxter tightened his hold on her shoulders. "We must remember that rules are set for a reason, and as temporary administrators, we have no right to question them."

"We might not have the right to change them," Cecily said crisply, "but I'll defend to my death the right to question them."

"Yes, I thought you might."

She shivered as a fresh gust of wind buffeted her body. "That wind is rather keen, don't you think? I had forgotten how cold it can be up here in the winter. I much preferred the summer, when we could linger in the warm breeze. I used to enjoy the scent of roses while we watched the fishing boats come home."

"Then we shall return to our suite." Baxter guided her toward the narrow door that led to the stairway. "I'm nursing the small hope that Raymond has by now delivered our luggage, and I can change into something a little more fitting for my position."

She eyed him as he paused to allow her to proceed him through the door. His best charcoal gray suit, worn with a light gray waistcoat and starched white shirt, fitted him perfectly. His silk gray and white striped tie was knotted precisely, and with perhaps the exception of his hair, which remained ruffled despite his repeated attempts to smooth it down with his hand, he looked regal enough to be presented at the royal court without raising an eyebrow.

"You look quite dapper, my love," she informed him as she raised the hem of her skirt to clear the doorstep. "I think the patrons of the Pennyfoot Country Club are fortunate to have such a debonair fellow taking care of their needs."

She had her back to him, and couldn't see his frown, though she heard it in his voice. "My instincts tell me that this abundance of compliments is leading up to something I don't care to hear."

"I can't imagine what that could be." She waited until they had descended the first flight of stairs before adding, "Unless, of course, you object to my plan to pay a visit to Dr. Prestwick later this week."

His groan echoed down the stairwell as they turned the corner. "I knew it. I suppose it's too much to hope that the chap has found a wife? I rather thought he was interested in Madeline Pengrath when we left Badgers End."

"I thought so, too." Cecily reached the bottom of the stairs and waited for her husband to join her. "I'll have to ask Madeline about that. I do hope she and Phoebe manage to visit soon."

Baxter started to answer, then stopped short at the sight of Raymond standing in front of their suite, surrounded by several bags and two large trunks.

"Oh, there you are, m'm," the young man exclaimed when he caught sight of Cecily. "I was just about to send one of the maids to look for you. I didn't want to leave your luggage out here in the hallway."

Baxter strode forward and unlocked the door for him. "Just drop them in the sitting room. I'll take care of them later."

"Yes, sir. Thank you, sir." Raymond struggled in with the heavy load, placing the baggage neatly side by side on the thick carpet.

"Here." Baxter handed him a folded note, but Raymond shook his head.

"That's all right, sir. I don't take nothing from the staff, especially the guv'nor. Mr. Wrotham never gave me nothing, and I don't expect it from you, neither. Wouldn't be right."

Watching the surprise on her husband's face, Cecily knew the young man had made a favorable impression. Pouncing on the opportunity, she said carefully, "I understand Mr. Wrotham was a very efficient manager."

Raymond's grin faded. "I s'pose you could say that, m'm. He was always barking orders, if that's what you mean."

"I'm sure you must all miss him very much. It must have been such a shock to hear about his accident. Such a tragic death." Cecily deliberately ignored the warning gleam in Baxter's eyes and kept her gaze fixed firmly on Raymond's face.

Raymond appeared to be concentrating

on lining up the luggage. "I don't know about missing him, m'm. It were a shock to find him like that, I can tell you."

Cecily caught her breath. "*You* found him? I didn't know that."

"Yes, m'm. Mr. Sandringham sent me out looking for him. I saw his bicycle leaning against the fence of that farm and I went in to look for him." Raymond wiped his forehead with the back of his hand. "I don't know what made me look in the well. Just a feeling, I s'pose. Anyway, I sort of glanced in as I passed and I saw something floating around down there. When I looked proper like, I could tell it was a man. Gave me a really bad turn, it did."

"I can quite imagine. So what did you do next?"

"I flew out of there and rushed back here to tell Mr. Sandringham. He rang for the constable. P.C. Northcott came up right away."

"Did you see anything unusual lying around the well when you found Mr. Wrotham?"

"No, m'm. Not that I can recall, any-how." He straightened his back. "Every-one's really happy that you and Mr. Baxter are taking over, m'm. We weren't that fond of Mr. Wrotham, if you know what I mean.

Bit of a bully, he was. Always swearing at the girls, and giving them a swipe with the back of his hand if they didn't mind straightaway. No one really liked him, except for Miss Bunkle, but then she didn't have to put up with his temper the way we did. To tell you the truth, I'm not really surprised he ended up in a bad way. I could see it coming, I could."

Baxter loudly cleared his throat. "Yes, well, that will be all, Raymond. Thank you. I can manage from here."

"Did the constable question all the staff?" Cecily persisted, at the risk of incurring Baxter's disapproval.

Raymond shook his head. "Nah, m'm, they didn't. P.C. Northcott, well, he's a bit of a duffer, ain't he. Said as how it were an accident, so there were no need to bother everyone with a bunch of questions."

"But you don't seem to think it was an accident," Cecily prompted.

Raymond looked uncomfortable. "It's not my place to say, m'm, but if you want the truth, there ain't that many people what do think it were an accident. Except for the bobbies. And no one's going to tell them any different, are they."

"Yes, well, that will be all, Raymond." Baxter strode to the door and opened it, looking pointedly at the young man until he disappeared. After closing the door, rather firmly in Cecily's opinion, he gave her one of his reproachful scowls. "Without any real effort on your part, I think you said."

She sent him a mischievous grin. "Did I? How very impractical of me." She sidled up to him. "Darling, how am I going to find out anything if I don't ask a few questions now and then?"

He was about to answer when a light tap on the door cut off his words. With a muttered exclamation, he opened it to reveal Moira standing in the doorway. Upon glancing at his face, the maid jumped backward as if she'd touched a hot stove, then stood there, apparently having forgotten why she was there.

Baxter, never having been one for patience with the staff, barked at her, "Well, girl, speak up! What is it?"

Cecily clicked her tongue and hurried forward. Gently ushering Baxter aside, she smiled at the terrified girl. "Moira, isn't it?"

The girl nodded, her eyes wide with apprehension.

"Did you have a message for me?"

The maid nodded again.

Baxter grunted, rolled his eyes at the ceiling, and much to Cecily's relief, backed away from the door.

Cecily tried again. "Did Miss Bunkle send you?"

This time the maid shook her head. Her mouth opened and closed, then she managed to stammer, "There's two ladies to see you, m'm."

"Did they leave their names?"

Moira looked stricken for a moment, then mumbled, "Mrs. Fortescue was one of them. Can't remember the other one. Sorry, m'm. I'm new here and things get sort of muddled in me 'ead sometimes."

"Is that a fact," Baxter muttered dryly.

Ignoring him, Cecily said quietly, "Please show the ladies up here, Moira, and then bring us a decanter of sherry, and some sliced apples with a variety of cheeses. Oh, and some cream crackers."

"Yes, m'm." The girl dipped her knees and rushed off.

Cecily closed the door and turned to regard her husband. "Bax, darling, you really should curb that sharp edge to your tongue when addressing the staff. You'll intimidate those poor girls."

"It appears that some of them need intimidating."

"That's as may be, but we don't want them taking fright and giving in their notice right before Christmas."

"From what I've heard, Wrotham was far more threatening than I could ever be. If they could put up with him, I have every confidence they will learn to abide my thoroughly charming nature. Debonair, didn't you say?"

She grinned at him. "*Touché*. Now, unless you want to listen to a lot of girlish gossip, might I suggest that you take this time to reacquaint yourself with your office while I greet Phoebe and, I presume, Madeline. Though I have to admit, I'm rather surprised to hear that the two of them arrived together. They never could be within a yard of each other without squabbling."

"Perhaps marriage to the colonel has mellowed the good lady." Baxter picked up a heavy trunk by its two handles and staggered into the boudoir with it. Raising his voice, he called back to her, "I just can't imagine those two living together. Can you imagine our ridiculously fussy Phoebe putting up with that befuddled fool? I don't think he's ever strung two complete sentences together, and when he does manage it, he doesn't make any blasted sense."

Cecily also raised her voice to answer him. "It's understandable, I suppose. The poor man had such dreadful experiences in the Boer War, it's not surprising he's a little strange in the head."

"Strange?" Baxter emerged from the boudoir, his voice still loud. "Fortescue is more than a little strange. He's positively *insane.*"

At that precise moment a light tap on the door announced the presence of visitors.

Cecily gasped, her hand flying to her mouth. "Do you think they heard?" she whispered urgently.

Baxter shrugged. "I'd say it's a trifle too late to worry about it now. Though I do suggest you open the door before your guests think you are ignoring them."

"Heavens!" Cecily flew to the door and flung it wide. There in front of her stood her two dearest friends in the whole world.

Phoebe's outfit, as usual, was impeccable, from the huge flower-bedecked brim of her hat to the elegant elbow-length gloves and the pearl-buttoned shoes peeking out from under the hem of her gray, heavy silk tea gown. A dainty parasol swung from her arm, and in the other she cradled a round tin of chocolate-covered biscuits — one of Cecily's very favorite treats.

By contrast, Madeline looked more like a woodland sprite, conjured up from the depths of the green forest. A crown of mistletoe covered her long, dark, flowing hair, and beneath her serviceable coat her soft muslin dress floated around her toes, which had been tucked into shoes that appeared too large for her dainty feet. She thrust a small delicate bouquet of tea roses at Cecily, who exclaimed in delight.

"Roses? At this time of the year?"

"From Porter's greenhouse. I ordered them especially." She flung her arms about Cecily, putting the delicate blooms in extreme danger of being crushed. "You look wonderful, Cecily. Marriage agrees with you."

She peered past Cecily's shoulder to where Baxter was still struggling with the luggage. "I'm happy to see you are taking such good care of my good friend, Baxter."

Baxter mumbled something and carried the last of the bags into the boudoir.

Not to be outdone, Phoebe stepped forward and kissed the air on each side of Cecily's face. "How absolutely divine you look, Cecily, dearest. I have missed you so much. This is going to be a magnificent

Christmas Season now that you are back in Badgers End. Here. For you and Mr. Baxter. An early gift."

Cecily took the tin of biscuits with a gasp of pleasure. "How thoughtful of you, Phoebe. Thank you both so much. The two of you look absolutely breathtaking. How wonderful it is to see you both again."

"Rather than intrude upon this somewhat cloying mutual admiration society," Baxter announced as he emerged from the boudoir, "I'll take my leave and allow you ladies to chatter to your heart's content."

Phoebe fluttered her eyelashes at him. "I do hope we're not chasing you out, Mr. Baxter."

Baxter allowed her a brief glance. "Not at all. I have work to do. Please excuse me, ladies."

Madeline waited until he'd opened the door, then said sweetly, "Should you find yourself in need of a potion while you are here, Baxter, I'll be happy to oblige. Free of charge, of course."

Baxter paused, and Cecily held her breath. There were those in the village who swore by Madeline's potions. There were even men who insisted that their virility in certain private matters was greatly enhanced by the strange concoctions of herbs and wildflowers. Baxter was well aware of this, though he was adamant in his disbelief that such powers as those attributed to Madeline actually existed. Nonetheless Cecily waited, half expecting him to make some derisive comment to offend her friend.

After a second or two, he said gruffly, "Thank you, Miss Pengrath, but I assure you, I have no need for such debatable assistance. You may ask my wife should you be in any doubt of that."

He closed the door firmly behind him, while Phoebe's shocked gasp was drowned out by Madeline's gurgling laugh. In a voice that always reminded Cecily of the wind in the bulrushes on Deep Willow Pond, she murmured, "You are a fortunate woman, Cecily. There goes a real man."

"Really, Madeline," Phoebe said crossly. "Have you no shame? What possesses you to talk so unbecomingly in front of a gentleman?"

"Perhaps if you had been half as bold, Phoebe dear," Madeline answered, "you might have landed yourself a gentleman instead of that buffoon with whom you are sadly saddled."

Phoebe drew herself up another inch

and glared at the other woman. "That buffoon, as you so crudely call him, is a prince in every way. He treats me in the manner to which ladies such as I have been accustomed, and he is delightful and entertaining company. At least he had the chivalry to ask for my hand in marriage. Perhaps, if you had been more of a lady and less of a hussy, you might have held the interest of a certain doctor, instead of losing him to that simpering fool, Winifred Chesterton."

Glimpsing the light of battle in Madeline's eyes, Cecily hurried to intervene. "How is Dr. Prestwick these days? I intend to visit him later this week. I do hope he's well?"

"Quite well," Madeline said shortly.

Phoebe's skirts rustled as she settled herself on the sateen couch. "He's doing very well," she said a trifle smugly. "His waiting room is constantly packed with patients, whether they are legitimate or not. Most of them are women, of course. Our handsome doctor always did have a way with the women."

Cecily, who had once been the object of the good doctor's affections, knew only too well how utterly devastating Dr. Kevin Prestwick's appeal could be to a vulnerable woman. She glanced at Madeline, who seemed unaffected by Phoebe's barbs as she floated across the floor in the direction of a comfortable royal blue armchair.

Seating herself, Madeline said blithely, "Dr. Prestwick bestows his good nature on everyone, man or woman. It's not his fault if some misguided ladies misinterpret a good bedside manner for something inappropriate."

Phoebe tittered behind a delicate gloved hand. "I don't think Winifred Chesterton is misinterpreting anything, judging by the way he was looking at her as she hung on his arm the other morning."

"That's a matter of opinion." Madeline's beautiful eyes narrowed. "I happen to know that Kevin is not in the least interested in that woman. He has said as much to me. He does, after all, spend most of his spare time with me, not with Winifred Chesterton."

"Yes," Phoebe allowed. "I suppose he does. Then again, since he has yet to ask for your hand in marriage, one has to wonder if his intentions are honorable. It's a pity you have no father to question the doctor's purpose in pursuing a relationship with you."

Madeline's lips curved in the smile that

always made Cecily nervous. "Phoebe, dear, I do believe that the doctor's purposes are none of your business. Perhaps you should keep a still tongue, lest you wake up one morning to find it transformed into that of a viper."

Phoebe pulled a lace-trimmed handkerchief from her sleeve and fluttered it in front of her face. "I was merely concerned for your welfare, Madeline. There's no need to become vindictive. Perhaps you should save your doubtful threats for Winifred, since she appears to be intent on ensnaring your prospective suitor."

"Don't think I haven't considered the prospect," Madeline said darkly.

Deciding that it was time to change the subject, Cecily said hastily, "Did either of you make the acquaintance of Mr. Barry Wrotham, by any chance?"

Madeline made a face. "Yes, he came to me about a month ago, looking for some of my potions. Quite an unpleasant man. I could sense a dark shadow hanging over him, even then. I thought about warning him, but his attitude was so offensive, I decided to let fate have its way." She looked directly into Cecily's eyes, and her voice changed to a low tone that Cecily knew well. "It wasn't an accident, you know," she said softly. "Someone pushed Mr. Wrotham down that well. Someone extremely dangerous. I have to warn you, Cecily. The shadow hangs over you, as well. Be very careful, for whoever killed Barry Wrotham could very well make you his next victim."

Chapter
4

Cecily was well used to her friend's dire warnings. Madeline's remarkable penchant for foreseeing the future was legendary, if somewhat unreliable. She had succeeded enough times, however, to give Cecily a decided chill at her words.

In an effort to lighten the moment, she uttered a breezy laugh. "Now, Madeline, what makes you think I have any intention of concerning myself with the death of a man whom I've never met."

The odd light still gleamed in Madeline's eyes. "Not only will you involve yourself," she said softly, "you will place yourself in grave danger. Please, my friend, beware of those who wish you harm. It could well be your undoing this time."

"Really, Madeline," Phoebe muttered. "You are positively macabre. Enough of this silly game."

Fortunately, at that moment a tap on the door announced the arrival of the cheese and sherry. The disruption managed to diffuse the somber atmosphere in the room, though Cecily could not quite rid herself of a vague sense of foreboding. She was thankful when the conversation turned to the upcoming Christmas Season.

"You really do need to do something more imaginative with the decorations," Madeline declared after sipping at her sherry. She placed the slim glass on the table in front of her. "The holly wreaths on the front doors are a nice touch, but the tree in the foyer is pitiable. I hope you have a larger tree in the library?"

"I haven't looked yet," Cecily admitted. "Hugh and I went up to the roof garden and then talked to Miss Bunkle in her room, but other than that, I haven't seen much of the hotel since I arrived."

Madeline looked surprised. "You call your husband Hugh now?"

"Only in company," Cecily confessed. "I gave him my promise. I must admit, it does sound rather demeaning to call him Baxter in front of everyone. It's not as if he's in my employ anymore. We are equal partners now."

Madeline nodded her approval.

"I thought the tree was very nice," Phoebe observed, having successfully ignored the exchange.

"Naturally you would think so." Madeline reached for the cheese knife and cut herself a square of Gorgonzola. "Judging from the meager decorations in the church, your taste is sadly lacking in the Christmas spirit."

She waved the knife at Cecily. "The Pennyfoot always looked so wonderful at Christmastime. There used to be garlands of holly and gigantic red ribbons adorning the bannisters of the staircase. Those lovely handmade ornaments you used to have on the trees in the foyer and library. Candles to light in the evening, and enormous swaths of ribbons and velvets in red and green sweeping across the ballroom. Huge bunches of mistletoe everywhere."

"I wondered when we were coming to that," Phoebe muttered nastily. "In my opinion, any woman who walks around with mistletoe in her hair is begging to be ravished."

"Really," Madeline murmured. "What an utterly delicious thought."

"As a matter of fact," Cecily said firmly, "I was intending to ask if you would be willing to see to the decorations for us, Madeline. I'm sure they are in storage somewhere in the hotel . . . I mean club."

"I'd be delighted." She grinned at Phoebe. "You can help if you promise me faithfully you will not complain every five minutes."

"Actually, Phoebe," Cecily said before that lady could deliver the retort hovering on her tight lips, "I was rather hoping that you might be willing to put together a pantomime for us. Since the men will be off on their traditional hunt for pheasant on Boxing Day, I thought it would be nice to entertain the ladies with their special event. Though no doubt the gentlemen will join them. Everyone seems to love a pantomime at Christmastime. I know it's terribly short notice, of course, but —"

"Oh, I'd adore to help!" Phoebe clapped her hands in delight. "It's been simply *ages* since I've organized anything more challenging that a christening at the church. Algie is such a bore when it comes to events. He simply refuses to allow me to put on a revue at the church hall. He keeps insisting it's immoral, no matter how much I try to explain that everything would be in good taste."

"I would imagine your habit of creating disasters has more to do with his reluctance," Madeline said. "I still haven't forgotten the fiasco of the lost python, or the time a member of your dance team did her best to stab one of the guests through the heart."

Phoebe visibly bristled. "It wasn't the girl's fault. Her foot slipped during the sword dance. Accidents happen in the best of productions. Even on the London stages, so I've been told."

Cecily loudly cleared her throat. "Well, I'm sure things will work out beautifully for the pantomime. I suggest we all meet at Dolly's Teashop the day after tomorrow to discuss the plans. I can't wait to sink my teeth into one of Dolly's exquisite Banbury cakes."

The ladies readily agreed and, accepting the hint, rose to take their leave. Cecily offered to show them around the newly renovated Pennyfoot before they left, then accompanied them as far as the main doors before heading toward the narrow hallway to her husband's office.

As she approached the staircase, she saw a couple descending to the foyer. It wasn't often she was struck by a woman's beauty, but the lovely creature on the arm of the distinguished-looking gentleman was the sort of woman who would attract attention everywhere she went.

Instead of a hat, she wore a band of

cream velvet fastened with a white silk camellia around a mound of luxurious dark brown curls atop her head.

Cecily's mouth positively watered at the sight of the woman's exquisite gown. It was the color of champagne, composed of panels of Swiss eyelet embroidery, which were divided by tiny insertions of gorgeous French Val lace. Her Gibson collar accentuated the woman's long, slim neck as she swept down the stairs with the air of one accustomed to grandeur and the services accorded by it.

Guessing that these were two of the "toffs" Jeanette was talking about, Cecily hurried forward to greet the pair as they reached the bottom of the staircase.

"Welcome to the Pennyfoot Country Club," she said as the couple paused in front of her. "May I introduce myself? I'm Cecily Baxter, the present manager of this establishment. If I or any of my staff can be of any service to you, please don't hesitate to ask."

The gentleman raised his eyebrows, looking down at her as if she were a vagrant who had wandered in off the street. "A woman manager? How very droll."

"Temporary manager, actually," Cecily corrected, deciding that she didn't like the man. "My husband and I are helping out the owner of the Pennyfoot, Edward Sandringham, who happens to be my cousin. As a matter of fact, I sold the hotel to him two years ago."

If she'd hoped to impress him, she was disappointed. "Really," the gentleman answered, sounding bored. "Well, I am Sir John Gilroy, K.C. Permit me to introduce my wife, Lady Lucille."

Cecily smiled at the woman. "I'm delighted to make your acquaintance, your ladyship."

"*Merci.*" Lady Lucille stared at a spot slightly above Cecily's head. "It is our very great pleasure to return to the club. I can only hope that the service is as impeccable as always."

Even without the thick French accent, Cecily would have guessed the lady's origin. She positively breathed Paris. "We shall do our best," she said, a little miffed at the suggestion that the new management might not come up to snuff. "This is not your first visit to the Pennyfoot Country Club, I assume."

"On the contrary. We come here quite often," Sir John said, answering for her. "In fact, we were here quite recently for the hunting season."

"Then you should enjoy the pheasant hunt on Boxing Day."

"I'm looking forward to it."

"Ah, there you are, John, old boy." The voice boomed down the staircase, startling Lady Lucille to the point of bringing a flush to her cheeks.

Cecily watched the portly gentleman rapidly descend, one hand on the bannister, the other clasping the arm of a scowling woman who was doing her best to keep up with him without tripping over the hem of her ruffled satin skirt.

"Evening, Lionel," Gilroy muttered.

The newcomer seemingly ignored him, his avid gaze instead devouring the delectable Lady Lucille. "Thought we'd join you for supper, old chap," he said a trifle breathlessly as he reached the bottom of the steps.

Gilroy nodded. "This is Mrs. Baxter, the new manager of the club. Mrs. Baxter, may I present Lionel Fitzhammer, K.C., and his wife, Barbara."

Fitzhammer held out his hand and Cecily reluctantly put hers into it, doing her very best not to visibly recoil when the scarlet-cheeked gentleman pressed his rubbery lips against her fingers.

"Charmed, I'm sure," she muttered, and

withdrew her hand rather smartly.

"Have you met the others yet?" Lionel asked, standing close enough to Lucille that his wife was forced to hover in the background. "They should be down shortly. Though Percy's a bit of a slow-coach. He'll probably be late to the table. He usually is."

"No, I haven't met the rest of your party yet." Cecily tried to sound fascinated. "I understand that all four of you gentlemen are members of the King's Counsel."

"You are correct," Fitzhammer said, his gaze once more fastened greedily on Lucille. "Percy Chatsworth, K.C., and his wife, Amelia, and Roger Peebles, K.C., with his wife, Gretchen. We are all Masters of the Bench, here to enjoy the Christmas Season in this excellent establishment."

"Then we shall do our best to make your stay a memorable one. We are honored to have you all as our guests." Cecily met the wary gaze of Barbara Fitzhammer and smiled at her. Although the woman's lack-luster brown hair and pleasant looks were vastly overshadowed by those of the flamboyant Lucille, her eyes were cornflower blue and quite beautiful.

"Jolly good," her husband muttered. "The Pennyfoot has always been one of our favorite places to stay, wouldn't you say, John?"

"Quite, quite." Gilroy pulled a fob watch from the pocket of his waistcoat and flipped open the lid. "I suppose we should make our way to the dining room."

"Oh, please, don't let me detain you." Cecily backed out of the way to allow them to pass. "I trust you will enjoy your evening meal."

"Bound to, madam," Fitzhammer boomed. "What with that excellent French chef of yours. Can't beat the French for knowing how to tickle a man's palate, eh, what?"

He gave Gilroy a sly dig with his elbow, his gaze riveted on Lady Lucille's face. The lady lifted her chin in a haughty gesture of contempt, yet her glance slid sideways at her husband, as if concerned the comment would offend him.

Sir John, however, merely grasped his wife's elbow, muttered his excuses, and steered her down the hallway, leaving a trail of expensive perfume behind. Fitzhammer barely took the time to bid Cecily good evening before charging after them with his unfortunate spouse in tow.

Left alone, Cecily breathed a sigh. It had been a long day and she was hungry. All she could think about now was retiring for the evening and enjoying a quiet meal alone with her husband in their suite. After spending two years in the quiet peace of her London town house, she found the bustle and noise of the club to be oppressive. It would take some time to accustom herself to all the upheaval again.

Feeling just a little depressed, for whatever reason she couldn't be sure, she made her way down the hallway to Baxter's office. Tomorrow would be another day. Her pulse quickened at the remembrance that she had an appointment with Wrotham's widow in the morning. She could hardly wait to find out what it was the late manager's wife had to tell her that was apparently so urgent.

If there was one thing that was clear after her discussions with Raymond and Jeanette, it was that quite a few people believed Wrotham's death was not an accident. She couldn't help wondering if Wrotham's widow shared that belief and, if so, might perhaps shed some light on what really happened. In any case, the meeting should prove to be quite interesting.

The following morning, Cecily arose feeling somewhat lethargic, thanks to a restless night in a strange bed. Baxter, apparently, had no trouble sleeping, and in fact, his snoring had been part of Cecily's problem — a fact she kept to herself. In the past Baxter had emphatically denied that he snored, and she had given up trying to convince him otherwise.

After a light breakfast of poached eggs and haddock in their suite, Baxter announced he had work to do. He kissed his wife and left, leaving Cecily to wait for the arrival of Barry Wrotham's widow.

Emily Wrotham arrived midmorning, just as Cecily returned from inspecting the accommodations for Mrs. Chubb, Gertie, and her family. Jeanette ushered the woman into Cecily's suite, and waited for her to remove her navy blue coat, which reminded Cecily of a military uniform with its large buttons on the shoulders.

Underneath, Emily Wrotham wore a serviceable skirt and a plain white shirtwaist relieved only by tiny rows of tucking down the front. Although she was young in appearance, her shoulders were bowed, as if she were too weary to raise her head.

Reminding herself that the poor woman had recently lost her husband, Cecily invited her to sit, and ordered Jeanette to have coffee and currant buns brought up to the room.

"I am so sorry to hear of your loss," Cecily murmured as the widow seated herself on the very edge of the couch. "It must have been a dreadful shock for you."

"Dreadful." Emily's thin voice wavered, and she sought in her sleeve for a large white handkerchief. After dabbing at her eyes, she said tearfully, "The police constable insists that Barry's death was an accident." She gulped, cleared her throat, loudly blew her nose, then added, "They are mistaken, Mrs. Baxter. Someone pushed my Barry down that well. I'm quite sure of it."

Cecily lowered herself onto the comfortable armchair. "That's a rather serious statement, Mrs. Wrotham. What makes you so certain that the constables are mistaken?"

Emily blew her nose again, with more delicacy this time. "Barry hadn't been himself for quite some time before that day. I knew something was wrong, but every time I asked him about it, he insisted all was well. In the end he got quite cross with me for asking him about it. So I had to give up asking. Then, on the day he . . . he . . . died, Sunday it was, he told me he would be working all afternoon here at the club. Stocking the wine cellar, he told me.

I was upset because it was his afternoon off, but he said it couldn't wait and he had to take care of it right away."

She paused, and Cecily waited a moment or two before prompting, "But you found out he wasn't stocking the wine cellar?"

Emily Wrotham nodded her head. "He'd been giving me that story about working late so many times, he must have forgotten he'd used the one about the wine cellar just two weeks before. I knew he wouldn't have to restock it that quickly, so I came here to see for myself."

"And he wasn't here."

"No, he wasn't." Emily's pale gray eyes filled with tears again. "I thought he was with another woman. I'd had my suspicions for a long time. Working at a place like this, he was bound to meet a hussy or two. I suppose I was expecting it in a way. He'd grown tired of me a long time ago. I could tell." A sob escaped, and she quickly smothered it with her crumpled handkerchief.

"I'm so sorry, Mrs. Wrotham." Anger burned in Cecily's breast when she saw the misery etched on Emily's once pretty face. Any sympathy she might have had for Barry Wrotham's ignoble fate was immediately erased. In her opinion, men who cheated on their wives ought to be horse-whipped. The pain and misery they caused while indulging in their selfish whims could not be measured.

"In any case," Emily said, still fighting tears, "I was really angry. I wanted him caught with whoever he was with, to bring shame on her and to put an end to it. So I told Mr. Sandringham that Barry was missing. I told him he'd never come home and I was afraid something had happened to him. I could tell Mr. Sandringham didn't care that much, but he knew I was worried about Barry, so he sent Raymond out to see if he could find him."

"Ah, yes. Raymond told me about finding your husband's body."

Another sob escaped her lips. "Yes, well, Raymond saw his bicycle leaning against the fence and went in to the farm to look for him. He found him . . . floating . . . in the well." This time her sobs overcame her.

Cecily was thankful to hear Jeanette's light tap on the door, thus giving Emily a chance to compose herself while she took charge of the refreshments.

After serving both women with a steaming cup of coffee and a buttered bun, Jeanette left the room, though not without raising a questioning eyebrow at Cecily as she passed by her chair.

Cecily pretended not to notice. That young maid's curiosity would no doubt get her into trouble one day, she thought, as she took a sip of her coffee.

Within a few moments, Emily Wrotham appeared composed enough to continue her story. "What puzzles me," she told Cecily, "is why my husband was on that farm in the first place. The land is being offered for sale, I understand, but Barry had no money to buy a place like that, and in any case, he's no farmer. I can't imagine what he'd be doing, wandering around an abandoned farm all alone."

"Perhaps, if your suspicions about another woman are justified, your husband might have intended to meet someone there."

Emily nodded her agreement. "That's what I think. It's the only answer, really. I think someone lured him there in order to kill him. And it's my thinking that perhaps the husband or suitor of whomever my husband was dallying with had a hand in it. Why else would someone want to kill a man like my Barry? He wasn't perfect, by any means, but he never harmed anyone in his entire life." Her words ended on a burst of weeping that took some time to dissolve.

Cecily let the woman cry, understanding that she needed to indulge in her grief. While she waited for Emily to control her sobs, she thought about what she'd heard. There was a ring of plausibility to the widow's words, though she had to admit that until now she hadn't thought about there being another woman involved. It would seem there was much more to Barry Wrotham than she'd realized.

When the widow seemed to have found her composure again, Cecily asked gently, "Have you spoken to the constable about your suspicions?"

"Oh, no." Emily dabbed at her pink nose. "I couldn't, Mrs. Baxter. For one thing, I don't know for sure that Barry was seeing someone else. I wouldn't want that sort of thing spread all over town if it isn't true. I have my children to consider. It's bad enough they lost their father. I don't want them thinking ill of him if I'm wrong about him."

"I see." Cecily's heart went out to this poor woman who had been left to raise her children alone. "Then why have you come to me?"

Emily leaned forward, her eyes glittering, her voice a low, fierce whisper. "I do believe, Mrs. Baxter, that the answer to it all lies somewhere right here, at the Pennyfoot Country Club. Someone either staying here or working here knows something, I'll stake my life on it. I want to know the truth. If someone did kill my husband, I want to know who it is and I want him punished. No one should be free to take a life without paying for it. I can't rest easy until I know the truth and see that justice is done."

"You do know that if your suspicions prove to be correct, then people will eventually be aware that your husband was being unfaithful to you."

Emily raised her small pointed chin. "If it's the truth, then I'll tell the children myself. I can't stay here anyway without Barry. I'll be taking the children back to London for Christmas, and we won't be coming back. We'll be living with my parents. I just can't leave until I know what really happened to him. I asked Mr. Sandringham to help me, but he was too busy getting ready for his trip. He told me to talk to you. He said you were very good at that sort of thing."

Cecily leaned back in her chair. So that was why Edward had told Baxter he thought there was something odd about

Wrotham's death. Dear Edward. Had he mentioned the fact that Barry's widow suspected foul play, Baxter would have adamantly refused to put a foot in Badgers End.

"I really can't promise anything," she said, reaching for her currant bun. "But I'll certainly look into it, if you like. Is there anything else you can tell me? Did your husband ever mention another woman by name? Or even a man's name you didn't recognize?"

"No, nothing. It was just a feeling I had, really. I know that's not much help, but believe me, Mrs. Baxter, when your husband is straying, somehow you can tell. Just little things. Like the way he avoided looking me in the eyes when he left for work."

She uttered a shuddering sigh. "He used to talk about his job all the time at first, then he got so he didn't want to talk about it at all. He was always in a hurry to get out of the house. Sometimes he didn't even bother to kiss me goodbye. He never used to be like that." She looked down at her hands, twisting the handkerchief around her fingers. "As I said, just little things."

"Well, I'll do my best to find out what I can." Cecily rose to her feet, and Emily followed suit, tucking her damp handkerchief back into her sleeve.

"I am much obliged, Mrs. Baxter. I know I can trust you to be discreet."

"Of course." Cecily tugged on the bell rope to summon a maid. "Though I have to warn you again, the truth will most likely come out in the end."

"If it *is* the truth. Then so be it."

Moira arrived a few minutes later to help the widow on with her coat, then escorted her out the door. After they'd left, Cecily wandered to the window to cast a wary eye on the darkening sky.

The clouds looked heavy and gray, and dried leaves drifted and swirled across the manicured lawn. It would seem that Baxter had been right in his prediction, for even as she watched, scattered snowflakes began to dance in the wind.

Mrs. Chubb and Gertie would be arriving soon. She could only hope that their stay would be uneventful. Much as she had missed the excitement of chasing after criminals, she had to admit, nothing would spoil Christmas more than the ugliness of murder once more invading the walls of the Pennyfoot.

Chapter
5

Gertie and her family arrived that afternoon in a flurry of excited greetings, hugs, and tears. The snow had begun falling quite heavily, coating the Esplanade and the roof of the Pennyfoot like a soft white coverlet.

Holding a hand of each twin, Cecily lead the party inside the warm foyer of the Pennyfoot, marveling at how big the children had grown. Their excitement at the sight of the Christmas tree was so infectious Cecily rashly promised them they could help Madeline decorate it.

"You'll be bloody sorry you did that, m'm," Gertie said, removing the tartan wool scarf she'd wrapped around her hat. "If I know these two, they'll have the bleeding tree upside down before you can blink."

"Gertie," Mrs. Chubb said sharply. "You promised. Not in front of the children."

"Sorry." Gertie grinned happily at

Cecily. "I promised I wouldn't use them words. I'm getting better at it, but now and again they slip out." She stopped short, staring at her feet. "Crikey, look at this carpet. Must have cost a bleeding fortune."

Mrs. Chubb rolled her eyes and groaned, while Cecily laughed. "It is such a joy to see you all again," she said. "You have no idea how much I've missed you. Especially my godchildren." She beamed down at the twins, who were staring wide-eyed at the sweeping staircase as if they'd never seen one before.

"Are we going up there?" Lillian asked, pointing a chubby finger at the stairs.

"What have I told you about pointing, girl," Mrs. Chubb said sharply.

"It's rude," James said loudly. He gave his sister a shove. "Lilly's rude . . . Lilly's rude . . . Lilly's rude."

Gertie raised her hand. "Shut up, you two, or I'll box your bleeding ears."

The twins dived behind Cecily and clung to her skirt.

"I'm sure she doesn't mean it," Cecily said, laughing.

"Be the death of me, they will," Gertie said darkly. "I never thought —" She broke off, staring at Miss Bunkle, who was making her way across the foyer toward them.

"Blimey, who the heck's that? Does she know she's got a knitting needle stuck in 'er hair?"

When the housekeeper reached them, Cecily hastily made the introductions. "Mrs. Chubb used to be the housekeeper here," she informed Miss Bunkle. "And Mrs. McBride was our chief housemaid."

"Really." Miss Bunkle sniffed, and looked down her nose at the twins. "And I suppose these were footmen?"

No doubt it was supposed to be a joke, but Gertie's chin shot up. "If you must know, these children were born right here in this hotel," she said, emphatically sounding her aitches. "That was in the good old days, when this *was* a posh hotel, not a bleeding country club for roadhogs."

"Gertie!" Mrs. Chubb gave her a horrified glare. "Mind your manners."

Miss Bunkle seemed unaffected by Gertie's scathing comments, dismissing them with a haughty toss of her head. "Your rooms are ready," she said, "if you care to follow Jeanette." She gestured at the maid hovering at the base of the staircase. "I'll have Raymond bring up your luggage as soon as possible."

"Blimey," Gertie murmured. "I never thought I'd end up being waited on at the

Pennyfoot. It don't seem right, some'ow."

"I know what you mean." Mrs. Chubb slipped her hands out of her muff and glanced in the direction of the kitchen stairs. "I feel as I should be going downstairs, not up them."

"I'm sure you'll soon get used to it." Cecily beamed at them both. "Come on, I'll show you to your rooms myself." She smiled at Miss Bunkle. "There's no need for Jeanette to go up with us."

Miss Bunkle dipped her head. "Very well, Mrs. Baxter." She raised her hand. "Come along, Jeanette."

The maid scuttled forward, giving Gertie a curious stare as she drew close. "Did you really used to be the chief housemaid here?" she asked in a loud whisper.

Gertie grinned. "You bet your bleeding boots I did. I was bloody good at me job, too. Best housemaid around, you just ask madam, here. Why, I could tell you stories —"

"Jeanette, stop bothering the guests and get down below stairs," Miss Bunkle ordered, raising her voice just enough to sound assertive.

Jeanette scurried off toward the kitchen stairs, while Gertie watched her go, an almost wistful expression on her face. "I dunno," she said softly, "but them days seemed so simple then. Nothing to worry about except getting the tables laid proper and the meals served."

Mrs. Chubb huffed out her breath. "And the ovens stoked with coals, the grates blackened every day, the floors washed, the sinks cleaned, the laundry done, the carpets swept, the beds made, the furniture dusted, the silver polished —"

"Heavens!" Cecily laughed. "You're making me feel tired, Mrs. Chubb."

"Me, too." Gertie dug an elbow in the stout lady's ribs. "Come on, Chubby, get up to your room before you feel tempted to go down there and start bleeding ordering everyone about."

Mrs. Chubb wagged a finger in Gertie's face. "I told you not to call me that."

"Oops!" Gertie grinned at Cecily. "Got a blinking memory like a sieve, I do."

Muttering under her breath, Mrs. Chubb grabbed each twin by the hand and headed for the staircase.

"Don't take any notice of us, m'm," Gertie said as she followed behind with Cecily. "Me and Mrs. Chubb get along really well. A lot different from the old days when she used to box me ears for talking back to her. She's more like me mum now.

Still tries to tell me what to do, but she knows I'm old enough not to care."

Cecily sighed. "It's hard to think that things have changed so much when everything looks so familiar."

"It do, indeed, m'm." Gertie looked earnestly at her. "I wanted to say, m'm, it's really, really nice of you to invite us like this. As guests, I mean. Though I have to admit, it do feel strange."

"I hope not too strange for you to enjoy your visit. Since you are my guests, I think we can dispense with you referring to me as 'm'm' while you are here."

"Oh, no, m'm, I couldn't." Gertie gave her head an emphatic shake. "It wouldn't seem right. Me and Mrs. Chubb talked about that on the way down on the train. We both agreed we couldn't stop addressing you the way we've always been used to, that's all. I hope you don't mind."

"Of course not. You must do whatever makes you the most comfortable." Cecily smiled at the sight of the twins dragging Mrs. Chubb up the stairs. "I just want everyone to enjoy the Christmas Season."

"I'm sure we will, m'm. Is Michel still here?"

"Yes, he is. And delighted at the thought of seeing everyone again."

"Go on with you, m'm." Gertie lifted her skirts as she began to climb the stairs. "I bet he didn't bleeding tell you that."

Cecily laughed. "No, he didn't. He made some vague comments about his peace being shattered and the reputation of the country club being forever sullied. But I could tell he was excited at the news."

"Hope he's got a good supply of brandy. He's going to need it with all of us around. What about the twins, Daisy and Doris? Are they coming?"

"Daisy will be arriving with Samuel to-morrow. Doris won't be here until later. She has a theatrical engagement to finish before she can leave London."

"I can't wait to see them again." Gertie heaved a sigh. "I really miss them. Daisy especially. She was always so good at taking care of me own twins. I wonder if they'll remember her." Gertie hugged her-self in her excitement. "This is going to be the best bleeding Christmas ever."

"What about Ross? When will he be ar-riving? I was hoping he'd come down with you."

"So was I." Gertie paused for breath at the first landing. Mrs. Chubb and the twins had already disappeared around the curve of the next flight of stairs. "To tell you the truth, m'm, his business ain't doing that well. Not much call for gardeners in Scotland nowadays. Most people take care of their own, and those what don't buy their vegetables from the greengrocers. He doesn't say much, but I know he worries about it. He stayed behind to finish up with the customers he's got for Christmas stuff, but I don't know what he's going to do after that."

"I'm sorry to hear that," Cecily murmured. "It must be a worry for you."

"It's his health I'm worried about, m'm." Gertie began climbing the second flight of stairs. "Got this awful cough, he has. Reminds me of when Ethel got ill with hers. I'll be glad if he does give up the gardening. The weather in Scotland is bleeding shocking in the winter. It's blinking cold enough to freeze the —"

She broke off as a man and a woman appeared on the stairs above her on their way down.

The woman's hair, visible beneath the upswept brim of her hat, was an exquisite shade of auburn, and her pale skin seemed colorless in comparison. She wore a fashionable suit of dark gray, with a silver soutache braid trimming the coat and the hem of the gored skirt. Her gloved hand clung to the bannisters as she paused to allow Cecily and Gertie to pass.

Her companion was dark in complexion, as if he had spent a good many weeks in the glare of the sun. His comely features were perfectly arranged on his face, and he gave both of them an engaging smile as they passed by him, then continued on down the stairs with the elegant woman.

"Flippin' 'eck," Gertie said when they were out of earshot. "Now there's a good-looking chap. Bet that suit cost a bob or two."

"I think the gentleman must be one of the Benchers staying here," Cecily said as they reached the next landing. "I met the other two and their wives last night, but there are two more I haven't met as yet."

"Benchers?" Gertie looked puzzled. "I'm not sure I know what you mean."

"They are barristers," Cecily explained. "The highest ranked of the judicial office. They sit on the Bench at the Inns of Court. Most prestigious position. Some members of the royal family have been Royal Benchers, including Prince Albert and King George the Fifth, I do believe."

"Blimey," Gertie said, sounding impressed, though it was obvious by her expression she didn't have the slightest idea what Cecily was talking about. "Right posh toffs, then. I reckon the country club doesn't do that bad after all."

At least she had that right, Cecily reflected as she joined Mrs. Chubb and the impatient twins on the landing.

The next few minutes were spent getting everyone settled. Then Cecily left them alone to relax after their long journey and went down to the kitchen to order up a tray of refreshments.

Mrs. Chubb had elected to keep the twins with her in her room, so that Gertie and Ross could have some privacy, an arrangement of which Cecily heartily approved. Having completed her mission in the kitchen, she then went in search of her husband. It had been far too long since she'd had a word alone with Baxter. She had forgotten how much time could be taken up with the business of managing a hotel. Country club. Try as she might, she could not think of the Pennyfoot as anything but a hotel. And she probably never would.

"She don't look like no housemaid to me," Jeanette said as she lifted a cauldron of hot water from the stove. "I ask you, what's a housemaid and a housekeeper doing staying as guests at the very hotel what they worked at once? Don't make any sense, do it."

Moira shrugged, her fingers busy peeling the shell from a hard-boiled egg. "It's not our place to say, is it."

Jeanette dumped the water into the sink and carried the empty pot back to the stove. "Oh, don't be such a ninny. Who's going to know if we talk about them?" She nodded her head in the direction of the ceiling. "I wish I could be a spider on the wall in some of those boudoirs. I reckon I'd see enough to make me eyes bulge out."

Moira's cheeks flamed, and she lowered her chin. "It's none of our business what goes on upstairs."

Jeanette stomped back to the sink and began slipping soiled dinner plates into the water. "Maybe not, but I reckon I could tell you a thing or two that would shock the living daylights out of you."

Moira raised her chin. "Like what?"

Jeanette grinned. "See? I knew you were just as nosy as me. What if I was to tell you I knew something about Rotten Wrotham that no one else knew?"

Moira's eyes grew wide with apprehension. "What do you mean?"

"Can't tell you, can I. But I can tell you this, them toffs upstairs aren't all that blinking perfect, neither. You'd be shocked if you knew what I know."

Moira went back to shelling her eggs. "I don't believe you know anything. You're just making it up to sound big, that's all."

"Am I then?" Jeanette swished the dishes in the hot water and stacked them onto the draining board. "Well, I wouldn't be too sure. You know the really handsome one? The one with the dark curly hair and the suntan? His wife is the one with all that red hair?"

"You mean Mr. Peebles?"

"Yeah, that's his name. Roger Peebles. Well, he's no angel, that's for sure."

"Go on!" Moira's eyes gleamed with excitement. "Did he make a grab at you?"

"Maybe he did and maybe he didn't." Now that she had Moira's full attention, Jeanette was thoroughly enjoying herself. "All I can tell you is, there's a lot more to him than meets the eye."

"You got a crush on him, then?"

Jeanette wiped her hands on her apron and glanced over her shoulder at her friend. "So what if I have?"

"You'd better not let your Wally know that." Moira looked worried. "You know what a temper Wally's got. He's likely to do something bad to Mr. Peebles if he thinks he's after you."

"He wouldn't have no say in it." Jeanette grabbed a dishcloth in one hand and a wet plate in the other. "He's only me blinking boyfriend, not me husband."

"Don't matter." Moira carried the broken shells over to the oven and opened the door. A blast of hot air erupted from the searing red coals inside as she threw the shells into the furnace, sending sizzling golden sparks dancing up the chimney. "Wally thinks you belong to him, and he won't take kindly to another man mucking about with his girlfriend."

"Here, I never said he —"

Jeanette snapped her mouth shut as Miss Bunkle sailed into the kitchen, flapping her apron in front of her face to cool it off. "Great heavens it's hot in here. Did someone forget to close the door on the oven again?"

"No, Miss Bunkle." Moira scraped her hands down the front of her apron. "I've just been burning the egg shells, that's all."

"Well, get that door shut, girl, before we lose all the heat out of that stove. Michel will be here at any minute to start the evening meal. He won't be too happy if his oven's gone cold."

"Yes, Miss Bunkle." Moira slammed the heavy door shut and returned to the table, where the newly skinned eggs waited to be chopped.

Jeanette went on drying the dishes, her mind conjuring up a vision of Mr. Peebles chasing her around the bedroom, and her running slow enough for him to catch her.

The next morning Baxter seemed anxious to get back to his accounts, which according to him, had been badly mismanaged. He seemed in a sour mood, and barely acknowledged Cecily's reminder that she was meeting Phoebe and Madeline later that morning at Dolly's Teashop. Which, she told herself, gave her justification for neglecting to tell him that she planned to pay Dr. Prestwick a visit on the way. There was no sense in aggravating his temper. She would simply tell him about it later, when he'd recovered from whatever was displeasing him.

After giving him a loving kiss on the cheek, she left him to his work. Raymond was waiting for her outside when she emerged into the cold, clean sea air, and she was glad of her black marabou stole snuggled warmly around her shoulders as she settled down in the carriage.

Raymond had suggested they use one of the motor cars, but Cecily had declined. It was difficult enough getting used to the noise of the dratted things. She just hated the thought of riding in one. Although Baxter had hinted more than once that he would like to own a motor car, so far when he'd brought up the subject, she'd managed to steer the conversation to another topic.

Sooner or later, she knew she would have to accept the fact that this was the modern mode of transportation. But right now, she was determined to enjoy the steady jogging of the carriage wheels, and the soothing clip-clop of horses' hooves on the snow-dusted street.

The Esplanade always looked so deserted in the winter. Stretching in a graceful curve along the seafront, with only a low barrier of railings separating the street from the smooth golden beach, it seemed to be mourning the warm summer days when the tiny shops were bustling with customers and children with kites soaring behind them raced across the sands.

Right now the dismal row of shops huddled behind ugly boards that sheltered the windows from the winter storms. Few people braved the seafront in winter, and those who did hurried to their destinations, rather than dawdle and browse as they did in the height of the season.

The brisk tattoo of the horses' hooves kept up a steady pace as they turned up the hill into the town. Cecily's pulse quickened, her gaze eager to settle on fondly remembered places. Saint Bartholomew's, where the vicar, Phoebe's son, Algie, conducted his services in his stuttering, stammering manner that sent most of his parishioners into a doze before he was halfway through.

Cecily smiled, wondering how Algie was tolerating his new stepfather. Colonel Fortescue had been a regular guest at the Pennyfoot Hotel before he married Phoebe. Although most people held the opinion that the colonel's mind had been severely diminished by his earth-shattering experiences in the Boer War, a view that Cecily reluctantly shared, apparently the colonel had been astute enough to propose marriage to Phoebe Carter-Holmes. No doubt in the secure knowledge that the lady would take great pains in taking care of him as efficiently and as selflessly as she did her bumbling son.

Cecily was looking forward to hearing

more about Phoebe's union with the bizarre retired soldier. But first, her meeting with Dr. Prestwick demanded her attention.

As they reached the High Street, she was overjoyed to find that here the spirit of Christmas prevailed with a vengeance. Huge boughs of berry-laden holly and fir adorned just about every shop front in the High Street. Paper chains in red, green, yellow, and blue, cut into delicate and intricate patterns, graced windows full of seasonal fare. Rows of plucked ducks and geese hung by their feet in Abbitsons the Butchers, while Harris the Drapers had clothed its mannequins in swathes of red and green velvet.

By the time they reached the doctor's house, Cecily was thoroughly imbued with the spirit of the season. She was relieved to note that the usual row of carriages had not yet arrived when Raymond reined in the horses in front of the neat front garden. She had deliberately left early, hoping to arrive before the office opened. By the looks of things, she had succeeded.

After asking Raymond to wait, she rapped on the front door, her heart leaping with expectation at the thought of seeing the handsome doctor again. She had refrained from her customary habit of sending a calling card in the hopes of surprising him. She wanted to catch him off guard, so to speak. He was more likely to tell her what she wanted to know if he was unprepared for her visit.

She was most anxious to know exactly what Dr. Prestwick's opinion was of the death of Barry Wrotham. No doubt the good doctor would be hesitant to tell her anything at first, but in the past she'd been able to persuade him otherwise. She could only hope that she was still able to do so. So far, all she had were vague suspicions and theories. Nothing substantial upon which to base an investigation that, if she didn't take care, could very well lead her into a great deal of trouble.

She needed the doctor's complete cooperation. And if she was to solve this case before Mrs. Wrotham left for London, she needed it now.

Chapter 6

The front door of Dr. Prestwick's house opened abruptly to reveal a gray-haired woman wearing a cap and apron, her lined faced creased in a frown. "The doctor's not ready yet to receive patients," she said crisply, and started to close the door.

"Oh, I'm not a patient," Cecily called out. "I'm an old friend of the doctor's, here to pay him a short visit."

The woman peered around the door with a suspicious look on her face. "Do you have an appointment, madam?"

"Well, no," Cecily admitted. "But I'm quite sure if you tell the doctor that Mrs. Baxter is here to see him . . . no, wait. Perhaps you'd better tell him Cecily Sinclair."

The housekeeper's expression darkened. "Perhaps you should come back later," she said. "*After* you have made an appointment."

Right on the heels of her words came another voice, smooth and mellow, yet filled with surprise. "Cecily? It can't be." The housekeeper disappeared and the door was thrown wide.

The man who stood on the doorstep stared at Cecily as if she'd materialized out of thin air. "Good Lord. It is. I'd heard you were coming down to Badgers End, but I had no idea you were already here."

Cecily laughed up at him. "Kevin! You don't look a day older."

"And neither do you, my dear." He held out his hand. "In fact, if anything, you look younger. Do come in. This is such a pleasant surprise. At least, I hope it is." His piercing blue eyes narrowed. "You're not here as a patient, I trust?"

Putting her hand in his, Cecily allowed him to escort her into the narrow hallway. The familiar smell of disinfectant and furniture polish brought back so many memories. She looked about her, noticing at once that the walls of the waiting room had been papered with an embossed design of milkmaids and cows in shades of cream and brown. Rather pleasing, especially when one had to sit and wait with nothing better to look at.

"I'm quite well," she told Prestwick, in a delayed answer to his question. "I happened to be coming into town today to meet with Phoebe and Madeline, and I thought I'd take the opportunity to stop by and visit with you awhile."

At the mention of Madeline, she thought she saw a shadow cross the doctor's face.

"Ah, yes. Madeline. How is she? I haven't seen her in quite a few days."

"Really?" Cecily followed him into his office and took the chair he offered. "Then you must not have had much time to spare lately."

Prestwick's expression was evasive. "Do I detect a note of disapproval in that remark?"

Cecily laughed. "It's not my place to pass judgment on you. It's just that I thought you and Madeline . . . well, you know."

"Do I?" Prestwick shuffled some papers on the desk in front of him, his expression carefully bland. "Madeline and I are good friends, that's all. I enjoy her company. I trust she enjoys mine."

"I'm quite certain of that." Cecily hesitated, then added recklessly, "She cares about you a great deal. I do hope you don't do anything that will bring her pain. She's had a hard life. She deserves some happiness."

Prestwick's eyebrow twitched. "I have no

wish to hurt anyone, Cecily. But I'm sure you didn't come here to talk about Madeline."

Accepting his effort to change the subject, she said brightly, "No, of course I didn't."

"I didn't think so." Prestwick tilted his chair back and crossed his slender hands across his chest. "If I were to wager a bet, I'd say you're here to inquire about the recent death of one of our citizens, are you not?"

Cecily did her best to look offended. "Why, Kevin, whatever do you mean? I stopped by to visit with an old friend, that's all."

He bowed his head. "Then I misjudged you, my dear. Please accept my apologies."

"Of course."

"So you have no interest at all in the death of the late manager of the Pennyfoot Country Club."

She tilted her head to one side. "Should I?"

He threw back his head, and a roar of laughter erupted from his throat. "Cecily, Cecily, Cecily. You are as transparent as a pane of glass. How can you sit there and tell me you're not gasping to know every single detail of Barry Wrotham's premature demise."

She grinned happily at him. "Well, I must admit, my curiosity is somewhat piqued. After all, there does seem to be strange circumstances surrounding the accident. If it was an accident."

Prestwick shook his head, his mouth still curved in amusement. "You will never change, my dear, I'm happy to say. But I'm afraid this time you will be disappointed. There is no murderer lurking about Badgers End. I'm afraid you will have to curb your investigative instincts for a while. Barry Wrotham's death, sinister as it may appear, was an accident, pure and simple."

"May I ask how you arrived at that conclusion?"

Prestwick shrugged. "I don't see why not. There were no marks on the body indicating foul play. Death was by drowning. Wrotham was a regular visitor at the George and Dragon, and more than once left there with more in his belly than he could handle."

"You're saying he was intoxicated and fell into the well?"

"That's the official verdict, yes. P.C. Northcott ruled it as accidental and I signed the death warrant. Wrotham was buried a week or so ago."

"Do you have any idea of the time he died?"

Prestwick's eyes narrowed. "Cecily, if you know something I don't, perhaps you should tell me now. It could save us both a good deal of trouble later on."

Cecily folded her hands in her lap. "I don't know any more than you do, which is why I'm asking the questions. I simply want to settle things in my mind, nothing more."

Prestwick picked up a pencil and tapped it on the desk before answering. "As far as I could tell, Wrotham had been dead less than two hours before he was found."

"On Sunday afternoon?"

"Yes. Several people saw him in the George and Dragon at midday. It was his habit to stop there on his way home, since Sunday was his half-day off."

"Did anyone mention that he'd had too much to drink, or that he appeared to be intoxicated when he left?"

"Not as far as I know. As I said, there was no investigation."

"And no one has questioned why Barry Wrotham should be wandering around an abandoned farm all alone on a Sunday afternoon? He must have known it was deserted . . . how long has it been since the owner left?"

"At least a year, so I believe." Looking

serious now, Prestwick leaned forward. "If you want my advice, Cecily, let things be. There's no reason to suppose this is anything but an accident, and if you start poking around and asking questions, you're likely to raise the wrath of a few people, including our good friend, Inspector Cranshaw. I doubt if he'll have much patience with you, after all the trouble you caused him in the past."

Cecily raised her chin. "I solved more than one case for the inspector and P.C. Northcott. More often than not by asking questions and using my brains to sift out the truth. He should be thanking me, not condemning me."

Prestwick's lips twitched. "I doubt that will happen. But in this case, you are looking for something that isn't there. Tell me the truth now, isn't this just a case of you having missed all the excitement of tracking down villains? Aren't you trying just a little too hard to make a mountain out of an anthill?"

"I thought that was molehill."

"I like anthill better. Never could stand moles. They can do more damage to a garden in one night than a midwinter hailstorm."

Aware that he was deliberately changing

the subject again, Cecily gave in. "Very well, Kevin, if you are so certain this unfortunate event was an accident, I suppose I must accept it. But it was very nice to see you again. You must join us for dinner at the Pennyfoot soon." She rose from her chair, and straightened her hat with both hands. "I should take my leave before you are deluged with patients all clamoring for your attention."

Prestwick jumped up and hurried around the desk to her side. "It was a very great pleasure to see you, Cecily. I trust your husband is well?"

"Very well, thank you." Cecily moved to the door and waited for him to open it. "I hope we shall see you again soon?"

"Just as soon as I can find the time." He opened the door for her and stood back to let her pass. "I mean it, Cecily. Forget about Wrotham's death and just enjoy the Christmas Season. I'm sure you have more than enough to worry about with all the responsibilities of taking care of the Pennyfoot guests."

"I do indeed." She smiled up at him. "Thank you, Kevin. I'll remember you to Madeline. I'll be meeting with her in a few minutes."

Prestwick tightened his lips ever so

slightly. "Please, give her my regards."

Outside in the cruel bite of the wind, Cecily hurried down the path to where Raymond waited with the carriage. The horses stamped with impatience, steam drifting from their nostrils as they tossed their heads.

"Straight to Dolly's Teashop, Raymond," she told him, and tugged her stole more securely around her shoulders. She was looking forward immensely to Dolly's warm tearoom, a very hot cup of tea, and a warm, luscious Banbury cake.

For the time being she would try to forget about Barry Wrotham's bizarre death, though she had no intention of giving up on it. Too many people had their suspicions about the accident. In any case, she was a great believer in hunches, and this time the tingling in her bones was so acute she could feel her flesh creep.

There was something else bothering her at that moment, however. Something that demanded her immediate attention. There was no doubt in her mind that all was not well between Dr. Prestwick and her dear friend Madeline. And right then that was more important to her than the death of a man whom apparently no one liked.

Arriving at Dolly's Teashop, Cecily

paused in front of the square-paned window and gazed in admiration at the magnificent Christmas cakes on display. The center one was raised above the others, and had been painstakingly decorated in glittering white royal icing. Tiny silver sugar beads nestled in the thick white swirls circling the top and bottom, and red and green sprinkles dusted the smooth shell pattern around the edges. Miniature sprigs of holly had been piped at intervals in the border, and a green paper sleeve wrapped around the sides of the cake. It made Cecily's mouth water just looking at it.

The familiar tinkle of the bell as she opened the door warmed her instantly. She was pleased to see nothing had changed. The familiar fragrance of newly baked bread blended with the exotic aroma of ginger and nutmeg, every bit as heavenly as she remembered.

The china jugs and vases shared space with boughs of fir and mistletoe on the wide mantelpiece, the decorative plates still balanced on the picture rail, and the large copper coal scuttle stood guard in the hearth as always. Even the polished brass fender with the dent in the right-hand corner had not been replaced, much to her delight.

The room was crowded, as usual, and the air hummed with lowered voices and the occasional titter of laughter. To Cecily's delight, Madeline and Phoebe were already seated at their favorite table close to the fireplace, where enormous flames leapt and sputtered up the wide chimney.

Phoebe's face was partially hidden beneath the brim of her hat, which tilted at an alarming angle, threatening to dislodge the mound of fruit and feathers adorning it. Madeline, as usual, was hatless, and gloveless, and as always, the target of many disdainful stares which she blithely ignored.

Madeline's presence in the village had always been clouded with controversy. Most people were afraid of her, intimidated by tales of her mystic powers, which were mostly embroidered with half-truths. There was no doubt Madeline was capable of some things that defied explanation and, at times, had unsettled Cecily quite considerably. It was doubtful, however, if Madeline had half the capacity attributed to her . . . magical or otherwise.

Nevertheless, her reputation exceeded her abilities, and most people tended to avoid her whenever possible, unless desperate enough to brave her cottage in search of a potion to cure their ills.

Apparently blissfully unaware of the sensation she caused, Madeline waved vigorously at the sight of Cecily, while tapping Phoebe smartly on the arm to get her attention.

Cecily was halfway across the room, threading her way delicately between the tables, when a strident voice rang out, easily overwhelming the quiet voices around her.

"Mrs. Sinclair! I don't believe it! Whatever brings you back here?"

Cecily smiled at the woman lumbering toward her, her massive bosom narrowly missing the heads of her customers as she squeezed by them. "Dolly! How lovely to see you again!"

"Well, this is a surprise." Dolly's florid face was wreathed in smiles as she held out her two chubby hands and grasped Cecily's. "Let me look at you. Well, looks as if the Smoke hasn't done you any harm, that's for sure."

"Not at all." Cecily withdrew her hands and edged over to the table where Phoebe and Madeline were waiting. "And I see the teashop is still doing a wonderful business."

"Aye, that it is, thank the good Lord. How's that handsome manager of yours? No, wait. He's your husband now, isn't he." Dolly's rolls of fat jiggled as she uttered a deep belly laugh. "Can't call you Mrs. Sinclair now, can I. It's going to take some getting used to, remembering to call you Mrs. Baxter and that's a fact."

"It took a great deal of time before I was used to it." Cecily wiggled her gloved fingers at Phoebe and Madeline and sat down on the empty chair. "I do hope you still make those sublime Banbury cakes, Dolly. I've had the taste in my mouth for them ever since I arose this morning."

"That I do, Mrs. Sinclair. Oops!" Dolly's double chin wobbled as her hearty laugh rang out again. "There I go again. Mrs. Baxter, it is. I'll remember eventually. I'll send Letty in with the cakes right away. These ladies wanted to wait until you arrived." She wagged a thick finger at Madeline. "Shame on you for not telling me it was Mrs. Sinclair you were waiting for."

Madeline shrugged. "We thought you would enjoy the surprise."

"You mean Mrs. Baxter." Phoebe snickered behind her hand. "You should have seen your face, Dolly. You looked as if you'd seen a ghost."

"I thought I had for a moment." Dolly clamped her pudgy fingers down on Cecily's unsuspecting shoulder. "Come back here to live, have you?"

"Oh, no." Cecily smiled with genuine regret. "We're just here for the Christmas Season. Baxter and I are helping out at the Pennyfoot until Edward finds another manager."

"Ah, yes, after that poor bugger fell down the well. Serves him right, that's what I say. Never had a good word to say to anybody. That's what you get for drinking on an empty belly. Should have been looking where he was going. Pity, that it is." She shifted her huge body around and pointed it in the direction of the kitchen. "Hope you enjoy your tea and buns, ladies. Come and see me again, Mrs. Sin . . . Baxter, before you leave. And bring that nice-looking husband of yours with you the next time."

Phoebe simpered as Dolly strode off, bumping chairs with her hips as she went. "Can you imagine Baxter in here sipping tea and nibbling on Dolly's pastries?"

"He'd far rather be at the George and Dragon enjoying a pint of ale." Cecily glanced at Madeline. "I've just had a nice visit with Dr. Kevin Prestwick. He asked to be remembered to you."

A faint pink hue crept over Madeline's alabaster cheeks. "Thank you," she murmured.

Phoebe pounced immediately. "You haven't seen him lately? Didn't you tell us that he spent every moment of his spare time with you?"

Wishing she hadn't mentioned it, Cecily hurried to change the subject. "What is the colonel doing with his time while you are enjoying Dolly's delectable baking?"

Ignoring her, Phoebe leaned toward Madeline, her eyes probing the other woman's face. "He's seeing that hussy, Winifred Chesterton, isn't he."

Madeline's expression froze. "I haven't the slightest idea whom Dr. Prestwick is seeing, nor do I care."

"I knew it!" Phoebe sat back with a look of triumph. "I saw them together just the other day."

Giving Phoebe a reproachful frown, Cecily laid her hand on Madeline's arm. "I'm so sorry, Madeline. I had no idea."

Madeline lifted her shoulders. "I just didn't want to talk about it. That's why I didn't tell you. The doctor and I had a disagreement. I haven't seen him in quite some time."

"I'm so sorry to hear that. He didn't say anything . . ." Cecily let her voice trail off, not knowing quite what to say.

Even Phoebe had the grace to look contrite. "I'm sorry, too, Madeline. If I'd known this was serious, I would never —"

"It's quite all right," Madeline said, interrupting her. "Kevin has never made me any promises and I didn't expect anything from him."

"But you wanted to marry him," Phoebe said with her usual lack of tact.

"Phoebe —" Cecily began in protest, but Madeline raised her hand.

"No, she's quite right. I was rather hoping. It just didn't happen, that's all."

"What happened?" Cecily asked, abandoning all efforts to mind her own business. "When I left Badgers End, I was so sure you and Kevin were becoming close."

Madeline gave her a brave smile. "It wasn't meant to be, that's all. We have such differing views. He won't accept my methods of curing ills, and I can't accept his rigid beliefs."

"You argued about medicine?"

"Yes, we did. There are so many kinds of herbal medicine, some of which have been successfully used for centuries. Kevin dismisses anything that hasn't been invented in a laboratory, and won't even consider that nature has its own powers of healing. Even though he is fully aware that a great deal of modern medicine is synthetic re-creations of plants. After a while, the arguments became tiresome. One day I attempted to treat his headache with a potion of herbs and he was quite insulting. I just couldn't fight him anymore."

"I find that most distressing," Phoebe said, dabbing at actual tears in her eyes with her laced-edged handkerchief. "How sad that two people with the same magnificent purpose, to heal the poorly, can be so contrary in their ways to go about it. It's a great shame that you cannot find some kind of compromise, so that the ill can benefit from both means of treatment."

Once in a while, Cecily thought, smiling at her friend, Phoebe had a way of putting her finger right to the heart of the problem. "Phoebe's right," she said, laying her fingers on Madeline's arm. "Both you and Kevin have a wealth of knowledge and experience that could be a tremendous benefit to everyone if only you could find a way to share and accept each other's beliefs."

Madeline's lovely face creased in a frown. "Perhaps you should talk to Kevin.

He's the one who's being stubborn. He just won't listen to reason and I am tired of talking to deaf ears. As far as I'm concerned, we will do better apart." She gazed out of the window, saying brightly, "I wonder if we shall have a white Christmas this year."

Cecily heard the slight break in her voice, and her heart ached for Madeline. Sensing that she had said more than enough at the risk of upsetting her friend, however, she accepted the change of subject and glanced in the direction of the kitchen. "Now where on earth is that girl with my Banbury cakes?" she murmured. "I'm positively starving."

Chapter
7

An hour or so later Cecily bade her two friends farewell and once more approached the carriage that Raymond had brought back shortly before the appointed time.

Instead of returning directly to the Pennyfoot, however, on an impulse she asked Raymond to drive her out to the abandoned farm where Barry Wrotham had met his untimely end. It had occurred to her, while listening to Madeline and Phoebe bicker about the arrangements for the pantomime, that as long as there had been no investigation into the accident, it was quite unlikely that a thorough search had been conducted.

"Tell me," she asked Raymond as he helped her into the carriage, "has anyone bothered to look around the abandoned farmhouse?"

"You mean the one where Wrotham died? Not as far as I know, m'm." Raymond waited while she settled herself on the creaking leather seat. "Don't s'pose the bobbies saw any need to muck about out there, seeing as how they all swear it were an accident."

"No, I don't suppose so." Cecily looked him straight in the eye. "I wonder if the house is securely locked."

Raymond's eyes brightened with the light of adventure. He pretended to consider the matter, stroking his chin in a purely theatrical gesture. "Hmmm. Well, I reckon there's only one way to find out, m'm."

Cecily beamed. "Exactly what I was thinking, Raymond. If we are to do a little snooping, however, there's one thing I must ask of you."

Raymond grinned. "I won't say nuffing to nobody, m'm. Though I daresay nobody would be surprised. After all, everyone's heard plenty of tales in the village about how you chased after murderers and whatnot when you was owner of the Pennyfoot. Almost got done in yourself now and then, so the stories go."

"Really." Cecily tucked her hands in her muff. "Well, don't believe everything you hear, Raymond. Village tales have a way of growing out of proportion when passed from one eager tongue to another."

"Yes, m'm. But don't you worry. Me lips are sealed." He tightened his lips and drew his thumb across them. "On me honor."

"Thank you, Raymond. I'm sure I can trust you to keep your word." She settled back to enjoy the ride.

The road they took wound up the cliffs to cross Putney Downs, giving Cecily a wonderful view of the bay. Though the heavy clouds had turned the sea a dull gray and a thin mist hung over the water, the entire sweep of the Esplanade as well as the tiny cottages lining the cove were plainly visible. Not at all like the dense fog of London that obscured anything farther than ten yards away.

She didn't miss the city at all, Cecily realized as she watched the warm walls of the George and Dragon appear through the haze at the foot of the hill. She was perfectly content to be back in her beloved Badgers End, where the peace and quiet of the countryside was undisturbed by the infuriating honking of horns and the constant explosions and ugly black smoke of the motor cars.

About a mile and a half from the pub, Raymond steered the horses onto a gravel road, where they jogged for a few more yards before coming to a halt in front of wide wooden gates. Raymond hopped down and pushed open the gates, then climbed back to urge the horses through before climbing back down to close the gates behind them.

Now they were on a rutted track than ran alongside a harvested cornfield. The cold weather had hardened the earth, and the wheels bumped and bounced as they made their way to another pair of gates, where Raymond went through the procedure of opening and shutting them once more. At last they arrived at a courtyard in front of what appeared to be stables, and the horses clattered to a halt.

Cecily climbed down from the carriage, shivering in the cutting breeze that chilled her bones. She followed Raymond around the side of the stables, picking her way carefully between the deep ruts dug by centuries of wagon wheels.

Raymond led her through another gate and up a winding garden path, lined with straggly weeds and long, unmown grass. The windows of the rambling farmhouse blinked ominously through their shrouds of dust, and a loose drainpipe rattled in the wind.

The heavy front door refused to budge when Raymond tried the handle. "Looks like it's locked tight, m'm," he said, his expression taut with anticipation.

"Well then, I suppose we shall just have to find another way in," Cecily said calmly.

Raymond's eyes lit up with delight. "Yes, m'm. That we shall." He stood back and studied the front of the house. "Can't see no broken windows or nothing. You just hang on here, m'm, and I'll take a quick gander around the back."

He disappeared, and Cecily huddled in the doorway in a vain attempt to escape the cold bite of the wind. The entire place appeared to be utterly deserted. A dilapidated broken-down wagon with one wheel missing sat in the courtyard, and several broken barrels lay on their side nearby. One of the doors to the stable must have lost its latch, since it swung dismally back and forth in the wind, its hinges groaning in protest.

Overhead, seagulls wheeled in search of food, their endless cries echoing across the rooftop of the decaying farmhouse. It was a mournful sound and tugged at Cecily's heart. A family had lived and thrived here once, until the encroaching industrial revolution had taken its toll on the farmers, robbing so many of their livelihoods.

She was a staunch advocate of modern

technology and the benefits it could bring. As she had argued with Baxter many times, sacrifices had to be made in the pursuit of progress. But there were times when it saddened her to think how much a modern society had cost in traditions and customs that had been an essential part of life for centuries. How unfortunate that in the interests of improving one way of life, another was forced to disappear.

A faint tinkle of glass somewhere in the distance interrupted her thoughts. She stepped out from the doorway, looking anxiously from right to left. It wouldn't do for her to be caught intruding on someone's property uninvited.

It only occurred to her at that moment that in her anxiety to search the farmhouse, she had broken her promise to Baxter. He would be most displeased with her if he knew she had ventured into forbidden territory without notifying him first.

To her relief, nothing moved but the leaves and a stray piece of paper tossed along the ground by the wind. Her curiosity aroused, she was about to go after it when the handle on the door rattled and the hinges squealed as it slowly opened inward.

Raymond's face peered out at her, one cheek smeared with dirt. "Funny thing, m'm," he murmured as he stepped back to let her in. "I was leaning me elbow against one of the windows and it sort of caved in."

"Goodness." Cecily peered at his elbow. "You didn't hurt yourself, I hope."

"No, m'm. You see, I was holding me coat over me elbow at the time."

"Yes, I do see." She straightened. "You must have leaned rather hard, Raymond."

He grinned with pride. "Yes, m'm. Reckon I did."

"Well, it can't be helped." She nodded her approval. "Thank you, Raymond."

"My pleasure, m'm." He turned and waved his hand at the darkened hallway. "Don't seem to be much in here, though. No furniture or nothing."

"Well, I suppose it won't cost us anything to look." Cecily moved down the hallway and peered into what once must have been the parlor. The room was quite empty, with just a small stove standing forlorn in one corner. Trying not to imagine a family huddled around its warmth, she turned her back on the desolate room.

"I think I'll take a look in the upstairs rooms, Raymond. Perhaps you should stay down here and keep an eye on the court-yard, just in case we should have a surprise visitor."

Raymond pulled his cap from his head and touched his forehead with it. "Right you are, m'm. I'll whistle if I see anybody."

"A good idea. Please do." She started up the narrow staircase, each one squeaking as she stepped on it. The dark clouds outside allowed little light to filter through the grimy windows, and she made her way carefully down the upstairs hallway, wary of stepping on a loose board in the gloom and turning her ankle.

She reached the door of the first room and peered inside. It was completely bare, and abandoning it, she moved on to the next room.

Stepping inside, she looked cautiously around. The bedroom was quite large, with a huge window overlooking the fields at the back of the house. She could see nothing in there but a rolled-up blanket against one wall and a tattered magazine lying next to it. The musty smell wrinkled her nose, and she could see her breath form in front of her face as she moved cautiously across the room.

The magazine bearing the previous month's date had a picture of the very latest fashion in outerwear on the cover. As she bent closer to peer at it, the floor popped loudly beneath her feet, making her jump. Her heart, galvanized by the unexpected sound, pounded with an urgency that made her uncomfortable.

Taking a last look around, she was about to leave when she spied something outside the window. An enterprising robin had built a nest on the broad windowsill. She smiled, imagining the tiny eggs hatching and each fledgling balanced precariously on the very edge of the carefully constructed nest, awaiting its first fluttering leap into the air.

She turned away from the window and was about to retreat from the room when she spied a tiny glint of light in front of the rolled-up blanket. She hurried toward it and crouched down, tilting her head this way and that to catch the sparkle again. Then she saw it. Half-hidden beneath the woolen blanket, a long pin lay caught between the floorboards.

In her attempt to pry it loose, Cecily thrust the blanket aside. As she did so, something fell out and rolled noisily across the floor, scaring her half to death. A long-necked bottle smacked against the opposite wall and lay still.

Leaving it for the moment, Cecily returned to her task. At last she pulled the pin from its resting place and examined it. No wonder it had sparkled in the light. It was a gold hat pin, adorned with a large diamond at one end. A very expensive hat pin. Certainly not the kind one would expect a farmer's wife to possess.

Her excitement rising, Cecily shook out the blanket. The quality of the material was excellent, and it appeared to have had little use. Hardly any dust rose from it, suggesting that it had recently been left there. Clearly not a year ago, when presumably the owners had left, according to Kevin.

Finding nothing more in the folds of the blanket, Cecily rolled it up again and left it where she had found it. The label on the bottle declared its contents to have been an excellent cognac. Again, not something one would normally find in a farmer's house.

Unless this particular farmer had been unusually wealthy, and that seemed unlikely judging by the general state of the house and the broken-down wagon outside, then it would seem that Emily Wrotham's suspicions could very well be right.

Her husband might well have been indulging in an illicit liaison when he visited the farm that day. If so, it was quite possible that a rival for the lady's affections had rid himself of his opponent. A just end, perhaps, but an illegal one, nevertheless.

Cecily rose to her feet. She had promised the grieving widow to find out the truth. She wasn't at all certain that Emily Wrotham would welcome evidence that bore out her suspicions.

After placing the bottle back behind the blanket, Cecily pinned the hat pin onto her bodice and covered it with her stole. Then she made her way down the creaking staircase to the hallway below.

Raymond emerged from the parlor as she reached the foot of the stairs. "Find anything, m'm?"

"Nothing of interest." She nodded at the rooms down the hall. "I'll just take a hasty peek down here."

"Very well, m'm. I'll wait on the doorstep if you don't mind. The smell in here is getting up me nose."

She could sympathize with him. The unpleasant odor of damp and mildew was much stronger downstairs. "Of course. I shan't be more than a minute or two." She hurried down the hallway and into each room, not really surprised to find nothing but more dust and cobwebs. Barry Wrotham had chosen well . . . a large, fairly comfortable room, certainly less damp, at the back of the house, hidden from prying eyes of anyone who might wander into the courtyard.

That's if it *were* Barry Wrotham, she reminded herself. It could have been anyone dallying with some dolly in an abandoned house. But then, why else would a man lie to his wife and visit a deserted farm, with seemingly no interest in buying it? It would seem that the Pennyfoot's ex-manager was hiding something, and another woman would appear to be the most likely answer.

Nevertheless, past experience had taught her never to jump to conclusions, and until she had absolute proof, she would have to keep her deductions to herself for the time being.

Raymond stood waiting for her when she stepped out onto the porch, his face pinched with cold. She could actually hear his teeth chattering as he handed her back into the carriage. "Straight home," she told him, "and when you get back, you may tell Michel I ordered a glass of brandy for you. It will help warm your insides."

Raymond touched the peak of his cap. "Thank you, m'm. Much obliged." He clambered up onto his seat and gave the impatient horses their reins. The carriage bumped and swayed across the rutted ground, crunched down the gravel path, and then they were off down the coast road to the Pennyfoot.

The midday meal had already been served when Cecily arrived back at the club. Miss Bunkle was in the foyer and gave Cecily a disapproving frown as she hurried through the front door.

"Mr. Baxter has been asking for you, madam," she said. "He sounded quite concerned. I told him Raymond had gone to fetch you from the teashop more than an hour ago. I've been expecting him back long before this."

"Thank you, Miss Bunkle," Cecily said brightly. "Please don't blame Raymond. It was my fault. I detained him. I'll have a word with Mr. Baxter right away."

"Thank you, madam." Miss Bunkle bowed her head, then glided away across the floor, her back as stiff as a ship's mast.

Cecily pulled a face. The woman performed her duties admirably, by all accounts, but Cecily much preferred the sometimes muddled, befuddled, but always well-meaning methods of Altheda Chubb. Life had been so much more fun in the old days at the Pennyfoot.

Aware that her disgruntled mood was due more to her imminent confrontation with her husband than any discord with Miss Bunkle, Cecily headed for Baxter's office.

He rose immediately as she entered after the briefest of taps on the door. Rounding the desk with an alacrity that surprised her, he grasped her by the arms and looked keenly into her face.

"Cecily, are you all right? Where the devil have you been? I've been half out of my mind with worry, imagining all sorts of dire calamities. What happened to you? Miss Bunkle said Raymond had left over an hour ago to fetch you back. What took you so long?"

She laughed up at him. "Dearest, if you would just stop firing questions at me, I'll do my best to explain."

He pulled her close and gave her a brief hug before letting her go. "Sit down, and tell me where you have spent the better part of this day."

She sat, wondering how she would find the words to explain why she had broken her word to him. "I don't suppose you have anything to eat in here?" She gave him her most appealing smile. "I'm quite cold and extremely hungry."

"I'm not surprised. You missed the midday meal." He reached for the bell rope and tugged on it. "I'll have the kitchen bring something for you."

"Thank you, darling. You are so incredibly thoughtful. I really don't know what I would do without you. I am such a fortunate woman."

His eyes narrowed in suspicion. "That sounds ominous."

She gave him an innocent stare. "What does, dearest?"

"All those expansive compliments. I fear you are leading up to something."

"Well, really." She managed a light laugh. "Can't a woman compliment her husband without risk of being accused of insincerity?"

"Oh, I don't doubt that you are sincere. It's your choice of time to compliment me that gives me reason to question your motive."

A sharp tap on the door saved her from answering. She waited while Baxter gave Jeanette his order, and tried not to notice the girl's curious glance directed at her as she turned to leave.

The door closed behind her, and Cecily

braced herself for Baxter's inevitable inquisition.

"All right," he said. "While we are waiting for your meal to arrive, perhaps you can enlighten me as to why you have been missing for the last several hours."

"I did tell you I was meeting Phoebe and Madeline for elevenses, did I not?"

"You did." Baxter returned to his chair and sat down, his hands folded across his chest. "But upon inquiring as to your whereabouts, I was informed that you had left here shortly after ten o'clock. Which meant you would have arrived in the town at twenty past ten. It is now —" He pulled his watch from his waistcoat pocket and examined it, then snapped it shut and replaced it in his pocket. "— a quarter past two. I hardly think it took you four hours to consume one or two of Dolly's buns and a cup of tea."

"Banbury cakes, actually."

His eyes narrowed. "Cecily, please tell me what are you keeping from me."

Although his attitude irked her, she could hardly ignore the warning in his voice. "Oh, very well. I took the opportunity to call on Dr. Prestwick before I went to the teashop. I wanted to ask him a few questions, that's all."

"I thought as much." His voice was perfectly calm, but a pink patch on each side of his face made Cecily uneasy. "Why didn't you mention to me that you intended to see him?"

"I meant to, but you charged off to the office with no more than a faint peck on my cheek, and didn't give me time to tell you anything."

"So you thought you'd punish me by sneaking off to see an ex-suitor of yours."

She stared at him, her resentment fading. "Why, Hugh darling, I do believe you are jealous."

He drummed his fingers on the table. "Do I have reason to be?"

She burst out laughing. "Of course not. You know very well how much I adore you. No man could ever live up to you. I simply wanted to ask Kevin some questions about Barry Wrotham's accident. I swear."

To her immense relief, his stern features relaxed. "I see. So you do agree Wrotham's death was an accident, then."

"I didn't say that."

"No, you didn't." He sighed. "I don't know why I live in such hopes."

She laughed. "Come now, darling. We agreed that I should look into this, did we not?"

"We also agreed that you would not conduct an investigation without informing me about it first."

"You are quite right. I'm sorry. But you really were in rather a hurry this morning."

"Very well. I'll accept that."

"Good." She took a deep breath. "Then I hope you'll also accept the fact that I acted purely on impulse when I left the teashop and went to search the farmhouse where Barry Wrotham died."

His expression worried her. Perhaps this time she had gone too far. She closed her eyes and waited for the inevitable explosion.

Chapter
8

A deep flush consumed Baxter's cheeks. He half rose from his chair, then sat down again. "You did *what?*"

"I just thought I'd have a quick look around," Cecily said hurriedly. "No one was there and Raymond accompanied me so I was perfectly safe."

"That's not the point, is it." His disapproving gaze seemed to pierce her heart. "We specifically agreed —"

"You're right, darling. I'm most terribly sorry. But I really didn't see any danger in it."

"You never do. What about the time you visited a certain dentist without telling me why you were going? You didn't see any danger in that, either. I almost lost you that time."

"Well, yes, I do admit, that was rather a mistake."

Baxter muttered an oath under his breath and buried his forehead in his hands. "Cecily, what is the point of promising me something if you don't intend to keep it? I thought I could trust you."

"And you can, darling. Really. You know how I am. I get an idea in my head, and before I know it, I've popped off to take care of it."

"You will very likely pop right off this earth if you cannot control your wickedly impulsive streak." He lifted his head. "What do I have to do to make you understand that I am responsible for your welfare, and by breaking your promise to me, you are making my task terribly difficult, if not downright impossible?"

Cecily bent her head and tried to sound suitably contrite. "I do understand, Hugh, really I do. I swear it won't happen again." She laid a hand against her breast. "Upon my heart, I swear."

He was prevented from answering by the arrival of Jeanette bearing a tray loaded with cold chicken and ham, wedges of cheddar cheese, slices of apples and pears, pickled onions, and crusty bread. The meal was accompanied by a jug of cider and two glasses. The maid waited for Baxter to clear a space on his desk before laying down the tray.

Baxter sat in silence until she'd left the

room, then filled both glasses with cider, one of which he offered Cecily. "This should help warm you. You still look pinched with cold."

"I am." She took the glass and sipped the golden liquid. "I told poor Raymond to ask Michel for a brandy. He was chilled to the bone."

"No wonder Michel has ordered such a large supply of brandy. It's bad enough he drinks the stuff all day long, but if he's giving it to the staff as well, we shall soon see our profits disappearing in a haze of alcohol."

Cecily wrinkled her nose at him. "He had to order extra brandy for the Christmas puddings. He told me he would begin steaming them this week. Besides, Raymond had to wait quite some time in the cold air for me. I thought he well deserved a brandy."

"Raymond is young. His body can adapt much more efficiently than yours."

"Are you suggesting I am old?"

"I wouldn't dare."

"Good. I would hope that you are far too much of a gentleman to remind me that I am older than you."

"Are you? I'd quite forgotten that."

She beamed at him. "Darling Hugh. You

always know exactly the right thing to say. No wonder Miss Bunkle gazes at you with such adoration in her eyes."

His contemptuous snort delighted her. She reached for a wedge of cheese and a hunk of bread. "This is so much fun. Like picnicking, only more comfortable. I never did see the enjoyment in sitting in a field tormented by ants and bees."

Baxter munched on a slice of apple before replying. "I remember quite well that you used to adore sitting in a field with me."

"Ah, yes, well . . . I wasn't thinking about the ants and the bees then."

"Am I to take it that the bloom has gone off the romance now?"

She grinned happily at him. "Nothing could ever take the bloom from my passion for you, my love. But you must admit, this is so much more cozy than sharing your meal with a herd of curious cows."

"Indubitably."

"By the way, you seem to be enjoying my lunch. Did you not eat in the dining room?"

"I didn't have much of an appetite. I hate dining alone. I did far too much of it in my life."

"I'm sorry, darling. From now on I'll

make every effort to be here at mealtimes. Now let me tell you about our plans for the pantomime. Which reminds me, we need to order a large tree for the library."

Baxter munched in companionable silence while she divided her time between elaborating on her conversation with Madeline and Phoebe and avidly devouring the delectable offerings on the tray.

After a while, Baxter leaned back with a satisfied sigh. "Well, did you find anything at the farmhouse to justify your visit?"

She struggled with her conscience for several seconds before finally blurting out, "I found a hat pin. That's all. Oh, and an empty bottle of cognac."

He sighed. "Well, I hope you're satisfied. If the constables couldn't find anything to indicate a murder had been committed, I'm sure you won't find anything either."

"Perhaps, but I don't intend to give up just yet." She dabbed at the corners of her mouth with her serviette. "After all, I promised Emily Wrotham I would find out why her husband lied about working on his afternoon off when he was actually wandering around an abandoned farm for no apparent reason."

Baxter's eyes turned rather bleak. "Why is it you have no trouble keeping your promises to everyone except me?"

She rose at once and hurried to his side. After placing a kiss on his cheek, she murmured, "Because, my darling, sometimes you extract promises from me that are miserably challenging to keep."

"Only because I care about your safety. I would be lost without you."

"And I you. So please don't fret so much. I'm really quite good at taking care of myself."

"I'll remind you of those words the next time you find yourself in dire peril."

"Piffle. I learned my lesson long ago. I watch my step with the utmost vigilance now."

"As you have demonstrated today."

She straightened. "There are times, Baxter, when I'm quite tempted to poke a finger in your eye."

To her immense satisfaction, he laughed out loud. "There, you see? You are still playing with fire."

"Then perhaps I'd better leave before I'm burned."

"Well, before you go, I have some news for you. Samuel and Daisy arrived earlier."

"Bax! Why on earth didn't you tell me before!" Cecily glanced at the pendulum clock on the wall behind him. "How long ago? Where are they now?"

"I didn't tell you because I didn't want you flying out of here without putting some food in your stomach. Besides, I believe they have taken our godchildren for a walk along the beach with Mrs. Chubb and Gertie."

"In this weather?" Cecily hurried to the door. "I do trust they wrapped up those babies warmly enough. That wind is so bitter."

"I imagine Gertie knows how to take care of her children by now."

She looked back at him. "We are talking about *Gertie*."

"Ah, yes. I see what you mean." He smiled. "Perhaps you should go after them and make sure all is well."

"Exactly what I had in mind." She blew him a kiss. "Until later, my love."

"Very well, and please, do try to stay out of trouble."

If she hadn't felt so guilty about breaking her promise to him, she would have made some sharp retort. There were times when Baxter made her feel as inadequate as a juvenile. On the other hand, it was rather comforting to know he worried about her so.

She left him frowning over his ledgers,

and went in search of her special guests. After checking with the desk clerk to make sure the party hadn't yet returned, she made for the front doors.

The clouds had thinned when she stepped outside again, and patches of blue sky promised a clear, cold evening with the nip of frost in the air.

Apart from the holly wreaths on the hotel doors, there was little to indicate the festive season as Cecily made her way down the Esplanade. Yet the very essence of Christmas was in the air, so prevalent, yet also elusive and impossible to define. It was more a feeling, she decided. An air of expectancy, as if everyone knew something very special was forthcoming, and the whole world was full of excited anticipation.

The dusting of snow had melted, leaving a sparkling dry pavement to walk on. Guessing that her visitors had headed toward the town, Cecily hurried in that direction, and it wasn't long before she spied the straggling group in the distance.

The twins hopped excitedly from one side of the pavement to the other, while Mrs. Chubb did her best to restrain them from darting out into the street. Gertie and Daisy appeared to be deep in conversation, while Samuel, who looked exactly the same as he had the last time Cecily had seen him, gazed out to sea as he lagged behind the rest of the group.

Mrs. Chubb saw Cecily first, and lifted her gloved hand in greeting. The twins rushed headlong toward her, and Cecily leaned down to catch them both in her arms. She gave the two wriggling bodies a hug, then let them go, envying them their abundance of energy.

Daisy dipped a curtsey as she reached her and Samuel pulled off his cap. "It's lovely to see you, madam," Daisy said, her dark eyes alight with excitement in her pretty face. "I can't tell you how good it is to be back in Badgers End."

"Yeah," Samuel agreed. "I forgot how good it smells down here. A lot different than the Smoke. You can breathe deep without choking."

Cecily laughed. "How wonderful to see you all. Just like old times. All we need now are Doris and Ross to complete our reunion."

"Doris will be down by the end of the week, m'm," Daisy said, grabbing hold of James, who seemed intent on climbing over the railing to the beach.

"I want to dig in the sand!" James

howled in protest.

"Me, too. Me, too!" Lillian jumped up and down, dislodging the bright red tam-o'-shanter from her head.

"They're tired," Mrs. Chubb said. "All this excitement is wearing them out."

"When's Father Christmas coming?" James demanded, dragging his boots as Daisy pulled him along.

"He don't come to naughty boys and girls," Daisy told him sternly. "So you'd better be good."

"Don't want to be good." James dug in his heels, jerking Daisy to a halt.

"Come 'ere," Gertie said, taking his hand. "If you don't behave, I'll tell your papa what a bad boy you are when he gets here."

The threat had the desired effect, and the twins allowed themselves to be led by the hand once more.

"Let's all go back to the hotel," Cecily suggested, "and we'll have tea and crumpets in the library by the fire."

Gertie fanned herself with an imaginary fan. "Blimey! Fancy me taking tea and crumpets with madam in the library. I never would have imagined it in the old days."

Cecily laughed. "Well, don't tell anyone,

but according to the rules, which are ridiculously strict, none of us are supposed to be in the library unless we have membership in the club. Then again, some rules are just begging to be broken."

Mrs. Chubb looked worried. "We don't want to get anyone into trouble. Perhaps we should have tea in the kitchen instead. After all, that's where we're used to having it."

"Nonsense," Cecily said briskly. "As long as I am managing the hotel, I'll entertain my guests where I please. Now come along, everyone. It's really getting quite cold out here."

"Looks like snow again," Samuel observed, his gaze on the clouds gathering over the turbulent ocean.

"Well, I hope it waits until my better half gets down here." Gertie made a grab for Lillian's hand. "I don't want him stuck on the train halfway between here and Edinburgh."

"Or Doris on the way down from London for that matter." Cecily smiled at Samuel. "I'm sure you must be anxious for her to arrive. I'm really looking forward to seeing her myself. I want to ask her to help us with the Christmas pantomime. Do you think she'll agree?"

Samuel shrugged. "I reckon she will. That's all she ever thinks about these days, is her singing. Never has time for me no more."

"Samuel's just about given up on Doris, m'm," Daisy put in. "Can't say as I blame him. He never sees her anymore. She's always busy with the theater."

"And her admirers. Lined up at the stage door, they are. I don't get a look-in these days."

"I'm sorry to hear that," Cecily said in dismay. "I always thought that you and Doris were meant for each other."

Samuel gave her a trace of a grin. "Ah well, I'll survive. Lots more fish in the sea, so they say."

Disturbed by the news, Cecily led the group back to the Pennyfoot. First Madeline and Kevin, now Doris and Samuel. They had all seemed so happy with each other just a short two years ago. She was so fond of them all, it was sad to see them break apart. It would seem that everything was changing after all.

She'd taken a special interest in Doris and Daisy ever since the girls had arrived at the Pennyfoot, looking far too young and fragile for the heavy work of a scullery maid. At first it had been impossible to tell them apart — but it soon became obvious that Daisy was by far the stronger and couldn't sing a note in tune, while her more delicate twin had the voice of an angel.

Cecily had been happy for Doris's success on the stage, but she could only hope that the child hadn't sacrificed her future happiness to follow her dream.

By that evening the delectable aroma of Michel's Christmas puddings permeated the entire first floor of the Pennyfoot. The fragrance of nutmeg, lemon rind, and allspice even reached to the second floor, causing Cecily to pause with her nose sniffing the air as she emerged from her suite behind Baxter.

"Now it really smells like Christmas," she said, with a long sigh of satisfaction. "I just hope Michel remembered to put in the silver threepenny pieces. I can hardly wait for the dinner on Christmas Day. No matter how much goose and rib roast I eat, the second Michel carries in that pudding flaming in brandy, I'm hungry all over again."

Baxter gave her a fond smile. "Is there ever a time when you're not hungry? For a woman of your pleasing figure, you have a remarkable appetite and a capacity to satisfy it without any of it settling on your waistline."

She raised her eyebrows at him. "I'm not sure if you've just paid me a compliment or handed me an insult."

He placed an affectionate arm about her shoulders. "I would never have the audacity to insult you, my love."

"Or the courage."

He sighed. "That, too. I have no doubt as to who would fare the worst."

"I'm happy that you recognize the folly of such a hazardous venture."

He was about to answer when the sound of voices raised in harmony interrupted her. "Listen," she said, lifting her hand to her ear. "It sounds as if our carol singers have arrived."

"It does, indeed." He offered her his arm and together they descended the curving staircase to the first floor.

Ten or so carol singers stood formed in a semicircle in the foyer, while the beautiful refrain of "O Little Town of Bethlehem" echoed down the hallway.

Standing in the corner watching them, one hand possessively grasping his wife's elbow, Sir John Gilroy looked impressive in black coattails and a white bow tie. At his side, Lady Lucille was magnificent in pearl pink satin, the ostrich feathers in her hair matching exactly the shade of her gown.

Lionel Fitzhammer hovered just a little too close to her, while she quite obviously ignored him. Lionel's wife, Barbara, seemed to fade into the background as usual.

Catching sight of the couple she and Gertie had passed on the stairs, Cecily nudged Baxter's arm. "You haven't met our distinguished guests as yet. I think we should go over there so that I can introduce you."

Baxter cast a glance across the room. "I wasn't aware you had met them."

"I haven't met them all. But since they are all standing over there together, I think this would be a good time." Without giving him any time to argue, she skirted the carolers and headed for the group, who seemed on the point of leaving as she approached.

She greeted Sir John and his wife, then introduced Baxter to them. Sir John, in turn, introduced the Fitzhammers. The handsome gentleman from the stairs and his wife proved to be Roger Peebles and his wife, Gretchen, leaving the fourth couple, older than the rest by a good ten years Cecily judged, to be Percy and

Amelia Chatsworth. After exchanging some pleasantries, the group bade them good night and made their way to the front doors. As they left, Cecily glimpsed snow falling thick and fast, covering the roofs of a row of shiny motor cars lined up outside. No doubt the Benchers were seeking more excitement than the Pennyfoot offered that evening. She really needed to start working on the pantomime.

"They seem pleasant enough," Baxter remarked, just as the carolers began a rousing chorus of "God Rest Ye Merry Gentlemen."

"I suppose so, though I can't say I care for the way Mr. Fitzhammer leers at Lady Lucille."

Baxter stared at her in amusement. "You wish he paid a little more attention to you, perhaps?"

"Great heavens, no." Cecily shook her head in disgust. "I simply fail to see why the man can't be satisfied with the woman he married. It's obvious he ignores poor Mrs. Fitzhammer. If I were her, I'd be fluttering my eyelashes at the handsome Roger Peebles. That would give Lionel something to think about."

"And what about Peebles's wife? Don't you think she'd mind if Mrs. Fitzhammer ogled her husband?"

Cecily shrugged. "Mrs. Peebles appears quite able to take care of herself. I think the person who is made most uncomfortable is Lady Lucille. She pretends indifference, but I think she's wary of her husband's wrath over Fitzhammer's lechery."

"If you ask me, Gilroy seems unaware of anything amiss." Baxter gave her arm a little shake. "I think you are making far too much of all this. The four men are obviously good friends, and their wives seem happy enough. You have quite enough on your mind without concerning yourself about the private affairs of our guests."

She smiled at him. "You're quite right. Let us enjoy this beautiful singing, and when they are finished, we'll take them down to the kitchen to enjoy some hot cocoa and shortbread. I asked Miss Bunkle to order some in. It's a shame Mrs. Chubb is no longer the housekeeper. She made excellent shortbread. Michel is a wonderful chef but he can't make pastries as well as Mrs. Chubb."

"Perhaps we should hire a pastry chef," Baxter suggested.

"It's worth considering, I suppose." Cecily sighed, thinking of the days when she could enjoy her ex-housekeeper's fluffy cream slices and chocolate eclairs.

By the time the carolers had ended their recital, the foyer had become quite crowded with onlookers. Cecily spied Miss Bunkle at the head of the kitchen stairs and made her way over there with Baxter close behind her.

"I have invited the singers to the kitchen," Cecily told the housekeeper when she'd reached her. "I thought they might enjoy some hot cocoa and short-bread."

"Very well, madam. I'll see to it." Miss Bunkle peered at Cecily's chest. "It's none of my business, madam, but are you aware you have a hat pin lodged in your bodice? It doesn't look too secure. It wouldn't do to lose it."

Cecily glanced down at the hat pin, which had worked itself loose from the folds of her shirtwaist. She had quite forgotten she'd pinned it there. Until now it had been hidden under a pleat. "Oh, thank you, Miss Bunkle. You're quite right. I should hate to lose it." She could sense Baxter's intense gaze on her as she fastened the pin securely once more.

"Funny thing, madam," Miss Bunkle said, staring at the pin. "One of our guests asked me not too long ago if I had a hat pin she could borrow since she'd mislaid hers. I thought she might have dropped it somewhere here in the club. You didn't happen to find that one, did you?"

Cecily looked her straight in the eye. "I can assure you, Miss Bunkle, this pin was not lost in the Pennyfoot."

Miss Bunkle nodded. "Excuse me for asking, madam. I was just wondering, that's all."

"That's quite all right, Miss Bunkle. Please see that our carolers have their fill of refreshments." She turned to leave, then paused, looking back at the housekeeper. "By the way, do you happen to remember the name of the guest who mislaid the hat pin?"

She hoped that she was the only one to hear Baxter's sharp intake of breath.

"I remember very well," Miss Bunkle said, looking smug. "She's here tonight. It was Sir John Gilroy's wife, Lady Lucille."

Chapter 9

"It has to be mere coincidence, of course," Baxter said as he accompanied Cecily down the hallway. "I seriously doubt that the wife of a Master of the Bench would be visiting a farmhouse in this remote village. Especially since the house has been empty for a good many months. What would be her purpose?"

"What, indeed?" Cecily murmured. "Unless she had an assignation with someone there."

"Are you suggesting that Lady Lucille was meeting a lover?" Baxter demanded, obviously put out by the very idea.

"Not at all," Cecily said innocently. "As you say, it was simply a coincidence. Lady Lucille lost a hat pin. I found one. It doesn't mean it's the same one."

"But you intend to ask her about it anyway," said Baxter, a little desperately.

"Well, there is something I'd like to look at first." She paused in front of Baxter's office. "I'd like to have a peek at the ledgers."

Baxter frowned. "May I ask why?"

"Certainly." She glanced down the hallway to make sure they were alone. "I noticed there was a fairly new register on the counter this morning. I assume you have the previous one in the safe?"

"Yes, I do. Jeanette brought it into me last night."

"Good." She looked pointedly at the lock. "You do have the key, I hope?"

"Of course." He drew a ring of keys from his pocket and fitted one into the lock. "You still haven't told me why you want to examine the register."

"I'm curious, that's all. I would just like to know when the Gilroys' previous visit took place."

He paused, one hand holding the door closed. "Cecily, I don't think I like this. I hope you're not imagining —"

"I'm not imagining anything, darling. I simply want to look. There's no harm in that, is there?"

He sighed and pushed the door open. "I suppose not. But I have that nasty feeling again that this is going to lead us right into trouble."

"Piffle. You worry far too much about things that might never happen."

She waited impatiently for him to retrieve the ledger from the safe. He laid it on the desk for her, and she opened it, flipping feverishly through the pages until she found what she wanted — the scrawled signature of Sir John Gilroy. Underneath, one below the other, lay the signatures of the other three Benchers. Apparently all four were accustomed to visiting the Pennyfoot together.

Cecily pointed to Gilroy's signature and slid her finger across the line, uttering a soft exclamation of triumph as she did so.

"What is it?" Baxter asked, leaning forward to peer over her shoulder at the page.

"Look at this." Cecily tapped the spot with her finger. "They were all here three weeks ago. The same time that Barry Wrotham met with his accident."

Baxter straightened. "That doesn't mean they had anything to do with it. Cecily, I must emphatically warn you. These people are extremely influential. They are Barristers-at-Law, for heaven's sake. The governing body of the Inns of Court. Think what it would mean if you even suggested they might be involved in something as ugly as murder. Not only would their reputation suffer, they could bring the entire world down on our heads. It could even mean the end of the Pennyfoot if they chose."

"You are dashing far ahead of me," Cecily said, closing the ledger with a snap. "I'm not going to rush up to them and accuse one of them of murdering Mr. Wrotham."

"Thank heavens." Baxter took out his handkerchief and dabbed his brow. "For a moment I thought —"

"Not without proof, that is."

Baxter's groan was heart-wrenching. "Cecily, for pity's sake. This time I beg you not to pursue this line of thinking. It can only lead to disaster for all of us."

"Not if I can prove that one of them is guilty." She laid her hands on her husband's shoulders and pushed him gently down on his chair. "Just hear me out and then tell me what you think about my theory."

Once more he groaned, lifting his hands in a gesture of defeat. "Very well. But I have to admit to a certain amount of skepticism."

"That's all right. I just want to voice my ideas, to get them set straight in my mind." She seated herself opposite him and folded her hands in her lap. "Supposing Lady Lucille were engaged in a liaison with one of the other Benchers. Since they are all staying at the Pennyfoot, she could hardly conduct that kind of relationship here in the club."

"It would be rather difficult, I agree."

"Quite. So, her lover discovers the abandoned farmhouse. The perfect place for a tryst. Wrotham suspects what is going on and follows them. A Peeping Tom, so to speak. Emily Wrotham thinks her husband was cheating on her, but I think Barry Wrotham might have become enthralled with watching the lovers. Perhaps this romance has been going on for some time. So, Wrotham spies on the happy couple, and then gets caught. Perhaps he threatens to tell all. The lover has to silence him. So he pushes our nosy manager down the well. It would be impossible for Wrotham to climb out, and no one is going to hear his cries for help. No one except his murderer, of course."

"And Lady Lucille," Baxter reminded her.

"She might not have known what happened." Cecily frowned. "Though she certainly would have guessed when Wrotham's body was found."

"Surely she would have told her husband about her suspicions?"

"Not if she'd been engaged in an entanglement with one of his associates. It certainly would explain that nervous little glance she's always directing at him."

Baxter shook his head. "All this is pure conjecture, of course. You have no proof that the pin you found in the farmhouse belongs to Lady Lucille. After all, you mentioned that Emily Wrotham suspected her husband of betraying her with another woman. The pin could belong to Wrotham's unknown paramour."

Cecily withdrew the pin from her bodice and twisted it around in the glow of the gas lamps. "I sincerely doubt it. This pin belongs to a lady of wealth. Look at how the diamond sparkles in the light. Wrotham was a man of modest means. No one with whom he would associate would ever be able to afford something like this."

"Well, until you know for certain to whom the pin belongs, it is dangerous to speculate. I must insist that you proceed with the utmost caution. If you are correct in your assumptions, whoever the culprit may be, he will go to great lengths to keep his secret. He has a great deal to lose."

"Indeed he does," Cecily murmured,

fastening the pin to her bodice once more. "But Wrotham lost his life. If someone killed him, then he should pay for it."

"Agreed. I would just prefer that someone else hand him the bill. I don't suppose you would consider talking to P.C. Northcott about your suspicions?"

Her glance of contempt was enough.

He sighed, and ran a hand over his hair to smooth it down. "Very well, but I am holding you to your promise, Cecily. I must warn you, if you violate my trust again, I shan't answer for the consequences."

"Don't worry, darling. I shall consult you before my every move. For instance, at the very first opportunity, I intend to show the pin to Lady Lucille, tell her Miss Bunkle mentioned she'd lost one, and ask her if this one belongs to her. She might not know where she lost it and will claim it. After all, it *is* a most expensive pin."

"She could deny it belongs to her."

"True."

"That's if it is hers, of course."

Cecily smiled. "If not, then I shall have to rethink my theory."

"And I shall be vastly relieved."

She rose, and held out her arms to her husband. "I think it's time we retired for the night. I'm weary, and we have a long day tomorrow."

He had risen with her, and moved around the desk to accept her hug. "You will take care, my love?"

"Of course." She drew back to look at him. "Did you order my Christmas tree for the library?"

"I did indeed." He dropped a kiss on her nose. "It will be here tomorrow."

"That's wonderful. Madeline will be here to begin the decorating, and Phoebe has promised to stop by with Colonel Fortescue."

Baxter lifted his chin and groaned. "As if we don't have enough bedlam to confuse us. It's been two years since we last saw the inimitable colonel. His brain must be even more addled by now."

"Not according to Phoebe." Cecily laughed. "I must admit, I'm amazed at how well that marriage seems to be working. Those two people are well suited to each other. They each bring something to the marriage that the other needs. And that is how a successful marriage should be."

He tilted his head on one side and gave her a quizzical look. "Is that how you see us?"

"Of course. You give me strength and

stability. I give you enthusiasm and drama in your life."

He grimaced. "Sometimes a little too much drama."

"Ah, my love, admit it. Excitement adds a little spice to life."

"You are all the excitement I need. I can manage very well without your adventures to enhance it."

Her protest was smothered by his kiss. Which, in her opinion, was a very satisfying ending to an interesting day.

It was late in the following day when Cecily found the opportunity to speak to Lady Lucille alone. Ross had arrived that morning, having spent the night in nearby Wellercombe. Thanks to the heavy snowfall, he'd been prevented from reaching the Pennyfoot when he'd arrived at the train station.

Gertie was overjoyed to see him earlier than she'd expected, and the twins raced up and down the stairs in their excitement, convinced that now Papa was there, Father Christmas would arrive any minute.

In desperation, after the midday meal, Gertie and Daisy had left Ross to rest in his room while they took the children outside to build a snowman. Mrs. Chubb had asked to be driven into town, since she was anxious to visit with some of her old friends.

Samuel, meanwhile, had requested permission to examine the six motor cars belonging to the Pennyfoot. Much to Cecily's surprise, he'd explained that he was in training to be an automobile mechanic, and generously offered his services free as practice in overhauling the vehicles.

Baxter had seemed somewhat reluctant, but uttered no objections when Cecily accepted Samuel's offer. Baxter had retired to his office shortly after, leaving Cecily to pursue her quest, though not before extracting one more promise from her to watch her step.

As luck would have it, that afternoon the four Benchers had chosen to visit the card rooms where, according to Jeanette, they were engaged in a fiercely competitive game of baccarat.

"You should see 'em, m'm," she confided, having met Cecily in the hallway after returning from the card room, where she had been serving the four men the Pennyfoot's best scotch. "Money flying everywhere. I never saw betting go so fast. Look!" She pulled three silver florins from her pocket. "They gave me this, just for pouring them drinks."

Thankfully remembering that gambling was legal now that the Pennyfoot was a club, Cecily reminded Jeanette that gossip about the guests was strictly forbidden. "The Pennyfoot has always had a reputation for keeping silent about what goes on between these walls," she told the excited young girl. "I wouldn't want that trust violated. Our guests depend on us to respect their privacy."

"Oh, I respect it, all right, m'm. I'm very good at keeping me mouth shut about what goes on here." She glanced over her shoulder as if making sure no one could overhear her, then in a conspiratorial whisper added, "You wouldn't believe half of the goings-on I see, and that's a fact."

Well aware of what many of the "goings-on" entailed, Cecily hustled the girl back to the kitchen, again reminding her that it was none of their business.

In the days when the Pennyfoot had been a hotel, the illegal card rooms, hidden below in the wine cellar, had been bustling with notables. The boudoirs were notorious for entertaining the lewd assignations of various members of the aristocracy and the upper crust of London. Although the card rooms were no longer an embarrassment, the boudoirs apparently had lost none of their former notoriety.

The list of guests named Smith, Jones, or Brown was endless. In fact, as Cecily was well aware, it had become so common for such names to be used to conceal one's true identity, that persons with the legitimate name of Smith made up another one so as not to be suspected of philandering.

She was on her way to the library to inspect the new Christmas tree when she encountered Lady Lucille who, it seemed, was heading in the same direction.

The lady seemed disinclined to talk, making it clear she felt it beneath her station to be caught conversing with the hired help. Cecily had to remind herself that she was no longer the owner of the Pennyfoot, and was therefore relegated to the realm of the employed. Bearing that in mind, she was overly solicitous when she addressed the woman.

"I wonder if I might have a word with you, your ladyship," she said as she stood back to allow Lucille to enter the library ahead of her. "I have something that might be of importance to you."

Lucille looked at her with the expression of one who seriously doubted that such a lowly being could have anything to say that would be remotely worthy of her time. "And what might that be?"

Following her into the library, Cecily caught sight of the Christmas tree in the corner of the spacious room. She had no time to dwell on it now, however. Thankful to see they were alone in the room, she carefully removed the pin from the pocket of her skirt. "Miss Bunkle informed me that you had mislaid a hat pin when you were here last. I found this one and wondered if it might belong to you." She held the pin up to the light, so that the diamond glittered as it spun in her fingers. "It's awfully pretty. I'm quite sure anyone would hate to lose something as appealing as this."

She had been watching Lucille's face carefully as she spoke. The other woman's eyes had widened just a fraction, and she blinked rapidly as she raised a delicate hand to her throat. "It is indeed *très magnifique*, Madame Baxter. It is not mine, however. I found my missing hat pin later. I did not lose it after all."

"Well, how fortunate for you." Cecily replaced the pin in her pocket. "I shall have to ask the other ladies if the pin belongs to them. I was thinking perhaps it had been stolen, since I found it in rather an unusual place. It was on the floor of a bedroom in an abandoned farmhouse."

Lucille's eyelashes fluttered again and a slight flush spread over her cheeks. "Is that so." She'd managed to put a great deal of disgust into those words, obviously hoping to imply she wouldn't be caught dead in a farmhouse. Abandoned or not. She turned away, and moved toward the bookcases, indicating that the conversation was over.

Cecily was not that easily dismissed, however. She followed Lucille to the racks of books. "Strangely enough, it was the same farm where poor Mr. Wrotham met his end."

Lady Lucille kept on moving down the shelves, but Cecily noticed that the woman's hand shook quite visibly as she reached for a book.

Pressing home her point, Cecily said quietly, "One has to wonder if Mr. Wrotham wandered into a situation he wasn't supposed to see. Two lovers enjoying a secluded hideaway, perhaps. Having witnessed a scene that could cause a great deal of trouble for the pair involved, it could well have become necessary to make sure Mr. Wrotham did not pass on his discovery to anyone else. After all, when one is in a position of eminence, one can sometimes be forced to go to extraordinary lengths to protect one's image, wouldn't you say?"

Lady Lucille spun on her heel so sharply a hairpin slipped from her tightly bound hair and bounced off her shoulder. "Madame Baxter, I have not the least idea what your babbling means. I have many excellent works of fiction from which I can choose right here on these shelves. I have no interest at all in your stories. If you will excuse me, I should like to examine these shelves without you here to bother me."

Cecily lowered her gaze before the other woman saw the resentment smoldering there. "My apologies, Lady Lucille. I shall go in search of the other ladies and ask them if the pin belongs to any of them. I'm sorry to have disturbed you."

She headed to the door, and had reached it when Lady Lucille said sharply, *"Attende, s'il vous plaît!"*

Cecily turned, waiting expectantly as Lady Lucille moved toward her, her hand outstretched.

"The pin. Give it to me," she said, obviously making an effort to sound more amicable. "I will ask my companions if it belongs to any of them. I am quite sure you have enough to do with the work of running such an excellent establishment, *non?* I will be happy to relieve you of an extra burden."

Cecily smiled. "That is most kind of you, your ladyship. But I couldn't possibly trouble you with any of my duties. Enjoy your reading. Good day."

Just before she escaped through the door, she glimpsed Lady Lucille's narrowed eyes, and the expression in them sent a nasty chill down her back. There was no doubt in her mind that, given enough reason, the elegant lady could be a formidable foe.

What also seemed apparent, Cecily reflected as she hurried down the hallway, was that Lady Lucille was vastly disturbed by the discovery of the pin and where it was found. Either the pin did, indeed, belong to her, or she knew who was the owner.

What's more, Cecily was convinced her theory was on the right track. It seemed highly possible that one of the ladies was engaged in an illicit alliance with one of the Benchers, and that Wrotham found out about it. It also seemed feasible to assume that Lady Lucille was the lady involved, since she had mislaid her hat pin when she was visiting the Pennyfoot the same week

Wrotham died. Which left one large question looming in Cecily's mind: Which of the Benchers would be foolish enough to dally with Sir John Gilroy's wife?

She broached the question to Baxter when she joined him in his office a short while later.

Her husband seemed distracted, and was rather short with her. "You are assuming all this, Cecily. You don't have an ounce of justification for your suspicions. It's no wonder Inspector Cranshaw becomes so incensed when you interfere in his investigations."

"Inspector Cranshaw is a fool," Cecily said mildly. "He wouldn't leave a dunderhead like P.C. Northcott in charge if he had any brains. Here we have a situation fraught with unanswered questions and ominous possibilities, and Northcott is ignoring the whole thing."

"Well, while I have to agree with your assessment of the police constable, have you considered at all the possibility that you are simply overreacting to an unfortunate circumstance simply because there is an element of mystery about it?"

Cecily leaned two hands on his desk. "Baxter, dear, I love you dearly, but sometimes you can be deliberately obtuse.

169

Wrotham's body was found floating in a well on abandoned farmland where he had no good reason to be, several yards from a farmhouse that is supposed to have been uninhabited for at least a year, yet the magazine I found there was dated just a month ago, and a very expensive diamond pin, which no farmer's wife would ever be able to afford, was found lying next to a fine, pure wool blanket that showed no sign of wear. Not only that, I'm convinced that Lucille was lying when she denied the pin was hers. If that doesn't add up to ominous possibilities, then you are right, I am overreacting."

Baxter blinked. "Well, when you put it like that . . ."

"Thank you. I'm pleased that you see my point. Now, as I said before you so loudly voiced your skepticism, which one of the Benchers would you suppose would risk his career to spend an afternoon with Lucille in a deserted farmhouse?"

"If it were Lucille who had been there, her lover could be anyone. It doesn't necessarily have to be one of her husband's associates, does it?"

"No, but it seems the most likely answer. If it were someone else entirely, why meet him here with so many witnesses about?

Why not meet him in London, which after all, has a great many more places to offer seclusion and a great deal more comfortable at that. No, I think that Lucille and her lover took the opportunity where they could, when they could seize the moment to slip off together without being missed. Or perhaps the whole affair exploded into passion for the first time while they were here at the Pennyfoot together, and their assignation was purely on impulse."

"Well, we all know where impulses tend to lead us, don't we."

She wrinkled her nose at him. "Come now, Bax. If you had to choose one, which Bencher would you select for Lady Lucille's lover?"

"I haven't the slightest idea. By the way, did you happen to notice if the Christmas tree had arrived in the library?"

"Yes, it has. I caught a glimpse of it but I didn't have time to examine it closely. Don't change the subject. I really would like to know your opinion. It's important to me."

Baxter leaned back in his chair, a perplexed frown marring his face. "Oh, very well. Though I can't say that I've paid much attention to the group. That handsome chap, I suppose. The one with the flame-haired wife."

"Ah, you managed to pay some attention, I see." She grinned at his expression of discomfort. "It's all right, I'm teasing. Roger Peebles is certainly a possibility. The sort of man a woman like Lucille would enjoy conquering. Then there's Fitzhammer, who is obviously infatuated with the lovely Lucille. Though I do believe she regards him with contempt. I wonder —" She broke off as a sharp tap sounded on the door.

After a short pause, during which Baxter raised his eyebrows at her in question, he called out, "You may come in!"

The door opened and Miss Bunkle's head appeared in the gap, the knitting needle in her hair scraping against the doorjamb. "Oh, I'm sorry to disturb you, sir . . . madam. I thought you'd be alone. That is . . ."

"Come in, Miss Bunkle," Baxter said impatiently. "You're not interrupting anything important." He ignored Cecily's meaningful look of indignation at his comment. "Is there something that needs my attention?"

"Yes, sir." Miss Bunkle edged into the room and stood wringing her hands for a moment before bursting out, "It's my pearls, Mr. Baxter. I'm afraid they've been stolen. There's a thief somewhere in the Pennyfoot and I believe it's one of the staff."

Chapter
10

It had taken quite a while to calm down the normally unflappable Miss Bunkle. After questioning her closely about where she had last seen her pearls, Cecily had promised to look into the matter. As she remarked to Baxter after Miss Bunkle had left, it wouldn't do to bring in the constable until they had at least attempted to solve the problem themselves. The last thing the Pennyfoot needed was for word to get out that a thief was loose in the building.

Much disturbed by the latest turn of events, Cecily began questioning the staff. Jeanette and Moira seemed vastly upset at the thought they might be accused of stealing the pearls, and Cecily had to assure them that she was simply exploring all avenues before calling in the constables.

Jeanette, especially, was quite beside herself. "No one's never called me a thief before," she declared, her cheeks red with indignation. "I never stole nothing in me life. I swear I didn't."

"No one is accusing you," Cecily told her, "or anyone else for that matter. We must ask everyone if they have seen or heard anything that might help us find the pearls."

"I reckon the old biddy lost 'em," Jeanette said, nodding her head at the parlor, where Miss Bunkle was fortunately out of earshot. "What's an old bird like her doing with pearls anyway? They'd look pretty daft strung around her scraggy neck."

"They were a family heirloom and of great sentimental value to Miss Bunkle. It isn't up to you to question why she has them, Jeanette. The point is, we need everyone to keep their eyes and ears open, just in case you should see or hear something that might help us find the pearls. If they are not found soon, we shall have to call in the constables."

"Yes, m'm." The girl stared down at her shoes, her bottom lip jutting at a stubborn angle. "All I know is, I didn't steal them."

Sighing, Cecily left the kitchen and made her way up the stairs to the first floor. It pained her to think that a trusted member of the staff had committed theft on the premises. The staff of the Pennyfoot had always been treated well, with generous pay and free time.

According to Baxter, Edward had been even more charitable than she had, thanks to the thriving business he had worked hard to build. To discover a miscreant among the carefully chosen workers saddened her as much as if it had been a member of her own family.

Deep in thought, she came close to colliding with the tall figure who had stepped out from the card room in front of her in the narrow hallway. She recognized Sir John Gilroy, and the handsome Roger Peebles hovering right behind him, as well as the older Bencher, Percy Chatsworth. Fitzhammer, the lecherous one as Cecily had dubbed him, apparently was still engrossed in a card game.

Cecily greeted the three men and added, "If you should happen to be looking for Lady Lucille, Sir John, I left her in the library about an hour ago."

Gilroy nodded, his expression somewhat forbidding. "Thank you, Mrs. Baxter. I believe she planned to take a book back to our suite. She has more than likely returned there by now."

He was about to move on when the impulse struck her. She pulled the hat pin from her pocket and held it up to the light so all three men could plainly see it. "I found this hat pin yesterday. I was wondering if any of you gentlemen recognized it as belonging to your wife."

Gilroy stared at her as if she'd committed a sin by mentioning the pin, while Chatsworth merely looked bored. Peebles, on the other hand, frowned at the pin as though he were trying to remember where he'd seen it before.

When none of them answered her, Cecily turned to Gilroy. "I understand your wife mislaid one during a previous visit, Sir John. Would you care to take a closer look, just in case it should belong to her?"

Rather impatiently he reached out and took it from her, squinting at it in the dim light of the corridor. Finally, he muttered brusquely, "I believe this might belong to my wife. I gave her one like it as an anniversary gift. I had no idea she had mislaid it. She'll be most relieved to have it returned to her. I'm very much obliged to you, Mrs. Baxter."

Elated at having her suspicions confirmed, Cecily beamed. "Not at all, Sir John. I'm happy to have been of service."

He stared back at her, his expression stony, as if a shutter had closed over his face.

Somewhat unnerved, she glanced back at Roger Peebles, and was intrigued to find him now watching Sir John with a furtive expression in his eyes. He seemed ill at ease, and fidgeted with his watch chain as if anxious to be somewhere else.

She watched the men move off down the hallway, wondering how Lucille was going to explain why she hadn't told her husband about the loss of his valuable gift, and what he would say if he learned where Cecily had found it.

She could at least be certain that it was Lucille who had been meeting someone in the farmhouse. If the pin had been stolen, like Miss Bunkle's pearls, or even found in the hotel and taken to the farmhouse by someone else, there would have been no need for Lucille to lie about the pin belonging to her.

Cecily uttered a heavy sigh. On the other hand, she was no closer to learning with whom the lady had taken such risks. Or if, indeed, the clandestine couple had anything to do with Barry Wrotham's death. Baxter was right. She had no proof that any of her theories were the right ones.

She had no time to ponder further at that moment, as a commotion at the front door suggested visitors had arrived. She recognized the strident voice at once and hurried forward to greet the newcomers.

Phoebe stood just inside the closed doors, her hand on the arm of a stout gentleman whose red face beneath the elegant top hat he wore contrasted sharply with his frost white whiskers. The colonel was talking loudly and with a great deal of agitation, brandishing his free arm as if staving off imaginary assailants and completely ignoring the quiet pleas of his wife.

Cecily crossed the foyer at top speed, conscious of the stares of several people standing at the reception counter. "Phoebe! And Colonel Fortescue! What a pleasure it is to see you both again."

The colonel mercifully stopped bellowing, his watery bloodshot eyes staring at her as if she had sprouted horns. "Cecily? Is that you? Good Lord, old bean, what the devil are you doing in this den of iniquity? Have you no blasted shame? What? What?"

Phoebe sent her a look of apology. "He thinks he's in a house of ill repute," she whispered from behind her gloved hand.

Cecily raised her eyebrows. "What on earth gave him that idea?"

"We passed a group of young ladies running down the steps outside. They were unescorted by gentlemen, and seemingly in high spirits. They called out to us, wishing us a happy Christmas, and I'm afraid that dear Freddie thought they were offering their services."

"Damn disgusting if you ask me," the colonel boomed. "Can't think why my wife would bring me here." He leaned over Phoebe, his eyelids flapping up and down in agitation. "Unless you're trying to get rid of me, what? What? Heaven knows what ghastly things happen to the poor blighters who get lured into this obscene harem."

"Oh, don't be such a dunce, Freddie," Phoebe said crossly. "This is a country club, and a very respectable establishment. Surely you remember the time when Cecily owned the Pennyfoot Hotel?"

The colonel blinked at Cecily. "The Pennyfoot Hotel. Why, by George, of course I remember! Jolly good show, old girl. Nice to be back in the old Pennyfoot. So where's Baxter then, the old goat? What have you done with him? Hope you haven't sent him packing, what? What?"

Aware of the odd glances being directed at them, Cecily said hurriedly, "Baxter is in the office. I'm sure he will be pleased to see you. You remember where it is, don't you?"

"Right ho, old bean. Think I'll toddle off for a quick snifter in the bar. Tell the governor to join me in there when he's ready."

"You're not toddling anywhere without me, Freddie," Phoebe said crisply. "In any case, the bar is not where it used to be. The drawing room is no longer there, either. You'll never find your way on your own."

"I'm afraid you won't be able to go in the bar with him," Cecily said. "Club rules, I'm sorry to say. No women allowed in the bar. Not even me."

"Whose rules are they?" Phoebe demanded. "Not that peculiar woman with a knitting needle stuck in her head?"

"I say, old fruit, bit painful what?" The colonel twisted the end of his mustache with a flourish. "Reminds me of the time I had an arrow shot right through my bloody pith helmet. Did I ever tell you —"

"A hundred times," Phoebe said rudely. She turned to Cecily. "Is Madeline here yet? I really need to talk to her about the backdrops for the pantomime. Are we meeting in the library?"

"I suppose we could," Cecily murmured. "Although it's not as private as it used to be. Perhaps it would be better to have our

181

meeting in my suite. At least we have no fear of being disturbed there."

"Good idea. I'll take Freddie to the bar and he can wait there for me."

The colonel's eyes lit up. "I say, jolly good idea, old bean."

"And you are to have no more than two glasses," she told him sternly.

"Oh, right, of course, old fruit. Anything you say."

"Then that's settled." Cecily glanced at the grandfather clock ticking away in the corner of the foyer. "I have one small errand to run, but it won't take me more than a minute or so. I'll meet you in my suite." She handed Phoebe the key. "I shan't be long."

She left Phoebe to explain to the colonel why the bar had been moved since he was last there. The last thing she heard him bellow before she passed out of earshot was an explosive, "Well, I never heard such blasted stuff and nonsense. Tell them to put the damn thing back where it belongs!"

Reaching the library door, Cecily turned the handle and entered the quiet room. She was thankful to see that Lady Lucille had left, and that no one else disturbed the peace of what used to be her favorite room in the hotel.

She wanted to take a closer look at the towering Christmas tree that she'd spotted earlier by the French windows. She was pleased to see that it was just as magnificent as her first impression of it.

The fragrance of it filled the room, and the thick branches laden with pine needles swooped down to the floor in perfect symmetry, leaving no unsightly gaps to be filled. The woodsman had done a fine job. Madeline would have a fine time decorating such a grand specimen.

Well content with the tree, Cecily wandered over to the fireplace. The portrait of James Sinclair, her late husband, had once hung on the wall overlooking the long Jacobean table where she had conducted so many committee meetings.

Now the portrait had been replaced by a turbulent seascape, and the Jacobean table with its constant vase of roses had been banished in favor of more armchairs and trestle tables.

Still, the memories could not be destroyed. It had been here in this room where she had once shared a cigar now and then with Baxter, and it had been here in this room where she had received her first inkling that his concern for her was something more than just a promise to her late husband.

She turned from the fireplace and gazed at the warm paneled walls and the shelves crammed with books that reached from the floor to the lofty ceiling. This was still her favorite room. Because it held so many wonderful memories. And because the spirit of everything that had mattered in her life still hovered within its walls.

She, Madeline, and Phoebe had spent so many pleasant hours discussing the frequent events that were held at the hotel to entertain the guests. Balls and tea dances, with Phoebe's sometimes bizarre presentations on the stage, were an integral part of the hotel's routine.

The tableaux, dances, plays, and even a magician were some of the most memorable events Phoebe had presided over, with the help of her inept, argumentative dance troupe, who invariably managed to bring disaster to the entertainment in some strange manner or other.

Much as Phoebe lamented each calamity, Cecily was of the private opinion that the guests actually adored the chaos that ensued, and would have been vastly disappointed had the performance been anything less than a catastrophe.

The door opened abruptly, shattering

her thoughts. Jeanette stood in the doorway, and she dropped a curtsey when she caught sight of Cecily. "Begging your pardon, m'm, but Miss Bunkle sent me to tell you that the last of your special guests has arrived."

"Doris is here?" Cecily hurried to the door. "How wonderful. Where is she?"

"Raymond took her up to her room, m'm." Jeanette waited for Cecily to exit the room, then closed the door and followed her up the hallway. "Is it true she's on the stage, m'm?"

"Doris is a professional performer, yes."

"In London?"

"Yes." Cecily paused. "Jeanette, I'd prefer that the guests didn't know that about Doris. I don't want her pestered by stage-struck admirers. I don't know who told you . . ."

"Samuel told Moira and she told me." Jeanette looked worried. "I haven't told no one else, m'm. Honest I haven't. I —"

Her sentence was cut off by a hefty sneeze that echoed up the wide staircase. Smothering her nose in a large white handkerchief, Jeanette ducked another curtsey and rushed off for the kitchen.

Cecily watched her go with a frown. The girl seemed unnecessarily agitated. This business of the stolen pearls must be making the staff uneasy. She would have to abandon her efforts to find out what happened to Wrotham for the time being and concentrate on searching for Miss Bunkle's pearls.

Sighing, she made for the stairs. She was looking forward to seeing Doris again. The young girl had been one of her favorites. It wasn't until she'd reached the first landing that she remembered Phoebe, who was no doubt waiting for her in her suite at this very moment. Her reunion with Doris would have to wait after all.

She found both Phoebe and Madeline ensconced in her living room engaged in a heated argument over where to hang the mistletoe.

"It would be inviting serious embarrassment to hang mistletoe in the main hallway," Phoebe asserted, wagging her finger at Madeline to emphasize her point. "It is too dark and too narrow to pass a person without coming within reach. Heaven knows what liberties some of these gentlemen might take at such an enticing opportunity."

Madeline rolled her eyes at the ceiling. "Just listen to her. As if a simple sprig of mistletoe would change a gentleman's character. People have been hanging mistletoe over their doorways for centuries at Christmastime and so far there have been no rumors of mass molestation."

"Just because we do not hear of such tales doesn't mean it doesn't happen. If you must hang the stuff somewhere, why not the ballroom, where any impertinent behavior can be easily detected and therefore avoided?"

Madeline fixed her with a baleful glare. "Has it ever occurred to your addled brain that some people welcome such advances? I seem to remember you being much less prudish when your colonel pursued you in the rose garden."

Phoebe's face turned scarlet. "I beg your pardon?"

Deciding it was high time to intervene, Cecily said hurriedly, "I think we can begin rehearsals for the pantomime tomorrow. Doris arrived a short while ago, and I'm hoping she'll agree to help us with the production. Phoebe, have you contacted your dance troupe? How many can we depend on to help us with our presentation?"

After giving Madeline a final lethal glare, Phoebe turned a cold shoulder on her and smiled at Cecily. "At least six of the girls are eager to participate. They've missed the excitement of performing in front of an audience."

"I hope Doris knows what's in store for her," Madeline murmured. "She's accustomed to professional performers. It's going to be something of a shock when she has to deal with the Troupe Fiasco."

"I've asked you not to call them that," Phoebe said sharply. "It demoralizes them."

"That's nothing compared to what they can do to an audience." Madeline gave Cecily a sly look. "Are you sure Doris wants to be associated with Phoebe's band of clumsy clowns?"

"Doris will be happy to donate her talents, I'm sure," Cecily said, crossing her fingers in her lap. "In any case, a pantomime is not exactly an opera. It's supposed to be a display of amusement, with lots of jokes and good humor and audience participation. Who's going to notice if things are not quite perfect? And even if they do, really, who is going to care that much? It's all in the spirit of Christmas, is it not?"

"Exactly my sentiments," Phoebe declared, giving Madeline a triumphant smirk.

Madeline threw her hands up in defeat.

"Very well. Don't say I didn't warn you."

"That's settled then." Cecily drew a sigh of relief. "When can you start the decorating, Madeline?"

"Right away, if you can tell me where to find the decorations." Madeline glanced at the clock on Cecily's sideboard. "Did you get another tree for the library?"

"I certainly did. I was just looking at it earlier. It's quite magnificent. I've decided to hold a private candle-lighting ceremony for my special guests in the library on Christmas Eve. You and Phoebe, and the colonel, of course, are all invited to attend. We'll have a wassail bowl and Christmas crackers, and roast chestnuts in the fire. We'll be hanging small gifts on the tree for the guests to be handed out on Christmas Day, so it will all look very festive with its candles burning."

"Oh, it does sound so heavenly!" Phoebe clapped her hands in delight. "I know dear Freddie will adore it." She glanced at Madeline. "I don't suppose you will be bringing the doctor, by any chance?"

Madeline's eyes were bleak when she answered. "For once you are quite correct, Phoebe. Dr. Prestwick will not be joining me this Christmas."

Cecily's heart ached when she saw the

despondency on her friend's face. "But you will join us, will you not?"

"I wouldn't miss it." Madeline rose to her feet, her peasant skirt fluttering in folds around her ankles. "I thought I'd ask Gertie's twins to help me with the decorating. It will give their mother a rest and keep them out of mischief."

"Oh, they'd love that, I know they would. If you ask Miss Bunkle where to find the decorations, I'm sure she'll be able to help you. Meanwhile, I'll talk to Doris and ask for her help with the pantomime."

Phoebe rose, too, smoothing her skirt down with her gloved hands. "And I must go in search of my husband. He is most likely getting lonely without me."

"If you've left him in the bar, he's most likely forgotten your existence by now," Madeline drawled.

Phoebe sniffed. "It won't take much to jog his memory. Pity you can't say as much for the good doctor."

Madeline smiled, though there was no humor in her eyes. "I can't imagine why you are so possessed with Kevin, Phoebe. Could it be that you are as enamored of him as half the female population of Badgers End?"

Phoebe tossed her head, at great risk of

dislodging her hat. "If I were, Madeline dear, I would do everything in my power to make sure his attention was on me, and not on half the female population of Badgers End."

"Better women than you have tried and failed," Madeline murmured.

Phoebe was about to answer when a light tap on the door caught everyone's attention.

Cecily opened it, surprised to see Moira bobbing up and down in an awkward curtsey. "I'm so sorry to disturb you, m'm," she mumbled, "but Lady Lucille sent me. She asked to meet with you right away." Moira's gaze slid past Cecily to the other two women. "She said it was important, m'm, that she speak with you in private."

"It's all right, Moira," Madeline said, gliding to the door. "We were just leaving." She transferred her smile to Cecily. "I will begin the decorating and I'll try not to get into anyone's way."

Caught up in wondering just what it was that Lady Lucille had to say to her, Cecily nodded absently. "Tell Miss Bunkle to give you enough candles to put on the tree in the library. I'd like a really good display of them."

Madeline nodded and passed through

the door, then came to a standstill so abruptly Cecily thought she had bumped into Moira, who still hovered outside in the hallway awaiting further instructions.

But then she saw Moira standing to one side. Madeline, it seemed, had been seized by one of her trances. She turned slowly to face Cecily, and the stark expression on her face sent a chill coursing through Cecily's veins.

In that ghostly voice quite unlike her usual throaty tone, Madeline said softly, "Beware the candles. They are burning too brightly."

Cecily stared at her, trying to make sense of the words. "What is it, Madeline? What are you trying to tell me?"

Behind her Phoebe uttered a shocked gasp as Madeline's eyes seemed to glow with an unearthly light.

"I see you playing with fire, Cecily," Madeline whispered. "Take great care, or you will be horribly burned."

Moira let out a whimper of fear, while Phoebe said harshly, "Madeline! Enough of this nonsense."

Madeline seemed not to notice. She simply wafted off down the hallway and disappeared from view.

"Well," Phoebe said, sounding shaken.

"What was that all about?"

Moira stared at Cecily with wide, frightened eyes. "M'm? Is the lady all right?"

Cecily pulled herself together. "Yes, I'm sure she's quite all right. Phoebe, you had better join your husband. It's getting late. Moira, please ask Lady Lucille to come here to my suite at her convenience."

Moira gave a frightened nod of her head and rushed off.

Phoebe left, too, shaking her head and muttering about Madeline not being right in the mind. Cecily closed the door and leaned against it.

There had been only a handful of times that Madeline had warned her in this way. And each time, she had found herself in deadly danger. She could only hope that this warning did not carry the same ugly threat.

Chapter
11

Less than ten minutes after Cecily had sent the message to Lady Lucille, a light tap summoned her to the door. Feeling somewhat apprehensive, she opened it and regarded the elegant woman, who stood looking down the corridor as if afraid someone might see her.

"Please, do come in," Cecily murmured, stepping back to allow her to enter. "Can I offer you some refreshment? I can have some tea sent up —"

"*Non, non, merci.*" Lucille trotted into the room in great haste. "I can only stay but a moment."

Cecily closed the door and indicated the nearest chair. "I hope there is nothing amiss with your room?"

"*Pardonnez-moi?*" Lucille turned anxious eyes on her. "Oh, not at all." She tugged at the fingers of her left glove, as if about to draw it off, then changed her mind and smoothed it down again. "Ma-

194

dame Baxter. I must ask of you a favor."

"Of course." Cecily waited until Lucille had seated herself, then took a chair across the room from her. "I'll be most happy to oblige if at all possible."

For a long moment it seemed as if the lady had trouble remembering what it was she had come to ask. Her hesitancy was such a marked change in her attitude that Cecily found it hard to realize it was the same woman.

Finally, Lucille lifted her chin and stared straight into Cecily's eyes. "My husband tells me that you returned the hat pin to him."

Having anticipated that Lucille's visit would have something to do with the hat pin, Cecily had prepared her reply. "Yes," she said smoothly. "I happened to be asking the other gentlemen if they recognized the pin when your husband declared that it belonged to you. It is rather distinctive, after all. An anniversary gift, I believe he said."

"*Oui.*" Lucille dropped her gaze. "You say you found it in the farmhouse?"

"Quite by accident, I assure you."

"You did not tell my husband where you found it?"

"No, of course not."

She looked up then, and to Cecily's surprise, her eyes filled with tears. "Madame Baxter, I know what you think of me. I am a weak woman, yes, but I have reason to seek attention elsewhere. My husband, he is a very busy man. He has many . . . interests that occupy much of his time. He does not have any time left for his wife. I might as well be a pretty picture on the wall for what little attention he pays to me."

"I'm sorry," Cecily murmured, at a loss as to how to respond to this outpouring of misery.

Lady Lucille shrugged. "He has a good position with the Inns of Court. Why is he not satisfied with that? I do not understand why he needs all this extra work and demands. I tell him over and over again, I wish the others would leave him alone. If he wasn't so busy all the time, I would have no reason to . . ." She caught her breath on a sob, and hunted for a handkerchief in her sleeve.

Instantly intrigued, Cecily would dearly have loved to know what extra demands were taking so much of Sir John's time, and who "the others" might be. She was far too polite to ask, however. In spite of her disapproval of the woman's infidelity, Cecily felt a modicum of sympathy for her.

It couldn't be easy to love a man and be ignored by him. Especially for a woman as seemingly passionate as Lucille. Sir John was making a grave mistake by neglecting his wife.

"Lady Lucille," she said softly. "It is not my place to pass judgment, nor is it any of my business. If you are asking me not to reveal to your husband where I found the pin, I assure you, your secret is quite safe with me."

Lucille pressed her handkerchief to her lips, her eyes still brimming. *"Merci, madame,"* she murmured. "You are most understanding."

Cecily studied her carefully. "Although, as I said, this is none of my business, I feel compelled to offer a note of warning. In view of the location where I found the pin, and since that is also the location where our former manager, Barry Wrotham, met his death, should there be an investigation forthcoming, I might have to mention it to the constables."

Lucille's eyes grew wide with apprehension. "An investigation? But I thought . . . I was told . . . Barry's death was an accident."

"It would seem that way, yes." Cecily deliberately paused, aware of the other woman's intense concentration. After a moment she continued, "There have been some questions raised, however, that need to be answered."

"Questions?"

"Yes. For instance, why Mr. Wrotham should be wandering around a deserted farm for apparently no good reason."

Lucille's expression was one of pure bewilderment. "But . . . I . . . I thought you knew. Mr. Wrotham, he came there to meet me."

Cecily felt her own eyes widen. "Barry Wrotham was your lover?"

"Mais, oui." Lucille lifted her hands and let them drop again. "I am sure you understand why I cannot tell the constables what he was doing there."

Cecily was still struggling with this latest revelation. She had been so certain that Lucille was involved with one of the Benchers. It had never occurred to her that this elegant, proud creature could have lowered herself to engage in an illicit alliance with Wrotham.

Apparently Lucille must have read her mind. "Madame Baxter, I have not always been a . . . how you say . . . member of society. When I met my husband, I was with the *Folies Bergère.* Sometimes, I miss the excitement of that time. Monsieur Wrotham reminded me of the woman I once had been." She raised a delicate hand to wipe her brow. "I do not expect you to understand."

"I understand better than you imagine," Cecily said dryly. "Lady Lucille, I can't promise that your . . . association with Wrotham can remain a secret. Perhaps if you tell me what happened?"

Lucille shrugged. "I do not know what happened to him. I left when he was still in the house. We could not take the chance someone might see us together. I walked all the way to the town. I was to meet a car that would bring me back to the club. The same car that had taken me earlier. I told Raymond I was visiting the shops."

"So the last time you saw Barry Wrotham, he was alive and well in the farmhouse?"

"*Oui.*" She sighed. "It grew dark as I left. Barry, he had been drinking the cognac, *n'est-ce pas?* I think he must have stumbled into the well and pouf!" She jerked a hand in the air. "He fell down it." She covered her face with her hands for a moment. "Imagine my great distress when I learned of Barry's death. I feel so terrible that this happened to him. If I had not responded to his attentions, he would remain alive to this day."

Cecily stared at her in silence, while outside in the hallway the jangling of a bell summoned the guests to dinner. "I see," she said at last. "Well, that would explain a great deal. I'm so glad we had this discussion, Lady Lucille."

"And you will tell no one what I have told you?" Lucille leaned forward, her hands outstretched in appeal. "You must understand . . . my husband . . . if he hears of this . . ."

"I see no need to inform the constables of our conversation," Cecily said slowly. "They have ruled Barry Wrotham's death an accident, and what you have told me seems to bear out that deduction."

"I am deeply grateful, *madame*." Lucille rose, looking more like her former self. "Now, if you will excuse me, I must join the others for dinner. I am sure they must be wondering where I am, *non?*"

Cecily got to her feet and walked with Lucille to the door. After seeing the lady out, she waited long enough for her to return to her suite, then headed down the stairs to the first floor. She couldn't wait to tell Baxter what she had learned. Nor did she have any qualms about discussing it with him. She had promised Lucille not to repeat anything that was said to the constables or to Sir John. She had not said anything about discussing the news with her own husband.

"You never did tell me how it was you got here a day early," Gertie said, bending down to unfasten the button on James's shoe. "I thought you said you still had a few customers to take care of."

"I did."

"So how did you get them all done so quick?" James kept kicking his feet so she couldn't get ahold of him. She made a grab at his pudgy leg and he let out a howl. "Oh, now, now," she muttered as she wrestled with the shoe. "Stop pretending that you're hurt. I didn't grab you that hard."

"Don't wanna go to bed," James yelled.

"Well, you're bloody going, so there."

Ross's voice, harsh with impatience, cut across the room. "For pity's sake, woman, can't you keep the bairn quiet for one minute?"

Gertie jerked her head up and stared at her husband. Ross was normally an even-tempered man, far less likely to get in a tizz than she was. This wasn't like him at all.

"Sorry, luv. I'll get him in bed in a minute."

"Don't wanna!" Jamie yelled.

"You'll do as I *say!*" Gertie carried the squirming child to the bed, where Lillian was already half asleep. She dumped James in beside her and pulled the covers over his flailing arms. "Father Christmas is not going to fill your pillowcase with toys if you don't go to sleep right now."

James stopped yelling and blinked sleepy eyes at her. "Father Christmas is coming tonight?"

"Not tonight, no. But soon," she added hastily as James opened his mouth to scream again.

James gave her a suspicious look. "He won't know where to find us. He'll go to our house an . . . an . . . we won't be there. He'll think we don't want any toys . . ." His voice rose on yet another wail.

Gertie frowned. "Of course he'll find you. He's watching you right now from the North Pole. He knows if you're being naughty and it all goes down in his little book. Look at Lillian. She's being good. Father Christmas will bring lots of toys for her."

James pouted. "I want lots of toys, too."

"Then you'd better go to sleep right

this blinking minute."

James turned immediately onto his side and closed his eyes.

Breathing a sigh of relief, Gertie crept over to where Ross waited for her by the door. "There, they'll be asleep any minute. Mrs. Chubb should be back soon. She went down to dinner an hour ago with Daisy and Samuel. Once she gets here, we can go down to dinner. I'm bloody starving, I am."

"Gertie." Ross sounded beaten, as if he'd been tramping Putney Downs all day instead of spending most of it resting in their room.

Gertie stared at him in concern. Now that she really looked at him, he looked really poorly. "Aren't you feeling well, luv?" She placed her hand on his arm. "What is it, then?"

"I've got something to tell you. I should've told you this morning, but I didna want to tell you in front of everybody."

His Scottish accent sounded even more pronounced than usual — a sure sign he was upset about something. Now she was really worried. "Tell me what, luv? What's wrong?"

He raised his chin to look up at the

ceiling, then looked down at her with such sorrow in his face she wanted to cry out. Fear gripped her with a cold hand, and her lips felt numb with cold.

"I've sold the business, lass," he said at last. "I just couldna cope with it anymore."

Relief made her weak. "Is that all? Blimey, Ross, don't frighten me like that again. Don't worry, luv. Something will turn up. You'll have to get a job, that's all. Plenty of work around for a strapping lad like you."

"I don't know about that. I'm no' such a lad anymore. More like an old codger."

"Don't talk rubbish." She shook his arm. "Why, you're twice as big and three times as strong as any young lad I know. And four times as blinking handsome, and all."

His eyes softened, and he pulled her into his arms. "Ah, Gertie, my sweet, adorable love. What would I do without ye. Any other woman would be weepin' and wailin' at the news."

"Yeah, well, I'm not any bloody woman, am I. Things always have a way of working out, that's what I say, so what's the bleeding use of worrying about it."

Mrs. Chubb knocked on the door at that moment and Gertie welcomed the interruption. She'd made light of the situation, but her insides were churning like a keg of butter. It wasn't so much that Ross had sold the business. She was happy about that. She'd worried about him working such long hours in the harsh Scottish winters. And she was quite sure he'd soon find work again.

It was more the fact that he'd given up. Ross didn't give up easily on anything, and next to his family, the business was his life. Something had to be really wrong for him to get rid of something that had meant so much to him.

Making up her mind to have a word with Dr. Prestwick just as soon as she could, Gertie said good night to her babies and Mrs. Chubb, then took her husband's arm. They could never afford to stay in a posh hotel like this one. This was the one and only chance of a lifetime to live like the toffs for a little while, and she was determined to enjoy every single second of it.

Putting her worries out of her mind for the time being, she walked with her husband toward the stairs. In spite of the battles she'd had with Michel, she knew quite well that he was one of the best chefs in the country. She was really looking forward to her meal.

They were halfway down the corridor

when she caught sight of someone moving in the shadows at the far end. The couple drew apart as they approached and the lady disappeared into a suite, while the gentleman turned his back and pretended to study a portrait hanging on the wall.

At the head of the stairwell, which was centered in the middle of the long corridor, Gertie glanced back at the lone figure farther down the hall. She'd recognized the woman as the French wife of one of the toffs. Lady Something-or-other. Now she recognized the gentleman. It was the handsome bugger whose wife had all that flaming red hair. Peebles, that was his name. Roger Peebles.

Intrigued, Gertie descended the stairs, wondering just what the Frenchie was up to lurking in the corridor with one of her husband's colleagues.

Jeanette grunted as she dumped the heavy tray of soiled plates onto the kitchen table. "Look at this lot," she mumbled to no one in particular. "It will take me all night to get these washed and drained."

"It will if you stand there talking about it," Miss Bunkle said sharply. "Moira will be back any minute with another load, so you'd better get started."

Muttering to herself, Jeanette rolled up her sleeves past her elbows and stomped over to the stove, where a cauldron of hot water sat bubbling and steaming. "All this soap and hot water is drying out me skin. Me hands look like they came off a crocodile."

Miss Bunkle grunted. "How would you know what a crocodile looks like?"

"I seen one of them toffs wearing shoes made from crocodile skin. Look just like me hands, they do."

Miss Bunkle gave her a sharp look. "I hope you haven't been poking around amongst the guests' personal belongings again. You almost lost your job the last time when Mr. Wrotham caught you snooping in the wardrobes. If you get caught again doing that, you can say goodbye to the Pennyfoot, that's for sure."

Jeanette sniffed, and wiped her nose with the back of her finger. "This ain't the only place around here. I could get a job anywhere doing what I do and getting better paid for it, too."

"That I doubt very much." Miss Bunkle shook a finger at her. "But you'll soon have the opportunity to find out if you don't get those plates in the sink this minute. And for heaven's sake, blow your nose. All that sniffing is driving me crazy."

"I'm getting a bloody cold, that's what." Jeanette grabbed the handles of the steaming cauldron and hauled it off the stove. She carried it to an empty sink next to the other two kitchen maids, who were feverishly plunging glasses, plates, and an assortment of cutlery in and out of the soapy water. "If I'm ill," she muttered, "you'll soon find out how much you'd miss me. What with all the guests here for Christmas and all."

"We'll cross that bridge when we come to it." Miss Bunkle picked up a fork from the other sink and examined it. "This fork isn't clean," she told the timid maid. "Make sure you scrub the prongs." She turned back to Jeanette. "Take some cod liver oil when you go to bed. That'll soon put you back on your feet. I'm going into the dining room. Make sure those plates are clean by the time I get back."

Jeanette waited until the kitchen door had swung to behind her before muttering, "Silly old cow." She mimicked Miss Bunkle's grating voice. "Take some cod liver oil."

The girl next to her giggled.

"I'd like to shove cod liver oil down her throat and see how she likes it." Jeanette swished a plate in the water and held it up to let the soap bubbles slide off it before placing it in the draining board.

The door swung open again and Moira staggered in, bearing the weight of yet another tray of dirty dishes.

"Blimey," Jeanette said as her friend dumped the tray on the table. "How many bleeding more are there out there?"

"That's the lot, I think." Moira swiped at her forehead with the back of her arm. "There's just the coffee cups and saucers now."

"Thank Gawd for that." Jeanette beckoned to Moira. "Here, I want to ask you a favor."

Moira came forward with a good deal of reluctance. "What is it? The last time I did you a favor, it got me in trouble."

Jeanette made a face. "It weren't my fault. How was I to know they was Miss Bunkle's knickers hanging on the line? I just wanted to have a bit of fun, that's all."

"Miss Bunkle didn't think it was funny when she saw her knickers hanging on the cherub's head in the middle of the fountain. She knew I knew who dunnit. I should've told her it was you. She knew I was keeping her busy so she wouldn't see who did it."

"Well, you didn't tell her it were me and that's why you're me best friend." Jeanette nudged her with her elbow. "You are me best friend, aren't you?"

Moira shrugged. "I s'pose."

Jeanette glanced at the other two girls, both of whom were busy chattering about what they'd like for Christmas. Drawing Moira to one side, she whispered, "I have to go out tonight."

Moira stared at her. "Tonight? But it's not your night off. You can't go out tonight. Besides, you went out last night."

"No, I didn't. I had a big row with Wally and he went off in a huff."

"I know. I heard you. I thought you'd made it up with him."

"Well, I didn't. I went to bed early 'cos of me cold."

"Well, that was your night off. You can't just go tonight instead. Not without permission from Miss Bunkle."

"I'm not going to be that long. I just have to meet someone, that's all."

"Who, Wally? You going to make up with him?"

Jeanette shook her head. "Not Wally. We broke up."

Moira gasped in dismay. "Then who?"

"Never mind who. I just need you to tell

Miss Bunkle that I'm not feeling well so I've gone to bed. I'll get these plates finished and then I'll leave."

Moira tightened her lips. "I'm not doing it unless you tell me who you're going to meet."

Jeanette glared at her in frustration. "I can't tell you, can I. At least, not now. I'll tell you later. I swear I will."

"Well, I don't know." Moira frowned. "I hope you're not getting yourself in no more trouble. You're in enough trouble as it is."

"Course not. I know what I'm doing. This is going to get me *out* of trouble, you'll see." Jeanette glanced at the clock on the wall. "And I'd better get on with these dishes or I'll be late. If you help me and tell Miss Bunkle I've gone to bed, I'll make it up to you. I'll do anything you want."

Moira sighed. "Well, all right. But you'd better be careful. If Miss Bunkle catches you, there'll be bloody hell to pay."

Jeanette grinned. "Don't you worry about that. The old biddy won't catch me. Thanks, Moira. I promise, I'll tell me everything just as soon as I know that everything's going to be all right again."

"Just be careful, that's all I ask." Moira turned back to the table. "Now we'd better get these plates washed, before we're both in trouble again."

Jeanette moved back to the sink and reached for another plate. She wished she *could* tell Moira who she was going to meet. It was so exciting, just thinking about it. But she'd promised, and until she was sure everything was going to turn out right, she had to keep that promise. She only hoped she wouldn't make a mess of things this time. Everything depended on what happened tonight. Everything.

Chapter
12

When Cecily arrived at Baxter's office, she was delighted to discover that he had completed his tasks for the day. "It would seem that you are finally catching up on all the work that Barry Wrotham's absence left behind," she said, giving her husband a warm hug. "I'm so pleased. I hated the thought that you might have to struggle with it all through the Christmas week."

"I would have put it all aside until after Christmas in any case," he told her.

"Piffle!" She smiled up at him. "You know very well you find it impossible to put aside work that has to be done."

"I seem to remember putting a great deal of my own work aside in order to come down here and manage this place for a month," Baxter said dryly.

"Ah, well, that was different." She glanced up at the clock. "In any case, since you are finished for the evening, what do you say to taking dinner in the dining room tonight? I'm tired of eating in our suite and snacking in your office. I would like to dine in style for a change."

"Anything you desire, my love. But I think it's a little late for Michel to cook us dinner now."

"Oh, they'll find something for us in the kitchen, I'm sure." She took hold of his arm. "Come, I have some delicious tidbits of news I'm just dying to share with you."

"Not gossip, I hope. You know how I abhor listening to gossip."

"Well, not strictly, no. This came straight from the horse's mouth. Besides, you'll be very pleased to hear that the mystery of Barry Wrotham's death has been explained. At least, I think it has. Though I can't help feeling that I haven't heard the whole story."

Baxter folded the ledger with a snap, then opened the door before turning out the gas lamps on the wall. "Well, my dear madam, you have succeeded in intriguing me. Let us proceed to the dining room this minute, so that we might satisfy both my curiosity and my appetite."

She accompanied him eagerly to the dining room, where to her delight, she found Gertie and Ross, still seated with

Samuel and Doris, enjoying a lingering cup of coffee.

The men rose as she approached the table ahead of Baxter, who had paused to give their order to one of the serving maids. After greeting them all, she concentrated her attention on Doris, whom she barely recognized.

A picture of elegance in a high-throated gown of pale pink batiste, generously trimmed in Point de Paris lace, the young lady seemed nothing like that frightened little scullery maid who'd dropped everything she'd picked up and had spoken only in whispers.

Now a seasoned performer on the London stage, Doris had grown into a poised, glamorous young woman. Still not a star, perhaps, but definitely on her way there. Only her shy smile reminded Cecily of the child she once was.

"Doris!" Cecily grasped both of the young girl's slender hands. "How utterly marvelous to see you again. You look exquisite. Quite the London celebrity. How are you enjoying the stage?"

Doris's eyes glowed with warmth. "It's wonderful, m'm. I've never been so happy in all my life." Her smile faded a little. "Well, except for when I worked here at the Pennyfoot, that is."

Cecily laughed. "Come now, Doris, we can hardly compare to the excitement and glamour of the stage. But I hope you miss us just a little bit."

"Oh, I do, m'm." Doris waved a hand at Gertie. "I miss Gertie and Mrs. Chubb. And especially you and Mr. Baxter. You were like parents to me. I'll never forget that. Never."

Cecily felt a warm glow herself. "We've always considered the staff of the Penny-foot our family. We miss you all very much."

Doris folded her serviette and placed it on the table. "Gertie was telling me you want to put on a pantomime."

"Yeah," Gertie said, laughing. "She asked me if I wanted to be in it. I told her I could be an Ugly Sister if we did *Cinderella*."

"I offered to be the prince," Samuel said, winking at Doris.

"Well, actually, I thought we might do *Aladdin*," Cecily said, looking hopefully at Doris. "Phoebe's dance troupe still have their *Arabian Nights* costumes. They were such a hit in the tableaux —"

"Except for the time Phoebe let a python loose on the stage," Baxter said dryly, having come up behind Cecily without her noticing. "I don't think the audience appreciated that little dramatic effect, judging by the amount of swooning ladies."

"Yeah," Samuel said with a grin. "The ballroom looked like a battlefield. After the python won."

They all laughed, greeting Baxter as if he were a long-lost friend. Cecily beamed on them all. It was so good to see her favorite people having such a wonderful time. It had been a good idea to invite everyone for Christmas, and now that the mystery of Barry Wrotham's death was solved, she could relax and enjoy the festivities.

Even so, as she preceded Baxter to a secluded table in the corner of the room, she couldn't quite dismiss the little niggling notion that Lucille had not been exactly truthful. Or perhaps she didn't want to pursue the possibility, just in case there was something sinister going on. Something that just might ruin Christmas for them all.

Right now everyone was happy and relaxed, looking forward with expectation to the big day. This was how it should be, and she could only hope that nothing would come along to spoil it all.

As for Madeline's dire warnings, she had

been known to be mistaken before. Cecily decided just to put the whole thing out of her mind. Nothing was going to interfere with this Christmas Season. Not if she could help it.

The very next morning Doris called a rehearsal for the pantomime. Having appeared in a production of *Aladdin* the year before, she was well acquainted with the music and the general story line. Since most of the speaking parts were ad-libbed anyway, it was just a matter of prompting and prodding the actors.

Motor cars had been sent out to the vicarage so that Phoebe could round up her dance troupe, and various members of the staff had been invited to join in the fun. Raymond, who had been following Doris around all morning, was given the part of the genie, and Cecily agreed to juggle his duties among the footmen in order to allow him to take part. Doris herself was to play Aladdin.

Phoebe was beside herself with excitement, especially when told that her dance troupe could perform their tableaux as part of the backdrop, and even the colonel was recruited to act as a palace guard.

Despite Doris's pleas, both Cecily and

Baxter declined to take part, citing their duties as being too numerous for them to spare the time. Gertie and Mrs. Chubb volunteered, however, and would be adding comic relief to the presentation. Though, as Baxter remarked in an aside to Cecily, just the appearance of Phoebe's dance troupe would provide plenty of amusement.

In all, the pantomime promised to be a spectacular addition to the Christmas events, and Cecily was well pleased with her decision. After leaving the excited cast to rehearse, she made her way to the kitchen. It had been some time since she had spoken to Michel, and she needed to go over the Christmas menu with him.

She was crossing the foyer when she spotted Percy Chatsworth entering through the front doors. He doffed his homburg at the sight of her, greeting her with a cheery "Good morning, Mrs. Baxter!"

She answered his greeting, and was about to pass him by, when she remembered something Lucille had said. *I do not understand why he needs all this extra work and demands . . . I wish the others would leave him alone.*

At the time, Cecily had wondered who "the others" might be, and what kind of business they were engaged in that Lucille found so distressing. It occurred to her now that Lucille might have been talking about the other Benchers.

True, it was none of her business, but curiosity had always been her downfall, and she really wanted to know what Lucille had meant by those words. Perhaps then she could finally banish that annoying little feeling that she had forgotten something that still taunted her mind.

Percy Chatsworth was a good deal older than his counterparts, and probably nearing retirement. It seemed a good place to start. "I trust you are enjoying your respite, Mr. Chatsworth?" She beamed at him. "Your work must bring such pressure to bear. It can't be easy to argue whether or not a man is guilty of a crime. It's a great responsibility."

"Indeed it is, Mrs. Baxter. Indeed it is." Chatsworth nodded his head emphatically in agreement.

"I imagine you are looking forward to your retirement. Your work must not give you time to enjoy much leisure. How fortunate that you are spared the time to visit with us here in Badgers End."

"Quite, quite." Chatsworth looked meaningfully at the grandfather clock. He was obviously in a hurry to be somewhere else.

"Though I suppose some of you manage to have business interests outside of the courts, wouldn't you say?" It was a shot in the dark, but she was hoping he might shed some light on Sir John's activities.

To her surprise, Chatsworth's eyes had narrowed to thin slits, and the muscles in his jaw were so tight she could see them twitch. "That would be quite impossible, Mrs. Baxter. Masters of the Bench are prohibited from owning or being engaged in outside businesses. One would be instantly disbarred for life. Now, if you will excuse me, I am late for an important appointment."

She watched him stride off, his cape flapping around his ankles like an angry dog. It must have been something she said, though she couldn't imagine what it was. In any case, it would seem that Sir John's added demands were not connected to business affairs. Which made his lack of attention even more unreasonable. It was no wonder his wife was so upset with him. Feeling decidedly sorry for the woman, Cecily continued on her way.

Long before she reached the kitchen door, she could hear the uproar ensuing from behind it. The crashing and banging of pans sounded ominously familiar as an irate voice strove to make itself heard above the racket. "*Sacre bleu!* 'Ow am I supposed to provide ze meal with ze excellence my patrons expect from me when I 'ave such incompetence from ze 'elpers? You are all 'elpless, *oui?* You do not know 'ow to serve ze rack of lamb, *non?* 'Ow many times I tell you . . . put ze little white frills on top ze feet, not around ze bottom!"

Michel was on the warpath again. Cecily pushed open the door to the kitchen, just as a saucepan lid crashed to the floor.

Miss Bunkle emerged from the pantry carrying a huge tray loaded with hams. Moira leaped to help her and instead bumped into her. The flustered maid jumped backward, stepped back onto the saucepan lid, skidded on it, and sent it clattering across the red tile floor.

Miss Bunkle, unlike Mrs. Chubb, who would have raised her voice to scold the maid, simply sat the tray on the huge butcher table in the middle of the kitchen and said coldly, "Do try to be more careful, girl. We don't want any more broken dishes."

"Broken dishes?" Michel swung around

from the stove, waving a wooden spoon in the air. "There'll be broken 'eads if I 'ave my way. I cannot work with such imbeciles —" Apparently catching sight of Cecily, he broke off, his eyes widening. "*Madame!* You are 'ere!" He swept her a flamboyant bow, sweeping yet another saucepan lid to the ground.

Cecily winced at the deafening rattle of its lopsided spin. Moira snatched it up before it could spin to a clattering stop. "Morning, m'm," she said, dipping a nervous curtsey.

"I'm sorry, madam," Miss Bunkle said, coming forward. "Things are a little disorganized this morning. One of our maids is ill and another has the half-day off and we are so busy we haven't had time to breathe."

"Oh, dear, we shall have to try to do something about that. Perhaps we should take on some extra maids over Christmas." Cecily smiled at Moira, who looked as if she were about to burst into tears. "It's all right, Moira. Get on with your work."

"Yes, m'm." The girl scurried over to the table and joined the other girls in polishing the silverware.

Cecily turned to the housekeeper. "Who is ill, Miss Bunkle?"

The housekeeper shook her head. "It's Jeanette, madam. She has a bad cold and went to bed early last night. The girl was sniffing all day yesterday. Now two of the others have started sniffing. If they go down with colds, we'll be in a right pickle."

"Has anyone attended to Jeanette this morning? Does she need a doctor?"

"I haven't had time to look in on her as yet, madam. I'll send someone to her room as soon as the midday meal is over."

"That won't be for another two hours or more." Cecily glanced at the clock. "I'll stop by there on my way out and see if she needs anything."

"Oh, no, madam, that won't be necessary. I —"

"Oh, *no, you can't!*"

Both Miss Bunkle and Moira had spoken at once. Or rather, Moira's protest had been more a cry of dismay. Everyone in the kitchen suddenly fell silent, as if sensing something important was amiss.

Cecily and the housekeeper stared at Moira, who appeared to be in great distress. She twisted her apron around her fingers as she stared wide-eyed at Cecily.

"What is it, girl?" Miss Bunkle demanded. "Speak up! Do you need to go to the lavatory?"

Moira's face flamed and she shot an embarrassed glance at Michel. "No, Miss Bunkle, it's just that, Jeanette, well . . ."

Cecily moved toward her, holding out her hand. "It's all right, Moira," she said soothingly. "What's the matter with Jeanette?"

"I don't know . . . that is . . . she's . . ." She sent a wild glance around the kitchen. Three of the maids stared back as if hanging on her every word, while Michel stirred a cauldron of soup with one hand and glared at the hapless girl.

"Perhaps we'd better step outside," Cecily said quietly.

At that Moira seemed even more agitated. "No, no, it's nothing, m'm, honest it isn't. Jeanette is quite all right, I know she is. She doesn't need nothing right now." She aimed a scared look at Miss Bunkle. "I can go and see her in a little while. She'll be all right until then. Honest. She'd rather be left alone."

Miss Bunkle walked right up to the maid and scowled at her. Although her voice was deadly calm, the knitting needle in her hair quivered as though attached to a rumbling volcano. "All right, my girl. *Where is Jeanette?*"

Tears welled up in Moira's frightened

eyes. "I don't know, Miss Bunkle. Honest I don't."

"I assume she's not lying down in her room."

"I don't think so, Miss Bunkle."

"You share the room with her, don't you?"

The girl nodded, dabbing at her nose with the back of her hand.

"Then you know where she is."

"No, I don't, Miss Bunkle. She never told me where she was going." Once more she sent a worried glance at the other curious girls.

"Stop your gawking and get on with your work," Miss Bunkle ordered, jerking a hand in their direction. "We're behind enough as it is. Moira, you come with me." She grabbed the girl's hand and marched her out of the kitchen, with Cecily following close behind.

Once outside in the hallway, Miss Bunkle pushed her face into Moira's, nose to nose. "Now you're going to tell me where Jeanette is and what she is doing, or I'll have you scrubbing floors every night for a week."

Moira promptly burst into a storm of weeping, making it impossible to get anything out of her.

"Perhaps I should talk to her," Cecily suggested. "I'm sure you need to be back in the kitchen taking care of your chores."

Miss Bunkle hesitated, then gave Cecily a sharp nod. "Very well, madam. But I have to tell you, I am not happy with the way the staff behaves here. The maids are impertinent, and as for Michel, he's a drunken lout with a filthy temper. The staff have been allowed too many liberties if you ask me. Discipline, that's what these people need. They need to be treated like servants, not like members of the family. It's no wonder the whole place is so disorganized."

Cecily suppressed her resentment as best she could, saying evenly, "I'm sorry you feel that way, Miss Bunkle. Please return to your work. I'll take care of this matter with Jeanette."

Miss Bunkle muttered her begrudging thanks and disappeared into the kitchen. Moira still sobbed into her apron and Cecily patted her on the shoulder. "Come along with me, Moira. We'll talk in my suite."

Moira gulped and sniffed, and blew her nose into her apron, making Cecily wince. She made a mental note to supply all the maids with handkerchiefs. No wonder they were passing colds around to each other.

"I'd better not, m'm," Moira said, her voice quivering. "Miss Bunkle is really cross with me. I don't want to make her any more cross."

"Very well." Cecily smiled encouragingly at her. "You can go back now if you feel better."

"Yes, m'm. I do. Thank you, m'm." She turned to go, but Cecily laid a hand on her thin shoulder.

"But first, I think it might be a good idea if you tell me when you last saw Jeanette."

Moira gulped again, then whispered, "I gave my solemn promise I wouldn't tell."

"When was that?"

Moira's lips trembled. "Last night, m'm."

Cecily felt a pang of apprehension. "Last night? That was the last time you saw her?"

Moira gave her a reluctant nod of her head.

"And she didn't say where she was going?"

"No, m'm. She didn't. She said as how it were a secret."

"She stayed out all night?"

"Yes, m'm."

Now Cecily was really worried. "Did she say anything else that might help us know where she is? Did she give you any idea she planned on leaving for good?"

"Oh, no, m'm. She told me she was meeting someone and she couldn't tell me who it was, but that she'd tell me all about it later. I think she meant to come back, m'm. That's why I'm so worried." Her bottom lip trembled again and she caught it under her teeth.

"Does she have a young man?"

"Yes, m'm. Wally Diggett. But she weren't going to see him. She told me they broke up."

"Perhaps she was going to mend their quarrel."

Moira gave a definite shake of her head. "No, m'm. She was going to meet someone else. She told me that much, but she wouldn't tell me who it was." She started to cry again. "She's going to hate me for telling you, I know she is."

"Please don't worry, Moira," Cecily said gently. "I won't let her know you told me anything. Which room are you in?"

"Number three, m'm. And thank you." The girl managed a weak smile. "I'm much obliged."

The door closed behind her, and frowning, Cecily made her way down the hallway to the maids' quarters. Reaching the door with a brass number three on it, she tapped, gently at first. When there was no answer from inside, she rapped loudly. "Jeanette? Are you in there?" After a moment's hesitation, she turned the handle and went inside.

She had forgotten how cramped the maids' quarters were. The room was barely big enough to hold the two cots, which sat close together with a gap just big enough for knees to pass in between. A small wardrobe took up the space in one corner, and a narrow dresser bearing a washbasin and jug stood in the other.

The only mirror in the room was a small oval one in a carved metal frame that hung on the wall over the dresser. The tiny window looked out on the kitchen yard, barely ten feet of paving before it reached the high wooden fence on the other side.

No wonder the young girls were leaving the service in droves to find jobs in the city. The pay for a servant was small, the hours long, and the work arduous. The compensation of having room and board thrown in was hardly an incentive anymore, when compared with the freedom of returning to one's own home at night in the city. Even if that home was no more than a cramped room in a boardinghouse.

Freedom, that was the key word. Freedom to come and go where and when one pleased, once the day's work was done. It made all the difference. Cecily sighed, and went to the wardrobe to open it. Two afternoon dresses hung there, and beneath them, two pairs of black patent leather shoes. On the top shelf sat two large traveling bags.

After closing the door, she wandered over to the dresser. A hairbrush sat on one side of the washbasin, together with a face flannel, a comb, and a toothbrush. It certainly would appear that Jeanette had planned to return to the Pennyfoot. So now the question was, why hadn't she?

Cecily left the room and closed the door behind her. She had a very bad feeling in the pit of her stomach. It would seem that the ill luck that had haunted the Pennyfoot ever since James's death was still with them. She could only hope that the girl was safe and sound.

Chapter
13

Baxter seemed less concerned with Jeanette's disappearance than Cecily would have liked. "She's probably gone off with her young man for a day or two," he said, looking disdainful. "You know what these young girls are like nowadays. Disgraceful, that's what I call it. I don't know what's happening to women lately. This blasted Women's Movement is causing more trouble than I ever imagined. What with women digging up golf courses, breaking windows, and starving themselves in prisons, the whole world is going to rot. And for what? What do they really hope to achieve?"

"The vote, for one thing," Cecily said mildly. "To be on an equal footing with men, for another. To be allowed to enter any room in any establishment, such as the card rooms and the bar of this country club. In other words, to be treated and respected as a human being."

"Are you saying I don't treat you with respect?"

"Of course not, dear. But then you are the exception." She smiled fondly at him. She had long ago learned that it was a waste of time to argue with his favorite grievance, much as she disagreed with his opinions. Ignoring his snort of exasperation, she poured out his tea from the silver teapot.

He had abandoned his office for a short while in order to take afternoon tea in the suite with her, a treat she truly enjoyed. Ever since they had arrived at the Pennyfoot, he had been closeted in his office for the most part.

Although he spent a great deal of time at home with his business, he'd at least had time to share meals with her, whereas here in the Pennyfoot, with the exception of a late supper at night, they were fortunate to snatch a few moments here and there over a cup of tea or a glass of sherry.

This afternoon, however, was a delightful departure from his normal routine, and she was determined to enjoy every moment. Even so, she'd deemed it necessary to inform him of Jeanette's unexplained absence.

"I'm particularly worried about

Jeanette," she told him, "because Miss Bunkle said that she was coming down with a bad cold yesterday. I do hope she hasn't fallen ill somewhere and is lying in a hospital bed. She'd be so miserable and lonely with no one to pay her a visit."

"I think we would have heard if that had happened. Someone would have notified us by now."

"Well, Jeanette might seem a little frivolous at times, but she doesn't seem the sort to simply take her leave without a word to anyone."

"Who knows what these young girls will do just to please a beau."

"Moira told me that Jeanette was planning to meet someone other than her young man. Miss Bunkle is convinced that Jeanette stole her pearls and has gone off to London to sell them."

"Well. There you are then."

"I don't believe that for one minute. Jeanette was quite indignant that we should even suspect her of stealing the pearls."

"That could have been a well-executed piece of acting. You'd be surprised what these girls are capable of doing."

"I suppose." She sighed. "I hate to think of a young girl like that involved in crime at such a tender age."

"Well, I suggest we let the constables take care of it. Has anyone reported her as missing?"

"Not yet. We're all rather hoping she'll soon return with a feasible explanation."

"I wouldn't wait too long on that expectation." He lifted a miniature mince pie from the tray of pastries. "This is what I enjoy most about Christmas," he added after taking a bite with a look of supreme pleasure on his face. "I really don't understand why we can't have Christmas food all year long. It seems such a waste to wait until the end of the year to enjoy plum pudding and Christmas cakes."

"Ah, but you wouldn't enjoy them half as much if you could have them anytime you wanted." Abandoning her concerns about Jeanette for the moment, Cecily helped herself to a mince pie. "Besides, it's a tradition, such as Easter eggs and hot cross buns."

"Another waste, if you ask me." He leaned back with his cup and saucer balanced on his knee. "To blazes with tradition, that's what I say."

She burst out laughing. "Why, Bax, I never thought the day would come when you would give up on tradition. You're always fighting progress and change. Except for the motor car, that is."

"Ah, well, that's the only sensible thing to come out of all this rush to modernize the world. I'm thinking of asking young Samuel to teach me to drive an automobile. I think it would be a great asset for getting around in my business."

Cecily regarded him over the rim of her cup. "You always meet your clients at the club, which is a twenty-minute walk from our house. By the time you managed to crank up the engine of a motor car, climbed in, drove it to the club, deposited it, and got out of it, you could have walked the distance in half of that time."

Baxter frowned. "It's not the time involved, Cecily, it's the impression one gives when arriving in an automobile. Prestige!" He wagged a finger at her. "That is the key to a successful business."

"Well, my love, no one can deny that you have a very successful business, so your prestige must be in excellent condition already, in which case, you do not need a motor car to enhance it."

He frowned at her for a moment, then his face softened. "Has anyone ever told you, Mrs. Baxter, that you have an infernal way of turning an argument in your favor?"

She grinned. "I learned from a master.

James could argue his way out of the dungeons in the Tower of London."

"Indeed he could." He studied her with a pensive expression. "You still miss him?"

"Not anymore." She got up from her chair, leaned over her husband, and kissed him. "How could I, when I have someone who fulfills me as you do?"

He sighed. "There are times when I feel I don't give you enough of myself. What with the business and now this . . ." He waved a vague hand in the air. "It seems we have so little time together these days. It was my biggest complaint when we worked here in the past."

She returned to her chair and reached for her tea. "Well, I must admit I was becoming a trifle bored at home, being left alone to my own devices. But now that I am back here at the Pennyfoot, I can find plenty enough to fill in my time. Though I will always welcome the chance to share a few minutes alone with you, my dear husband."

"It won't always be this way."

"I know." She sipped her tea, then replaced the cup in its saucer. "I am a patient woman, Bax. I know that one day we will have all the leisure time in the world together, and that is well worth the wait."

"I promise I will make it worth your while."

She smiled at him, content for now in knowing how much he cared for her. She was, indeed, a fortunate woman.

"It's very nice of you to invite us to help you decorate the tree, Miss Pengrath," Daisy said as she sat the twins down at a small table in the library. "The little ones have been looking forward to it all day, haven't you, ducks?"

Lillian nodded, while James looked bored. Daisy hoped he wouldn't give her any trouble. The twins had really grown up a lot since she'd last seen them. They were becoming quite a handful.

"I'm delighted to have the help," Madeline said in her low, musical voice. "It will give their mother and Mrs. Chubb some time to themselves."

Daisy wished fervently that she had a voice like Madeline's. She'd tried to speak like that now and then, but all she managed to do was sound as if she had a bad cold. "I know Gertie and Mrs. Chubb will like that." She beamed at the twins. "And it will be fun to help, won't it, luvs."

James pouted. "Don't want to," he muttered.

"Yes, you do," Madeline said firmly. She rummaged inside the large tapestry bag she'd brought in with her, and came up holding two peppermint sticks. "We'll have lots of fun, and this will be your pay for helping me."

Lillian's face lit up, and James held out a chubby hand. "I want it *now*," he demanded.

"Only when you've finished helping." Madeline dropped them back in the bag and pulled out a thick wad of paper strips. She laid them out on the table in piles of pink, blue, green, yellow, white, and red. Next she put out a large pot of paste with a brush fixed to the cap. "Now, this is how you make a paper chain."

Daisy watched her dab the paste brush on one end of a pink strip and fasten it into a circle. Then she threaded a blue strip through the circle and fastened the ends of it with the paste. "Now, do you two clever little people think you can do that?"

Lillian nodded eagerly and reached for a strip of paper. Even James seemed intrigued, in spite of his best efforts not to look interested. Daisy helped them put the paste on the strips and fasten the ends, then let them choose the next strip.

Out of the corner of her eye, she

watched Madeline hang the glass ornaments, hand-sewn lace-trimmed hearts,
and red velvet bows on the tree.

Seeing her at work, so graceful and se-
rene, Daisy found it hard to believe the
stories they told about Madeline in the village. In that white cotton dress with its
little red bows, she looked just like an
angel. A very beautiful angel. If she was
dressed in a proper gown, she'd put all
them toffs to shame. It didn't seem right
that she wasn't married. But then, not
many men would want to take the chance
of marrying a witch.

"James took my paper," Lillian wailed. "I
wanted that pink one."

"It's mine," James declared, holding the
strip to his chest, where it promptly stuck
to the bib of his apron.

Daisy peeled it off, tearing it in the pro-
cess. Both twins wailed and it took a
minute or two to restore harmony.

"Here," Madeline said as she lifted the
uneven chain of paper from the table. "You
can help me hang it on the tree now, and
then we'll put all the Christmas crackers in
between the branches."

"What are crackers?" James asked as he
draped one end of the chain over a low
branch of the tree.

"They have snaps inside them," Daisy explained. "You hold one end and I hold the other, then we pull and the cracker pops with a bang and a present falls out of it."

"And a hat," Madeline added. "Here, I'll show you." She hunted in her bag again, and then handed Daisy a box filled with long colored paper tubes, gaily decorated and frilled at each end. "Take one out and we'll let them pull it."

Daisy took a cracker out of the box and helped each twin grasp the end of it. "Now pull," she told them.

They both tugged hard and the cracker popped open with a loud snap that made Lillian jump. Something fell to the floor and both twins dove for it. James came up holding a tiny silver horse, and Lillian pouted.

"He always gets everything," she wailed.

Madeline unwrapped the remains of the cracker and pulled out a paper hat, which she placed on Lillian's head. "Ah," she said softly, "but you are the one who is crowned the queen."

Lillian's tearful frown vanished, and she floated around the room chanting, "I'm the queen, I'm the queen!"

"Now it's time to put the candles on," Madeline said, handing some of the tiny wax sticks to Daisy. "You two can tell us where we should put them."

"Why are we putting candles on the tree?" James demanded.

"We're going to have a candle-lighting ceremony," Daisy told him. "We'll all stand around the tree on Christmas Eve and sing carols, and then someone lights all the candles and we turn all the lamps out and everyone gets a present off the Christmas tree."

"Will Father Christmas be here?" Lillian wanted to know.

Madeline laughed. "Father Christmas won't come until everyone is asleep. So you must be sure to go to sleep really quickly that night."

"Will the candles be burning when he comes?"

"No, we have to blow them all out," Daisy explained. "It would be much too dangerous to leave them burning on the tree. It could catch fire."

"Then how will he see to come down the chimney?" James demanded.

"We'll leave a lamp lit for him," Madeline promised. She reached up to fasten a candle holder onto a branch. "Don't worry, Father Christmas is accustomed to moving around . . . in the dark. He —"

Her voice stopped abruptly, and she seemed to freeze, her hands so still that Daisy thought she could have been a statue. Even the twins were silent, staring at Madeline's still figure as if they had seen a ghost.

The eerie silence that settled over the room made Daisy's blood run cold, then Madeline spoke, and her soft words sent chills all the way down Daisy's spine.

"There is evil in this room," she said, her voice close to a whisper. "Danger lurking everywhere. You must beware. *You must beware.*"

The warning seemed to float in the air, cold and menacing. Frightened now, Daisy drew the children close to her. She stared at Madeline, wondering frantically for whom the words were meant. Was it her? Was she in danger? The twins?

Madeline dropped her hands and turned to face her. "You can start putting the candles on the other side of the tree," she said, her voice perfectly normal again.

Daisy blinked. It was over so quickly she wondered if she'd imagined it, but the twins still stared at the other woman as if afraid of her.

Daisy pulled them around the other side of the tree with her and started talking very fast about all the things the children had to look forward to during Christmas. Before long they were chattering and laughing with her, and even Madeline joined in their silliness.

Daisy gradually relaxed, though she knew that it would be a very long time before she forgot the strange moment when Madeline saw something that no one else could see. Something evil and frightening, and perhaps still lurking in the shadows of the quiet library.

By the end of the day Cecily had to accept the fact that Jeanette was probably not going to return to the Pennyfoot. Miss Bunkle expressed her displeasure by announcing that she couldn't possibly cope with the Christmas Season unless she had another pair of hands.

Cecily promised to see what she could do about hiring another maid, but when Miss Bunkle insisted that she report to the constables that Jeanette had stolen her pearls, Cecily put her foot down.

"You cannot accuse someone of a crime without good cause," she told the infuriated woman. "Just because Jeanette has apparently left our employ does not mean she's a thief."

"Why else would she run away?" Miss Bunkle demanded. "It looks awfully suspicious to me. If she didn't steal my pearls, then where are they? They didn't just simply walk off on their own."

"Well, perhaps I can find out what happened to them. Just give me a little time."

Miss Bunkle tightened her lips. "Very well, madam. But if they don't turn up in the next day or two, I'm going to tell the constables everything."

"If I can't find out what happened to them, I'll call the constables myself," Cecily promised rashly. The last thing she wanted right now was a full-scale investigation going on in the club. Edward would never forgive her if she allowed the Christmas Season to be spoiled by a petty thief.

On a hunch she stopped by Moira's room and tapped on the door. Luckily the girl hadn't yet gone to bed, though she seemed extremely disturbed by Cecily's visit.

"I don't know nothing more about where Jeanette is, honest," she said when Cecily invited herself into the room.

"Actually, I came to ask if you had any idea where Miss Bunkle's pearls might be," Cecily said, seating herself on the edge of Jeanette's bed.

Moira looked frightened. "I told you, m'm, I had nothing to do with the pearls."

"Miss Bunkle thinks Jeanette might have taken them and that's why she ran away. What do you think about that?"

Moira's cheeks grew red, and she stared down at her feet. "I don't know nothing about that, m'm. But I got to thinking about things and I think I might know who Jeanette was meeting last night."

Taken by surprise, Cecily said sharply, "Then I think you had better tell me."

Moira fidgeted with the strings of her apron, winding them around her fingers so tightly they turned white. "I don't want to get no one in trouble, m'm, but if something bad has happened to Jeanette . . ." Her voice trailed off miserably.

"I'm sure nothing bad has happened to your friend," Cecily assured her. "And I promise you that you won't be getting anyone into any more trouble than they are already in, so why don't you just tell me who you think Jeanette was meeting and we'll see what we can do."

Moira sank onto her bed. "Well, I do know that Jeanette was sweet on someone. She was always talking about him, and once I saw her talking to him in the corridor."

"Did she tell you she was fond of this person? She could have simply been having a friendly conversation."

"Well, the other night Jeanette had a terrible row with Wally over him. I heard them arguing about it in the kitchen yard. Wally told her that if he wasn't good enough for her, she could run right back to her pretty boy lover."

"I see," Cecily said slowly. "And what did she say to that?"

"She said that's just what she was planning to do, and that if Wally didn't like it, it was just too bad. Wally laughed at her, and said that no toff would ever be caught dead with her."

Cecily stared at her. "A toff? Are you saying Jeanette was romantically involved with one of the guests?"

"I think so, m'm."

"Do you know who he is?"

Moira pressed her lips together, then blurted out, "You won't tell anyone I said anything, will you? I don't want to get no one in trouble. I just thought he might know where Jeanette went."

"I won't tell anyone you told me," Cecily promised. "But I must know who it is, Moira. It could be extremely important."

"All right." Moira carefully unwound the

string from her fingers. "It were one of them barristers from London. The good-looking one. His name is Roger. Roger Peebles."

Cecily gaped at her. "Roger Peebles? Are you sure?"

Moira nodded. "Yes, that's him. Roger Peebles. He's the one. I think Jeanette was going to see him last night."

Cecily made an effort to collect her thoughts. The whole idea was so ludicrous. Jeanette was a nice young girl, but she was not exactly what one would call a beauty. She was certainly no match for Peebles's wife, Gretchen. Then again, there was no accounting for taste. Peebles wouldn't be the only one to turn to a serving girl to add a little spice to his life.

Making a mental note to talk to Peebles at the first opportunity, Cecily rose to leave. "Well, thank you, Moira. I appreciate you being so candid with me. You did the right thing by telling me what you know."

"Please don't be too angry with Jeanette, m'm," Moira pleaded. "After all, she's not the only one. I reckon all them barristers are the same. I saw the fat one, Mr. Fitzhammer, going into his room with a lady what wasn't his wife. I know that 'cos I saw his wife downstairs in the library right after I went downstairs again so it couldn't have been her I saw in his room."

What was the matter with these men, Cecily fumed inwardly. They had everything they could possibly want . . . money, prestige, a beautiful wife, and one would assume, a gorgeous home, and still it wasn't enough. As long as she lived, she would never understand the mentality of the human male species.

"I hope you won't repeat any of this to anyone else," she told Moira. "What goes on inside these walls must never be divulged to anyone. Is that clear?"

"Oh, I know, m'm." Moira nodded solemnly. "Me lips are sealed. I only told you 'cos I thought it might help find out what happened to Jeanette."

Cecily nodded. "Well, we'll have to see. Now get some sleep, Moira. You'll have a long day tomorrow if Jeanette doesn't return."

Moira's voice wavered when she asked, "What do you think happened to her, m'm?"

"I think she probably went off looking for adventure somewhere, and is probably wishing right now that she hadn't been so silly."

She closed the door behind her and

headed back to the stairs. The answer she'd given to Moira's question had been deliberately vague. The truth was, she was far more concerned about the missing maid than she was willing to admit. She could only hope that Jeanette wasn't in more trouble than she could handle. The sense of urgency that had bothered her earlier was even more intense now. It was imperative they find the girl as soon as possible. She could only hope it wasn't too late.

Chapter
14

"These two are driving me blinking bonkers," Gertie announced the next morning. She and Mrs. Chubb had taken the twins for a stroll along the sands after breakfast, hoping to wear down some of the boundless energy that kept the children ceaselessly on the move.

The cold wind from the sea had whipped their faces, turning their little cheeks bright red by the time they'd returned to the Pennyfoot. Gertie was now huddled in Mrs. Chubb's room, trying to thaw out her frozen bones, while Mrs. Chubb did her best to prevent the twins from ruining the bedsprings as they bounced up and down with a little too much exuberance.

"Why don't you take Ross into the town and enjoy some of Dolly's baking?" Mrs. Chubb suggested. "You two haven't spent more than an hour or two together since he arrived."

"We've spent all night together," Gertie

said, reaching out to break James's grasp on his sister's hair. She gave his hand a light slap. "Leave your sister alone or I'll tell your papa what a bad boy you are."

"I meant doing something outside the hotel. Go for a walk with him, or stop by the George and Dragon. Go and watch the ice-skating on Deep Willow Pond."

Gertie sighed. "I just been for a walk and my toes are ready to bleeding drop off with the cold. Besides, Ross is lying down. He don't feel very well."

Mrs. Chubb's eyes were full of concern when she looked at her. "He's not ill, is he?"

"I hope not." Gertie did her best to dismiss her pang of fear. "I think he's just tired, that's all. And fed up. I wasn't going to tell you this 'til after Christmas, but he's sold the business."

"Oh, my." Mrs. Chubb clutched her chest. "What is he going to do now?"

Gertie shrugged. "Oh, he'll find something, I know he will. It's just . . . it's not like him to give up like that."

Mrs. Chubb nodded. "He's not a young man anymore, Gertie. You have to remember that he's a lot older than you. He's ready to slow down a bit. And the business was taking its toll on him. I could tell that."

"Yeah, well, he'll be able to have a bit of a rest now, until he finds a job. The money he made on the business will keep us going for a bit. And I can always go back to work if needs be."

Mrs. Chubb grabbed Lillian's hand, just as she was about to pull the washbowl and basin off its stand. "It would be hard on you, Gertie, after all this time."

"I don't think so." Gertie winced as James fell off the bed. He started wailing and she scooped him up and sat him on her lap. "I've sort of missed working since I've been married to Ross. I know I have plenty to do in the house, and Gawd knows the twins take up enough time, but they're getting older and I miss the company of the other girls. Being back here has reminded me of all the laughs we used to have, and all the adventures."

"We tend to remember the best of times and forget the worst."

"I know. Still, I do miss it." Her gaze met Mrs. Chubb's, and the older woman's wistful expression made her smile.

"I miss it, too," Mrs. Chubb confessed. "I mean, I love helping you take care of the children, but soon now they'll be going to school. What will two grown women do all day long in the house together without the

253

little ones to worry about?"

Gertie shrugged. "Housework, I s'pose. Like we do now."

"Not very exciting, is it."

"No, it's not." She grinned. "Are you thinking what I'm thinking?"

Mrs. Chubb sighed. "It would be very nice to go back to work again, Gertie, but you know very well Ross would never allow you to go back to work and I'm getting too old for it now. Maybe we could take in some sewing or something, just to give us a little extra and keep us busy."

"Yeah, maybe." James wriggled off Gertie's lap and promptly ran up to his sister and tugged on her hair again. "All right, that's bleeding it." She sprang up and slapped James on his rump.

He opened his mouth and howled, still holding on to Lillian's hair. By the time Gertie had untangled the long curls from his fist, Lillian was howling as well.

"We've got to get them out of here," Mrs. Chubb exclaimed as she gathered Lillian in her arms and hugged her to her generous bosom. "The other guests will be complaining about the noise."

"Let's take them for a walk around the grounds. They can throw stones in the fish pond or something. With the trees sheltering us, it might not be as bloody cold as it was on the beach."

"Good idea." Mrs. Chubb reached for Lillian's tam-o'-shanter and pulled it down over her ears. Then she wound a scarf around the little girl's neck and buttoned her into a warm coat. The boots were next, and it took her several minutes to fasten all the buttons with a button hook. Meanwhile Gertie struggled with James, who was still sniffling.

Several minutes later they were ready, and holding each child by the hand, Gertie and Mrs. Chubb emerged into the hallway and headed for the stairs.

Snowflakes floated down like soft white feathers as they stepped outside. Gertie had elected to go through the French doors in the library and out through the rose garden. There were no roses in bloom this late in the year, so there was no risk of the children trying to pick the blossoms off the bushes.

The wind from the ocean barely penetrated the thick hedges in the garden, and the twins spent a pleasant few minutes exploring the new territory and throwing snowballs at each other, while Mrs. Chubb and Gertie sat on the wooden bench, enjoying the tranquil scene.

"These bushes look like they could use a bloody good trim," Gertie remarked, pointing at the rows of rosebushes on either side of the crazy paving path.

"They do look a bit ragged." Mrs. Chubb frowned. "What happened to the arbor? It used to be so pretty with its archway of climbing roses."

"I knew something was missing." Gertie shook her head. "These gardens haven't looked the same since poor John Thimble died."

"I thought Ross did a good job of taking care of them when he worked here."

"Yeah, he did. But he really didn't have the time to do much before we moved back to Scotland."

"I've really missed living here," Mrs. Chubb said softly. "Scotland is very nice, but it's not Badgers End."

"I know." Gertie stretched out her booted feet. "It's too wild, too lonely. I miss the sea, and the shops, and the cliffs."

"And the people."

"Yeah, 'specially the people."

"Mama!"

The bloodcurdling shriek brought Gertie to her feet. "It's time we moved on before these two kill each other. Let's go for a walk around the tennis courts. By that time it should be close to mealtime again."

Mrs. Chubb rose a little stiffly. "All I seem to do here is eat."

Gertie grinned. "So what's bleeding wrong with that?" She grabbed James's hand as he raced by her. "We have a rehearsal this afternoon. Daisy said she'd look after the twins. It will give us both a bit of a break."

"I'm surprised Daisy didn't want to be in the pantomime," Mrs. Chubb remarked as she dusted a smear of dirt on Lillian's coat.

"Nah, Daisy doesn't like to be on show in front of everybody. She says she leaves that sort of thing to Doris. You know, it's a funny thing. I always thought Doris was the shy one, and Daisy was always so sure of herself, always ready to stand up to anyone what gave her lip. Yet now it's Doris what loves the stage and performing in front of people, and Daisy would rather be on her own than in a crowd."

Mrs. Chubb nodded. "Just goes to show, you never really know people as well as you think you do."

They rounded the end of the rose garden and came out on the edge of the bowling green. The grass had been allowed to grow a little too long, and needed a roller across it. The brief snow shower had ended, and a watery sun peeked out from behind the ominous clouds. As they neared the tennis courts, James tugged on Gertie's hand, anxious to explore this new and unusual playground.

"What's it for?" Lillian asked when they reached the high fence that surrounded the courts.

Gertie explained as best she could the rudiments of tennis. "It's a game, and you have a racquet and you hit the ball to each other across the net."

"I wanna play tennis!" James announced.

"Me, too." Lillian broke free from Mrs. Chubb's hand and rattled the gate. "I want to go in there."

Gertie unlatched the gate and opened it. The twins raced onto the court and started chasing each other all around. "That'll get rid of some of that energy," she said smugly.

"You hope."

Even as Mrs. Chubb spoke, James came running back to them. "We wanna play the tennis game!"

"Well, you can't." Gertie waved a hand at the empty court. "Tennis is a summer game. You can't play it in the snow. Besides, there's no net, and no racquets and no balls. So you can't play tennis now."

"I wanna play!"

James stamped his foot, and Lillian joined in, chanting over and over, "Wanna play tennis! Wanna play tennis!"

"All right!" Gertie glanced over to the shed that housed the equipment for the tennis courts and the lawn bowls. "I wonder if the shed is locked."

"I doubt it. Judging by the way the grounds have been neglected." Mrs. Chubb looked at the expectant faces of the twins. "It's worth a look, I suppose."

"All right, you keep an eye on them while I go and look. If it's open, I'll just bring a couple of racquets back and some balls. They don't need a net."

"Wanna net!" James insisted.

Gertie rolled her eyes skyward and headed for the gate. After closing it carefully behind her, she crunched her way across the crisp, overgrown grass to the shed.

As Mrs. Chubb had predicted, the door had been left unlocked. It swung inward with a groaning creak that made Gertie wince. She stepped inside, holding her nose at the stench that greeted her. Must have been a skunk in there, she told herself as she glanced around.

Mounds of black tarpaulin hid the contents from view, and sighing, Gertie advanced farther into the evil-smelling shed, wary of spiderwebs and whatever else might be waiting to snag her hat. She lifted the hem of her skirt with one hand, conscious of the thick layer of dust covering the bare floorboards. They creaked and snapped as she moved forward, making her jump with every sound. Then, without warning, the door swung to, plunging her into darkness.

For a moment she stood, heart pounding, waiting for her eyes to adjust to the dim light struggling to penetrate the small grimy window. Finally the shadows separated themselves, and she was able to make out the shapes again.

She was tempted to go back and open the door wide so she could see better, but instincts told her to grab what she wanted and get out of there. The stink was overpowering.

She reached for a corner of the closest tarpaulin and dragged it aside. To her relief, she saw a stack of tennis racquets, lying on top of a folded net. She dragged them out to the middle of the floor. Now all she needed was a couple of tennis balls.

The mound next to the one she'd disturbed was smaller. It seemed a likely place to be concealing a box of tennis balls. She tugged on the tarpaulin, but it seemed caught on something, so she lifted it instead.

At first she thought someone had left a pile of clothes under there, but then she saw a pair of shoes sticking up on end. Something about the way they remained in that odd position made her go cold. They could only be that way if there were feet in them.

With a growing sense of horror, she tugged really hard on the tarpaulin. The thing under there rolled out into the open.

Gertie opened her mouth to yell, but no sound came out. Frozen with shock, she stared at the bone white face with its glassy sightless eyes. She barely recognized the maid, but there was no mistaking the uniform. The black afternoon dress was crumpled, and the white lace collar around her throat was soaked in something that was dark and horribly messy.

At last Gertie's voice exploded in her throat and her scream rattled the walls. It was the last thing she remembered as she fell to the floor.

Mrs. Chubb heard the scream and knew

at once something dreadful had happened. She closed the gate on the twins and, despite their howls of protest, stumbled across the grass to the shed.

The door was closed, and she couldn't open it all the way. Peering through the gap, she could see Gertie's boot sticking out from under a pile of skirts. The rest of her body prevented her from opening the door far enough to squeeze her tubby figure through the narrow space.

Afraid to push too hard in case she hurt Gertie, she tried to peer farther into the shed to see the reason for Gertie's scream. But the shadows were too thick, and all she could see were mounds of tarpaulin and some old clothes. Wrinkling her nose against the foul smell, Mrs. Chubb banged on the door with her fist.

"Gertie! Ger*tay!*"

A low moan answered her.

"What's the matter, duck? What happened?"

The boot moved, and the door gave a little under Mrs. Chubb's hand. "Get me out of here," Gertie moaned. "I'm going to be sick."

Thoroughly alarmed now, Mrs. Chubb leaned on the door. It flew open and she stumbled inside, coming up short when she saw the crumpled figure lying in the middle of the floor. "Oh, good God, who's that?"

"It's one of the maids."

"Is she . . . ?" Mrs. Chubb let her voice trail off.

"She's bleeding dead, ain't she," Gertie snapped. She got unsteadily to her feet. "Let's get out of here, quick. We've got to tell someone."

Mrs. Chubb spun around, gulping down huge breaths of air, which didn't help much, seeing as the smell was enough to kill an elephant.

Gertie tugged the door open, stumbled outside, and promptly got rid of her breakfast.

Moaning, Mrs. Chubb surged forward after her. Her foot struck something and sent it skidding across the floor. She caught sight of it as she barreled through the door, and her stomach heaved.

"There's a knife in there," she gasped as Gertie turned a chalk white face toward her. "A big carving knife. I think it's covered in blood."

Gertie moaned and turned away from her again. "Bloody hell," she muttered when she was finished. "I used to have a stronger stomach than this."

Mrs. Chubb kept on taking deep breaths until she was reasonably sure she wasn't going to follow Gertie's performance with one of her own. "Enough to make anyone sick," she gasped at last. "You'd better go back to the club and find Mrs. Baxter. I'll bring the twins back if I can get them calmed down." She sent an apprehensive glance over to where both children stood with their fingers entwined in the fence, wailing loud enough to wake the dead, which was an unfortunate choice of words, she realized.

She hurried back to the enraged twins. Poor little mite. Who in the world would want to harm a young girl like that? A lot of sick people in this world, that was for sure. Poor Mrs. Baxter. She'd be beside herself when she heard the news. Couldn't have happened at a worse time, being Christmas and all. Though there was no good time for a murder to happen. What a mess.

She tugged open the gate and the twins hurled themselves through it, grabbing at her skirts and howling in a mixture of outrage and fright.

"What the matter with Mama?" James demanded between sobs, pointing at Gertie, who was rapidly disappearing in the murky distance.

"I want my mama!" Lillian stamped her foot. *"I want my mama!"*

"Then let us go find your mama." Mrs. Chubb grabbed a hand in each of hers. She felt better now that she was in charge again. Worrying about the children made her forget the ugly thing she'd seen in the shed. Though she had a nasty feeling that once she got to bed that night, she'd be seeing it all over again in her dreams. The prospect was extremely unsettling.

"We shall have to notify the constables now, of course," Baxter said when Cecily gave him the bad news. "They are bound to call in Inspector Cranshaw."

Cecily sat glumly in his office, wondering if there was anything she could have done to prevent this awful thing that had happened to the young girl. "I suppose there is no way we can avoid involving the inspector."

"None at all," Baxter said firmly. "The sooner we get this into the hands of the police, the better. We don't need the Pennyfoot involved in an investigation. It's obvious the girl was involved with someone of ill repute. Someone willing to buy the pearls she stole from Miss Bunkle. Probably one of those louts who hang around the George and Dragon all night. The sooner the culprit is arrested, the sooner we can put this behind us. All they have to do is find someone trying to get rid of a string of pearls. That shouldn't be too difficult for Cranshaw to handle, you'd suppose."

"I don't think it was someone from the village," Cecily said unhappily. She told him what Moira had told her.

"I don't believe it for one minute," he declared when she was finished. "Peebles and a kitchen maid? Never. The scandal could finish his career, not to mention his marriage."

"Exactly," Cecily murmured. "Perhaps that's why he had to kill Jeanette. She could have threatened to tell his wife and he had to silence her."

The icy expression she knew so well frosted his eyes. "Cecily, I absolutely forbid you to pursue this line of thinking. To accuse one of our most important guests without justification could cause a ruckus that would ruin the reputation of the Pennyfoot once and for all. We simply cannot take that kind of risk."

"I agree. Which is why I shall not inform the inspector at this time of my suspicions."

His shrewd gaze bore right through her head. "It is my firm belief that the maid was trying to sell Miss Bunkle's pearls to a hoodlum who decided to rid himself of the need to hand over the money. That is what I shall tell the constables. I sincerely hope that you let the matter rest there and allow the constables to do their job."

She merely nodded, hoping he wouldn't insist on her word. She had no intention of allowing the matter to rest there. What Baxter didn't know, however, wouldn't concern him. At least for the time.

Apparently accepting her silence for acquiescence, he reached for the telephone. After a lengthy wait for the operator, he managed to get his call put through to the police station.

She listened with one ear while he explained the situation. The rest of her mind worked busily on this latest development. She'd accompanied Raymond to the shed, where he'd locked it securely in case someone else should stumble upon the body before the constables arrived for their investigation.

She would have liked to conduct a far more intensive investigation herself, rather than the quick glance around she'd taken. She knew better, however, than to intrude on the scene and arouse the inspector's wrath. He was quite capable of closing down the Pennyfoot at the slightest provocation, especially when he learned that she was back at the helm, albeit on a temporary basis.

She and the inspector had drawn swords too many times for her to take a chance on antagonizing him now. Edward would never forgive her if she caused the cancellation of the Christmas Season. As it was, things were going to be somewhat disrupted. Unfortunately there was no doubt about that.

Chapter
15

Cecily's worst fears were realized when the inspector arrived an hour or so later. In spite of Baxter's theories about Jeanette's involvement with someone from the village, Cranshaw insisted that no one be allowed to leave until he'd had a chance to question potential witnesses. P.C. Northcott was given access to the current register, and generally made himself a nuisance while he copied down the list of guests currently staying at the club.

Baxter adamantly refused to remain in his office while Northcott worked on the list. His feud with the police constable went back a good many years. He'd once told Cecily that Northcott had stolen the young lady he was courting many years ago, but Cecily had always felt there was more to it than either man would say.

In any case, she volunteered to stay with Northcott until he'd completed his task, a decision that made the constable very uncomfortable indeed.

"It's not proper," he explained in his huffy voice, "for a gentleman to be alone in a room with a lady."

"A married lady," Cecily reminded him. "And a mature one at that." Nevertheless, she left the door open just a crack. There were a few things she wanted to ask the constable, and it was best that she wasn't overheard by the inspector, who was roaming the halls of the club looking for clues.

Northcott sat in Baxter's chair, the register open in front of him while he laboriously copied the names down in his notebook. She'd given him permission to remove his helmet, and he'd sat it on the desk next to him. The glow from the gas lamp gleamed on his bald head and the shiny buttons on his coat. He'd had a lot more hair the last time Cecily had seen him, and his pudgy face had lost much of its ruddy glow.

He looked older, and seemed slower in his movements, which had never exactly been swift. Every now and again he licked the end of his pencil before scratching it across the paper, and he muttered each name under his breath as if that made it easier to write it down.

Cecily pretended to be busy at the filing drawers for a while, until she was fairly confident that Northcott had relaxed. Then she sat down in her favorite chair in front of the desk. "This is like old times, Sam," she said pleasantly.

He seemed startled by her words when he looked up. "Yes, m'm. I s'pose it is. I must say, it's a pleasure to see you back in Badgers End. Not a very good reason to meet again though, is it."

"No, indeed. The poor girl." Cecily uttered a loud sigh. "I wonder who would have had reason to do such a dreadful thing."

"Well, I really can't say, Mrs. Sinclair."

"It's Mrs. Baxter now," she reminded him.

"H'oh, of course. I forgot you married 'im."

The note of disgust in his voice was evident. Cecily tightened her lips, but managed to keep her voice even when she answered. "Does the inspector have any idea who might have been responsible for this dreadful act?"

Northcott's eyes grew wary. "Now, you know very well, m'm, I can't let on what the inspector knows. He'd have my guts for garters if I told you anything."

"He does have some clues then?" Cecily leaned forward. "What about the knife? Mrs. Chubb told me she saw a carving knife. I assume it came from our kitchen?"

Northcott's desire to seem important apparently overrode his fear of the inspector's wrath. He cleared his throat then, as if addressing a full court and jury, announced, "We 'ave h'ascertained that the lady in question did indeed h'observe a utensil wot turned out to be a carving knife. You are correct in assuming that said utensil originated in the kitchen of this 'ere h'establishment. A witness, who shall remain nameless, identified it as such."

"Miss Bunkle recognized the knife?"

Looking put out at her assumption, Northcott nodded reluctantly. "Proper mess she were'n all. Carried on something alarming, she did. Anyone would think it was her wot got knocked off, the way she was caterwauling. That's a fact."

Something else she would have to deal with later, Cecily thought ruefully. "The knife was used to kill Jeanette, I assume?"

Northcott twisted his florid features into a gruesome grimace and drew his thumb across his throat. "One quick slice and it were all over," he said with a relish Cecily found quite unnecessary.

"I see. I suppose the inspector will be questioning the staff?"

Northcott nodded. "And maybe one or two of your guests. He'll be conducting the interviews in the ballroom this afternoon."

Well, that would take care of the rehearsal, Cecily thought gloomily. Knowing the inspector, he would make a big production of it all.

"Well, it looks as if I 'ave all the names down now," Northcott announced. He gave his pencil a final lick and jammed it in the top pocket of his coat. "Thank you for your time, Mrs. ah . . . Baxter, and if the h'inspector should ask, I didn't tell you nothing. Mum's the word. All right?"

"Agreed," Cecily promised cheerfully. She was anxious for him to leave now. Ever since she'd spoken to Moira the night before, she'd been anxious to speak to Roger Peebles alone. So far she hadn't had that opportunity. All morning he'd been accompanied by his wife and one or another of his Bencher colleagues.

But now there was even more of an urgent reason to speak to him. Although well aware of her duty to pass on to the inspector what she knew, she was reluctant to do so until she'd had a chance to question the man herself. Baxter was right. There was no point in arousing suspicion of an esteemed guest if Moira had been mistaken.

She could only hope that if the girl was questioned by the inspector, she would keep silent about Peebles's possible involvement with Jeanette. At least until she'd had a chance to speak to him and, with any luck, learn exactly what Peebles was doing philandering with a lowly kitchen maid.

When Cecily went in search of Roger Peebles later, she was told that all four Benchers had retired to the card room for a game of baccarat. Resigning herself to a lengthy wait, she made her way to the library. She had promised Madeline and the twins that she would inspect their handiwork and no doubt they were waiting for her approval.

Upon entering the library, however, she found the four wives of the Benchers huddled around the fire, apparently engaged in deep discussion. They looked up as she approached, their faces lined with apprehension.

"Mrs. Baxter, is this dreadful news true?" Barbara Fitzhammer asked fearfully.

Cecily had hoped to keep the murder quiet for a little longer, but it seemed word had already spread among the guests. Even so, she was deliberately vague in the hopes she was mistaken. "I'm not certain to what news you refer, Mrs. Fitzhammer," she said cautiously.

"The death of that poor girl." Gretchen Peebles shuddered. "I heard that her throat was slit with a carving knife and that her frock was soaked in blood."

Cries of horror greeted that comment.

"What kind of establishment is this," Lady Lucille muttered, "that such an atrocity is allowed to happen?"

"Indeed." Amelia Chatsworth languidly waved a pink satin fan in front of her face. "Such a dreadful deed. I certainly hope the murderer isn't loose in this very club. We could all be murdered in our beds."

Barbara Fitzhammer shrieked so loudly it made Cecily jump in alarm. "I think we should leave at once."

Lady Lucille looked about to faint. "I think that is a very good idea," she declared. "All this has made me feel quite unwell."

The chorus of agreement worried Cecily. Hiding her concern, she announced firmly, "I can assure you, ladies, that everything is being done to ensure the safety of our guests. I doubt very much if the person responsible for Jeanette's death has lingered long in the area for fear of being discovered. In fact, the inspector and constables have already left to return to the police station. They are satisfied that there is no danger to anyone here at the Pennyfoot."

That wasn't strictly true, since according to Northcott's furtively whispered comments to her upon leaving, the inspector had not discovered anything that would lead him to the murderer. What's more, he planned to return to an urgent case in Wellercombe, leaving the investigation in the hands of his constables for the time being.

It was Cecily's considered opinion that had the victim been a member of the aristocracy, or perhaps one of these ladies who were staring at her with such apprehension, Inspector Cranshaw might have been a great deal more interested in hunting down the murderer. Obviously a common kitchen maid didn't warrant as much attention as the "urgent case" in Wellercombe — a fact that infuriated Cecily.

"But what about the Christmas festivities?" Amelia Chatsworth demanded.

"What effect will this tragic event have on everything?"

"Yes, indeed." Gretchen Peebles gazed up at Cecily with anxious eyes. "We wouldn't want to spend Christmas in a place of mourning. It would be far too demoralizing. It would completely spoil our Christmas."

"Perhaps it would be a good idea to look for a hotel in Wellercombe," Lady Lucille murmured.

"Yes, yes, do let's," Barbara Fitzhammer chimed in. "I just wouldn't feel safe here now."

Thoroughly alarmed now, Cecily hurried to reassure them. "I beg all of you to calm yourselves and try to put this incident out of your mind. As I've said, you are in no danger. The Pennyfoot Christmas Season will go on as planned. We have some wonderful festivities for you to enjoy, including a delightful pantomime and Michel is planning a spectacular Christmas dinner in the ballroom, with champagne and gifts for everyone. It would be a great shame to miss all that, especially when it would be most difficult to find room at another hotel this late in the Season."

"True," Amelia Chatsworth murmured. "And there isn't another country club within traveling distance, unless we return to London. Think how our husbands would feel if they couldn't spend their time in a card room. Everyone knows that it is illegal in a hotel to engage in such pursuits. It's the main reason my husband chooses to stay at the Pennyfoot."

"You're right," Barbara Fitzhammer said mournfully. "Lionel would never agree to go to a hotel now."

"Neither would Roger," Gretchen Peebles murmured. "I'm afraid we have no choice, ladies. We might as well make the best of it."

Having avoided disaster for the time being, Cecily left them chattering together and headed for the kitchen. It had occurred to her that the staff would also need some reassurance. Not to mention her own special guests.

Mrs. Chubb, the twins, and Gertie were lying down in their rooms, after having been questioned thoroughly by the inspector. Daisy, Doris, and Samuel had gone into town earlier that day, but would most likely have returned by now for the rehearsal, which would not now take place. Out of respect for Jeanette, Cecily had canceled everything for that day.

As she hurried down the steps to the

kitchen, she realized she still hadn't inspected the tree in the library. That would have to wait until later now. There was just too much to be done.

As she entered the kitchen, it was obvious that Jeanette's death had a marked effect on the kitchen staff. The maids were all huddled by the sink around Moira, who sobbed loudly into her apron. The potatoes hadn't been peeled, the carrots had not been sliced, and even Michel stood aimlessly stirring his soup in apparent ignorance that the lengthy preparations for the evening meal were not being executed.

There was no doubt that the discipline Miss Bunkle kept talking about was sadly lacking. Looking around, Cecily was surprised to find no sign of the gaunt housekeeper. She was not in the pantry or the scullery, or even in the kitchen yard outside.

Clapping her hands to gain the maids' attention, she called out, "I want everyone back at their post immediately. We have a meal to serve in less than three hours, and by the looks of it, you haven't even begun your tasks."

At the sound of her voice, Michel had snapped to attention. "Hurry up, hurry up, you nitwits," he yelled, forgetting his fabricated French accent in his agitation. "Get a bloody move on, all of you!" His tall hat slipped sideways, and he made a grab at it, seizing it just before it slipped into the soup.

"Where is Miss Bunkle?" Cecily asked him as the maids scurried back and forth. "Why isn't she in here taking care of all this?"

Michel shrugged. "She is in her room, *madame*. She refuses to come out." He jammed his hat back on his head and in a thick French accent added, "I do not know what is ze matter with her. She wail and cry and carry on . . . like a baby. I tell you, *madame*, this kitchen was a lot 'appier to work in when Mrs. Chubb was house-keeper. *Oui?*"

"Oh, dear." Cecily glanced at the clock. "Don't fret, Michel. I'll take care of it."

Michel went back to his soup. "Someone needs to take care of things. I cannot work with such imbeciles."

Cecily hurried over to Moira, who stood sniffing mournfully at the sink, every now and then wiping her cheeks with the back of her hand.

"I understand all this is a great shock to you," Cecily told her. "I'll need to talk to you later, but right now, do you think you

280

can manage to do your work? Michel really needs you now that Jeanette is no longer with us."

It was the wrong thing to say, Cecily realized as fresh tears poured down Moira's face.

"I *told* her not to go out," she sobbed. "She wouldn't listen to me."

Cecily patted the girl's shoulder. "I know, dear, I know. I'm sorry, Moira. Please try to manage as best you can this afternoon and we'll have a little talk this evening, all right?"

The girl sniffed, wiped her nose with the back of her hand, and nodded. "Yes, m'm. I'll be all right. Really."

Feeling only a tad reassured, Cecily left the kitchen and hurried down the hall to Miss Bunkle's room. There was no reply to her sharp rap on the door, and giving up, she returned to the foyer and climbed the stairs to Mrs. Chubb's room.

Gertie had apparently recovered from her ordeal and was visiting with Mrs. Chubb when Cecily arrived.

"I really can't dawdle," she told them after making sure that all was well with them. "Miss Bunkle has locked herself in her room and refuses to come out. With Jeanette gone, the maids are short-handed. I must go back there right away to attempt some order."

Mrs. Chubb and Gertie looked at each other. Apparently a silent message passed between them as they both nodded.

"I could go down there and take over until Miss Bunkle feels better," Mrs. Chubb said, getting to her feet.

"Oh, I couldn't possibly ask you to do that," Cecily protested. "This is your Christmas holiday. I didn't ask you down here to work."

"I know, madam, but I'm getting bored sitting around doing nothing, and it will take my mind off things."

"I could help, too." Gertie jumped to her feet. "It'll be fun. Really, m'm. Just like old times."

"But what about the babies?" Cecily nodded in the direction of the bed where the twins lay sleeping peacefully.

"Daisy could take care of them. She asked me if she could anyway. She said she misses them."

Mrs. Chubb nodded. "It will do us both good, madam, and it will only be for a short while anyway. We'd really like to help out."

"Yeah, m'm, really," Gertie said earnestly. "Please let us do it."

"Well, if you're sure . . ."

Gertie's whoop of delight woke up the

twins and they sat up, sleepily demanding something to eat.

"I'll go down there right away," Mrs. Chubb said, "just as soon as I can find an apron. Gertie, you talk to Daisy, and if she says it's all right, come down as soon as you can."

"Yes, Mrs. Chubb." Gertie headed for the door.

"And Gertie?"

She paused, looking back at the other woman.

"You should be able to find a uniform to fit you in the laundry room. Make sure you look neat and tidy. We want to set a good example to the rest of the staff."

"Yes, Mrs. Chubb." There was just a hint of irony in her voice as she rushed out of the room.

Cecily hid a smile. It was amazing to see the transformation in the two women. Up until this moment they had behaved more like mother and daughter, but now Mrs. Chubb was in charge again, and Gertie was once more relegated to the role of chief housemaid. Gertie was right. It was just like old times.

Cecily was on her way down the stairs to inform Baxter of the new arrangements with his staff when she heard the commotion in the lobby. At first she thought Colonel Fortescue had returned, but then she saw Raymond talking excitedly to the tall, stern figure of Sir John Gilroy.

Lady Lucille was at his side, leaning heavily on his arm, her face covered by a delicately embroidered handkerchief into which she loudly sobbed. She seemed not to notice Cecily, who had hurried over to them with a feeling of deep foreboding.

"Is something wrong?" she asked as Raymond turned his impassioned gaze in her direction.

"There's been an accident," he said, speaking so fast his words tumbled over each other. "The motor car went right off the cliffs. Landed upside down on the rocks, it did."

"Oh, my." Cecily's hand strayed to her throat. "I hope it wasn't one of ours."

"What the devil is all this racket about?" a deep voice demanded.

Cecily turned to see Baxter striding toward them, having apparently been disturbed by all the noise.

Lady Lucille was still weeping profusely, moaning something over and over that Cecily couldn't understand.

Raymond started chattering again, while

Sir John remained silent, his jaw set in a grim line.

"Slow down, Raymond," Baxter said irritably. "Tell us exactly what happened."

"I was on me way into the town," Raymond said, his voice still trembling with agitation. He gulped several times, then continued, "I was going to Abbitsons to get some more chickens for the dinner tonight. I saw this motor car in front of me and it were going really fast, at least twenty miles an hour I reckon. Then he went over the top of the hill and started down the other side. Never made the first bend. Sailed right off the cliff, he did."

Lady Lucille wailed louder, and Sir John put his arm around her. "My wife needs to lie down. This has been a great shock. I need to inform . . . though God knows how . . . excuse me."

Cecily's sense of dread intensified. "Of course. Please let me know if there's anything I can do to help."

He barely acknowledged her offer with a slight inclination of his head before helping his wife up the stairs.

Apparently Baxter had come to a similar conclusion as he demanded sharply, "Raymond, did you recognize anyone in the automobile?"

Raymond nodded. "Not right away, though I went for help when I saw him disappear over the cliff. The noise was something awful. It were right across from Jim Biscott's farm. Jim climbed down with me to see if the driver were all right." Raymond gulped again. "One look at him and we knew he was a stiffun."

"Oh, dear." Cecily clutched Baxter's sleeve. "Who was it, Raymond?"

"One of them Bencher blokes," Raymond said unsteadily. "I'm not sure, but I think his name were Peebles. Yeah, that's it. Roger Peebles."

Chapter
16

"Unbelievable," Baxter said, closing the door to his office sometime later. "We arrive back at the Pennyfoot after a two-year absence and in less than a week we have two deaths on our hands."

"Three, if you count Barry Wrotham." Cecily seated herself on her favorite chair and watched her husband take his usual place behind his desk.

"Well, Wrotham's death happened before we arrived. And at least two of them were accidents." He leaned back in his chair and passed a hand over his hair. "I suppose we should be thankful for small mercies."

"I'm not so sure of that."

He stared at her, his eyes wary. "What does that mean?"

"It means that I'm not convinced that the other two deaths were accidents."

He groaned. "I thought we'd pretty much established that Wrotham fell into the well."

"In view of what has transpired this day, I'm beginning to have second thoughts about that."

"What does Jeanette's unfortunate end or Peebles's accident have to do with Wrotham?"

"Suppose that Peebles's death wasn't an accident."

He stared at her for a long moment. "Are you saying that Peebles deliberately drove his car over the cliff? I know people sometimes become depressed at Christmastime, but Peebles didn't strike me as the sort to do himself in."

"No, I'm not saying that." Cecily sighed. "I went to offer my condolences to Mrs. Peebles. She was quite distraught, of course, poor woman. She did, however, tell me that Peebles had been extremely irritable and short with her lately. Apparently they had a quarrel earlier this afternoon, and he left here in a great hurry without telling her where he was going. According to Mrs. Peebles, his behavior recently has been quite out of character."

"Well, then, there you are. He went out in a fit of temper and drove too fast. The road over Putney Downs has some very sharp bends. It was never meant for motor cars. That's the trouble with them. If you don't treat them with respect, they can cause all kinds of problems. If you ask me —"

"I think Roger Peebles was murdered," Cecily said deliberately.

Baxter shut his mouth with a snap, then after a moment said in an unsettling quiet tone, "Just how do you come to that conclusion?"

Cecily leaned forward. "I think he knew who killed Jeanette. Whoever is the murderer had to get rid of Peebles because he could identify him."

Baxter's frown was formidable. "This morning you were accusing Peebles of killing the maid. Now you're saying someone else killed her? How many more of our guests are you planning to accuse of murder?"

"I'm not accusing anyone just yet."

"I'm glad to hear it. I —"

The jangling of the telephone interrupted him. He lifted the receiver from its stand and said cautiously into it, "The Pennyfoot Country Club. Hugh Baxter speaking." He listened for a moment then added, "Thank you, operator. Please put him through." Glancing at Cecily he whispered, "Northcott. I —" Once more he broke off, listened, then said irritably, "Go on, I'm listening." Another pause, then he added, "And what about the girl?"

Cecily watched his face closely, and saw relief creep into his eyes. Muttering his thanks, he replaced the receiver and looked at her. "I was right," he announced. "Northcott has completed his investigation and has ruled Peebles's death an accident. As for the death of our maid, he believes, as I do, that she was killed while attempting to sell the pearls she had stolen. Probably trying to extort too much money from the wrong person. They are currently questioning people in the village in the hopes of tracking down the culprit."

"But —"

He raised his hand. "I suggest we cease concerning ourselves about a nonexistent murderer among our guests and concentrate on the task we came down here to do, which is to conduct a successful Christmas Season at the Pennyfoot."

His pompous attitude infuriated her, but she curbed her resentment. It was pointless to argue when she had no proof to offer. All she had at that moment were suppositions and she knew better than to rely on such nebulous reasoning.

Rising to her feet, she murmured, "Very well. I shall go to the kitchen and see how things are faring under the new management."

"I think that's a very good idea."

After closing the door rather sharply behind her, she uttered a low growl of frustration. Her instincts told her that the deaths were connected in some way. Somehow she had to find out what that connection was, and who had reason to kill three people. And she knew just where to start.

She made her way to the foyer, but instead of going down to the kitchen, she climbed the stairs to the third floor.

As luck would have it, she found Samuel resting in his room. He opened the door with a book in his hand which, he explained, was helping him with his studies of mechanics.

"That's exactly what I came to talk to you about." Cecily glanced down the hall. "May I come in for just a moment?"

"Of course, m'm." He looked mystified, but stepped back to allow her to enter. Leaving the door slightly ajar, he beckoned a little self-consciously at the lone armchair in his room. "If you'd care to sit, m'm?"

"I won't take up more than a moment of your time," Cecily said, declining his invitation. "I need you to do something for me, if you will. Something that will have to be done with great discretion."

Samuel immediately looked interested. He threw his book on the bed. "Anything for you, m'm. You know you can always rely on me."

"Thank you, Samuel." Cecily lowered her voice. "I assume you have heard about the accident this afternoon."

Samuel nodded. "Moira told me. She was all upset about what happened to her friend, and now this. It took me a while to calm her down."

Cecily looked at him in surprise. "I wasn't aware you were acquainted with Moira."

He grinned. "Well, I wasn't when I came down here, if you know what I mean, m'm. But what with Doris not being around much anymore, well, a bloke has to take his chances where he can, so to speak."

"Oh." Cecily cleared her throat. "Yes, I see. Well, it's nice that Moira has a friend who can cheer her up. I'm afraid Jeanette's death has been a terrible shock for her."

"That it has, m'm. But I think she's getting over it a little now."

"Well, I'm glad to hear it. Now, about this little task I have for you." She quickly explained, and as she expected, Samuel was eager to help.

"I must ask you to keep all this in complete confidence for now," she said as she was leaving. "I don't have to tell you what this would mean if word got out."

"You can trust me to keep me mouth shut, m'm," Samuel promised her. "It wouldn't be the first time I had to keep a secret."

She smiled. "No, indeed, Samuel."

"Quite like old times, it is, m'm."

She was still smiling as she left, wondering how many times she would hear that phrase before this Christmas was over.

As she made her way down the hallway, she caught sight of Amelia Chatsworth ushering a weeping Gretchen Peebles into her room. Cecily waited until the door had closed behind the two women, then cautiously approached the Peebleses' suite. This was as good a time as any to put the second part of her plan into action.

After pausing to make certain she was unobserved, Cecily tried the door handle, uttering a little hiss of satisfaction when the door opened. This would save her the trouble of returning to her room for the set of master keys Baxter kept there.

She slipped inside the room and closed

the door. The suite was in great disarray, with clothes strewn haphazardly across the bed and shoes lying on the floor. In the middle of the room a trunk stood with its lid open. Apparently Gretchen Peebles planned to return to London. Cecily could only hope the rest of the group wouldn't return with her.

Moving about the room, she opened drawers, then carefully closed them again. She wasn't really sure what she was looking for, except for the vague hope that she might find something that would point to where Peebles was heading in such a hurry that afternoon.

She opened the wardrobe and peered inside. Two men's day suits and an evening suit hung next to several gowns. Quickly Cecily searched the pockets of the suits, trying to ignore her voice of conscience that told her she was behaving like a common thief.

The pockets were empty, and she was about to close the door again when she caught sight of a shoe box on the upper shelf. It rattled when she shook it, and intrigued now, she took it down and opened the lid.

Inside were several gambling chips, larger and a different design than those belonging to the Pennyfoot. A scrap of paper had been tucked underneath them, and she drew it out. Placing the box on the floor of the wardrobe, she unfolded the slip of paper.

It was an IOU in the sum of two thousand pounds. Printed across the top of the paper was a peculiar name. *Cureagambler.* The scrawl at the bottom was difficult to make out, but it could have been Peebles's signature. If so, then Roger Peebles was a lot more than a social gambler. What's more, he owed someone a very large sum of money.

She studied the printed heading again. Such an odd name. *Cureagambler.* She frowned. Spread apart, the words could read, *Cure a gambler.* Well, by the looks of it, Peebles certainly needed to be cured. Perhaps that was it. An organization that helped gamblers give up their addiction. Now, maybe if —

The sound of voices in the hallway outside startled her. After a moment's hesitation, she stuffed the note into her sleeve, then hastily replaced the box on the shelf before quietly closing the wardrobe door.

She had a nasty moment when she thought that one of the voices might be Gretchen Peebles returning to her room, but then the chattering guests passed by. After waiting another tense moment or two, Cecily slowly opened the door and peered through the crack. Once more the hallway appeared to be deserted. Holding her breath, she slipped out into the corridor and closed the door.

Her next stop was the kitchen, where she found a very different atmosphere than the last time she'd been there. Mrs. Chubb was bustling around, barking orders while maids scurried back and forth. Gertie stood at the table loading up a tray with crystal salt and pepper shakers.

She looked quite different in her black afternoon frock and a frilly white apron. Even her cap sat firmly on top of her head. In the old days it was always slipping sideways over her ear, while she constantly tucked stray strands of hair back under the pins.

She looked up as Cecily entered and gave her a lopsided grin. "I haven't forgotten nothing, m'm," she announced cheerfully. "It's all there in me head, just like I was here yesterday."

"I can't thank you enough, Gertie." Cecily picked up a fork and examined it critically. "Things have been a little slack in the kitchen. Miss Bunkle was always complaining about the lack of discipline but I don't think she had the gumption to enforce it."

"Not like the old battle-ax, anyway." Gertie jerked a thumb over her shoulder. "She'll soon whip 'em into bleeding shape. In her bloody element, she is."

Cecily managed a smile. "Well, it's a relief to know that things are under control in here again. After everything that's happened today, I need something to go right."

Gertie lowered her head toward her and whispered, "Terrible what happened to that toff, m'm. Raymond said he were crushed under that flipping motor car. Just goes to show what happens when you get careless in them things. What with that poor girl this morning and now this. Bloody terrible it is. Right before Christmas and all. Put a proper gloom around this place, it has." She jerked her chin at the rest of the staff, most of whom seemed to be tumbling over each other in their haste to follow Mrs. Chubb's orders.

The housekeeper caught sight of Cecily at that moment and came hurrying over. "There's nothing else gone wrong, I hope, madam?"

Before Cecily could answer, Gertie uttered a harsh laugh. "Gawd, I bleeding hope not. Two blinking deaths in one day is enough for anyone, if you ask me."

"That's enough, Gertie. Remember your place." Mrs. Chubb sent Cecily a look of apology. "Some things never change, I'm afraid."

"It's all right, Mrs. Chubb. It's a pleasure to have you both back at the helm."

"Yes, madam. We were sorry to hear of the motor car accident this afternoon. Though I can't say I'm surprised. The way some people go speeding around the bends in those things, I'm surprised there aren't more people dying in them."

"Yeah," Gertie said gloomily. "You'd think he'd know better. His poor widow won't have much of a Christmas this year, that's for sure. Though, mind you, it's no great loss in my opinion."

Cecily looked at her in surprise. "I wasn't aware you'd met Roger Peebles."

Gertie shrugged. "Bumped into him in the hallway. I don't like to speak ill of the dead, m'm, but he wasn't exactly the faithful husband, if you know what I mean."

"Gertie," Mrs. Chubb said sharply. "It's none of our business. I'm quite sure madam has better things to do than listen to idle gossip. I know I do."

"Don't let me keep you, Mrs. Chubb," Cecily said smoothly. "I'm sure you have plenty to do."

"Indeed I do, madam. And so does Gertie." She sent a meaningful look in Gertie's direction, then rushed over to the sinks, where two of the maids were arguing with each other in strident voices.

"I'd better get these bloody shakers into the dining room, m'm," Gertie said, lifting the tray. "Or the old girl will be getting her bleeding knickers in a twist."

Cecily followed her out into the corridor, holding the door open for her as she passed through with the heavy tray.

"Tell me, Gertie," she said as she followed her up the steps. "What did you mean when you said that Roger Peebles wasn't the faithful husband?"

Gertie paused, looking over her shoulder. "Well, m'm, don't tell Mrs. Chubb I told you, but I saw Roger Peebles taking a lady into his room. Yesterday it were. And it weren't his bloody wife."

"Did you happen to notice who it was?"

"Yes, m'm. It were that French toff, Lady Lucille."

Cecily stopped short, taken by surprise. "Are you quite sure?"

"Yes, m'm. Saw her plain as day, I did. Can't mistake her anyhow. All done up like a dog's dinner, she was."

At the top of the steps Cecily parted company with Gertie and walked across the foyer in deep thought. In her mind's eye she could see Raymond, arms waving in agitation as he informed a stern-faced Sir John Gilroy of Peebles's accident, while Lady Lucille wept profusely into her handkerchief.

Was she weeping for a lost lover, perhaps?

Still engrossed in her thoughts, Cecily paused by the Christmas tree, pretending to be interested in the delicate ornaments nestled among its branches. Did Lady Lucille tell her that story about Barry Wrotham being her lover in order to cover up the identity of her true lover, Roger Peebles?

What if her original theory were correct after all, and Wrotham had discovered the two meeting at the farmhouse, perhaps threatening to inform Sir John unless they paid him to keep quiet. If Peebles were already deep in debt, he would have no choice but to silence him.

Then again, where did Jeanette fit in all this? Did Peebles's philandering include her as well? That simply didn't make sense.

She heard her name spoken in a low voice and swung around to confront Samuel, who had crept up behind her.

"Sorry, m'm," he said softly. "I didn't mean to startle you."

"That's all right, Samuel." She drew him closer into the corner, where they had less chance of being observed. "Did you manage to examine Peebles's motor car?"

"Yes, m'm, I did. I told the bobbies that Mrs. Peebles sent me to see if it could be repaired." He sent a furtive glance around, then added in a loud whisper, "It were the brake shoes, m'm. Both of 'em, snapped right off."

"I see," Cecily said, not seeing at all. "Was the damage done in the accident, do you think?"

Samuel shrugged. "Hard to say for certain, m'm, but if I had to guess, I'd say someone helped them along a bit. Not likely they'd both go at the same time without a bit of nudging, if you get my meaning."

Cecily let out her breath. "Yes, I do. Thank you, Samuel. I'd had a feeling something like that might have happened."

Samuel glanced over his shoulder.

"Who'd want to hurt that toff, anyway?"

"That's something we'll have to find out. I must ask you not to say a word to anyone about this. No one at all, you understand? If we are going to catch this person, we mustn't let him know what we know."

"Do you think it's the same person what did Jeanette in?" Samuel asked fearfully. "What if he's still lurking about, looking for his next victim?"

Cecily sighed. "This is exactly why we have to keep quiet about this. We don't need our guests to fly into a panic. After all, we're not absolutely certain that someone did tamper with the motor car. Just keep your eyes open, and if you see anything at all that strikes you as unusual or out of place, come and tell me at once."

Samuel nodded. "Don't worry, m'm. You know you can count on me."

Cecily left him in the foyer and headed down the hallway to Baxter's office. She had promised to keep him informed, but she wasn't certain at this point how much she wanted to tell him. So much of it was still conjecture.

He looked up when she entered the room. "Ah, there you are. I was just about to send one of the maids to look for you. How are things in the kitchen?"

"Better." She sank onto her chair. "Mrs. Chubb and Gertie have pretty much taken over everything for the time being, and even Michel seems in a better mood. I don't know what we would have done without them."

"Well, we might have to rely on them for longer than we thought." Baxter closed his ledger with a loud snap. "Miss Bunkle has given in her notice."

Cecily gaped at him in dismay. "No! Why? Did she say?"

"Apparently three deaths in less than a month have totally unnerved her. She is packing her bags and expects to be on the train to London early tomorrow morning."

Cecily sank back in her chair. "She might at least have worked out her notice. What are we going to do now? I can't ask Mrs. Chubb and Gertie to work through the Christmas holidays and it will be impossible to find another housekeeper at this late date." She covered her face with her hands. "Edward will never forgive us."

Baxter cleared his throat. "Perhaps we can persuade Mrs. Chubb and Gertie to help us out awhile longer if we give them generous compensation for their efforts."

Cecily lowered her hands. "Can we afford to do that?"

"Yes, I think we can." He opened the ledger, studied it for a moment. "We can certainly add another guinea each to the salaries."

"Well, that is generous. In that case, I shall have a word with them right away. I'll tell them about your offer and see if they are interested." She started to rise.

"Did you have a reason for this visit?"

Having momentarily forgotten why she was there, she sat down again. "Samuel thinks that someone tampered with Peebles's car," she said without preamble.

As she'd expected, a frown appeared on his face. "How did he manage to arrive at that conclusion?"

"He examined the motor car."

"Why did he do that?"

"Because I asked him to examine it."

"I might have known." He pressed the fingers of one hand against his forehead. "I was under the impression you had given up chasing after murderers and were concentrating your concerns on our Christmas Season."

"As long as there is the possibility of a killer in our midst, you know very well that I cannot rest until he is apprehended."

Baxter sighed. "Very well. What did Samuel discover?"

"He said it had something to do with the brake shoes, whatever they are. Apparently they were damaged."

"The motor car went off a cliff, fell over a hundred feet, and landed upside down. I'm not surprised there was damage."

"Ah, but Samuel believes they were damaged before it went over the cliff."

Baxter's frown intensified. "What makes him think so?"

"Well, I really don't understand too much about motor cars, but I do know that if one cannot stop them, it's entirely likely they won't slow down to manipulate a bend in the road. Which is what appears to have happened to poor Mr. Peebles."

Baxter sighed and laid his pen down next to the inkwell. "That's not what I meant. Has he informed Northcott?"

"No, I told him to keep it to himself for the time being. You know how P.C. Northcott is, always bungling things. I think we should be more certain of our facts before we trust this investigation to him."

"Perhaps you're right. After all, Samuel could very well be mistaken." He gave her his piercing stare. "Just as long as you remember your promise. At the very first sign of danger, you will turn this over to the constables."

"Of course, darling." Cecily rose to her feet. This probably wasn't a good time to tell him she'd been snooping around in Peebles's suite. It could wait until later. "Now I had better run down to the kitchen and pray that Mrs. Chubb and Gertie will take us up on our offer. If not, we could be in a real pickle."

"If not," Baxter said dryly, "we had better prepare ourselves for a disastrous Christmas."

Chapter
17

To Cecily's intense relief, Gertie was delighted to accept Baxter's offer. "This couldn't come at a better time, m'm," Gertie told her when Cecily presented the idea to her. She had just returned to the busy kitchen from the dining room, where the guests were already seating themselves in anticipation of another delicious meal.

"I didn't say nothing before," Gertie added as she piled tureens of soup onto her enormous tray. "But Ross sold the business, so right now he's out of work. I'll carry on here for as long as you need me."

"Goodness!" Cecily exclaimed. "I had no idea. It must have come as quite a shock to you."

Gertie shrugged. "Can't say I'm really surprised. Besides, he needs a rest. He's been looking poorly lately. I think he should see a doctor."

"I'll ask Dr. Prestwick to stop by," Cecily

promised. "Now I must ask Mrs. Chubb if she'll be willing to help out until we can get another housekeeper."

"I don't think you'll have any bleeding arguments with her," Gertie said, jerking her head in the housekeeper's direction. "Look at her. Having the time of her life, she is."

Gertie was right. Mrs. Chubb eagerly accepted the offer. "Though I don't think we'll be able to do the pantomime as well, madam," she said, looking anxiously around her bustling kitchen. "We'll have our hands full getting this lot in shape."

"Don't concern yourself about the pantomime." Cecily sighed. "I'm not at all sure there will be one, after all. No one has had a chance to rehearse that much, and the performance is scheduled for tomorrow night."

"I thought we were going to have it on Boxing Day."

"Doris and I decided to bring it forward. In any case, after what's happened, perhaps it would be considered in bad taste to continue with it."

"Well, if you ask me, madam," Mrs. Chubb said, raising a cloud of flour as she vigorously dusted her apron, "I think it will take everything off the minds of everyone. Do them good to have a laugh, that it will."

"Perhaps you're right," Cecily murmured. "After all, I have more or less promised some of the guests that we will carry on the Christmas Season as planned. I'll have a word with Doris and see what she can do."

"Very good, madam. And don't worry about the kitchen. Everything's in order now. You won't miss that sourpuss with the knitting needle one bit."

" 'Ark at her," Gertie muttered as she swung by carrying the loaded tray above her head as if it were holding feathers instead of filled tureens. "All she has to do is yell bleeding orders. It's us flipping slaves what does the blinking work."

The door swung to behind her, and Mrs. Chubb winked at Cecily. "Business as usual, madam. Just like old times."

The next morning Cecily rang Dr. Prestwick and invited him to lunch at the Pennyfoot, then went down to the ballroom, where Doris was holding the rehearsal for the pantomime. Madeline was flitting around helping everyone with their costumes and giving instructions to Samuel and Raymond, both of whom had volunteered to set up the backdrops.

Doris assured Cecily that her cast would be ready for the big night, and that they could manage quite well without Mrs. Chubb and Gertie. Though she did warn Cecily not to expect a professional performance.

Having watched Phoebe struggling to control her unruly band of dancers, Cecily had already resigned herself to the usual comedy of errors. With any luck, the audience would be in a jovial mood and willing to accept a few mishaps.

Leaving Doris to cope with what seemed a dubious task, Cecily went in search of the Benchers. She spotted Lionel Fitzhammer in the smoking room, in deep conversation with Percy Chatsworth. Since this was yet another room where she was not allowed, she waited for some time before the two men emerged and she could talk to them.

"I wanted to offer my condolences for the loss of your colleague," she said after the two men greeted her with a polite nod. "It must have been a terrible shock to you all."

"Dreadful," Percy Chatsworth muttered. "I still can't believe Roger's gone. He should never have been driving while besotted with brandy."

Cecily stared at him. "Are you saying that Mr. Peebles was intoxicated when he left here in that motor car?"

"Of course he wasn't," Fitzhammer said curtly. "We'd had a couple of shots of brandy after lunch, but Roger could hold his damn liquor, that's for sure. Careless, that's what he was. Never did know how to take care of his automobile. I'll take a wager he didn't have his brakes examined before he left London. Some people shouldn't be allowed in the driver's seat, that's what I say."

"I still say he'd had one too many," Chatsworth insisted. "A little too fond of his brandy, was our Roger, if you ask me. And that French cognac they serve in the bar creeps up on you. Before you know it, it's hit you." He shot an apologetic glance at Cecily. "Not that I'm complaining, of course. Jolly good brandy, that is."

Cecily accepted this compliment with a smile. "Did either of you happen to know where Mr. Peebles was going when he left here yesterday?"

"Haven't the foggiest," Chatsworth muttered. "Bit of a dark horse, actually. Never did have much to say. Except in court, of course. Jolly good barrister, he was."

"He was, indeed," Fitzhammer agreed gloomily.

Cecily turned to him. "What about you, Mr. Fitzhammer? You were drinking with him before he left. Did he happen to mention anything to you about where he planned to go?"

Fitzhammer's beady eyes narrowed. "Not to me, he didn't. May I ask why you are so interested in Roger's appointment?"

"Just curious." Cecily gave him her most discerning smile. "He appeared to be in an enormous hurry. I was wondering if perhaps there was some emergency that needed to be taken care of, that's all. Mrs. Peebles didn't seem to know, so I simply wondered if you could shed some light on the subject. I mean, if he had an appointment, then someone must be wondering why he didn't keep it."

"As far as I know," Fitzhammer said carefully, "Roger wasn't planning on going anywhere in particular when he left here. He was in rather a snit, and I got the impression he needed a breath of fresh air. That's all."

"I see." Cecily smiled at both men. "Well, thank you for your time, gentlemen. I'd like to remind you that the pantomime will take place immediately after supper tonight, in the Grand Ballroom. I trust you and your wives will be there? It might help to alleviate some of the heartache for all of you."

"My wife and I will most certainly be there," Fitzhammer said heartily. "The show must go on, and all that rot."

"My wife and I plan to accompany Gretchen to the train station this afternoon," Chatsworth said, sending Fitzhammer a sour look. "She will be returning to London with her husband's body. But we should return here in time for supper, though whether or not Amelia will be in any mood for a pantomime, I can't say for sure. I had the devil of a time persuading her to stay for Christmas as it was."

"Make her go, old boy," Fitzhammer said, slapping Chatsworth on the back. "It will do you both good."

"I hope Sir John and Lady Lucille will attend," Cecily put in.

Chatsworth sighed. "I imagine they will. Lucille twisted her ankle the other day coming down the stairs, but she seems to be managing to get around on it."

A vision flashed into Cecily's mind of Lady Lucille leaning heavily on her husband's arm yesterday. "Oh, I'm sorry to hear that," she said quickly. "Please tell her to let me know if there is anything I can do. The village doctor will be having lunch here today. I'm sure he will be happy to take a look at Lady Lucille's ankle if needs be."

"I'll convey your message to her." Chatsworth took out his pocket watch and flipped open the lid. "Now I have some business to take care of, so if you'll excuse me?"

"Of course." Cecily watched both men leave, then headed for the foyer. Just as she reached it, the front door opened to admit Dr. Prestwick.

He spotted her at once, and gave her an expansive grin, which she returned. He then doffed his trilby hat and offered her a low sweep of his arm. "Mrs. Baxter. You look as exquisite as always."

He was dressed in a dark gray lounge suit under a black topcoat and looked both debonaire and handsome. Cecily responded to his greeting by fluttering her eyelashes at him in mock adoration. "And you, my dear Kevin, are every bit as utterly engaging."

Moira, who was crossing the foyer at that moment, shot a curious stare at each of them before scurrying for the steps to the kitchen.

Cecily pulled a face. "Oh, dear, I'm afraid we might have generated some unwelcome gossip below stairs."

Prestwick chuckled. "That will teach you to trifle with my affections. How is that handsome husband of yours?"

"Hale and hearty the last time I saw him." She glanced at the grandfather clock, just as the Westminster chimes began to strike. "Your timing is perfect, Kevin. Lunch will be served shortly. Let us retire to the dining room, where I can offer you an aperitif while we wait to be served."

"My pleasure, madam." He offered her his arm and accompanied her down the hallway to the dining room. "Baxter won't be joining us?" he exclaimed in surprise when they were seated at Cecily's favorite table set for two.

"He's taking his meal in the office," Cecily said a little guiltily. She hadn't had a chance to tell Baxter she was dining with the good doctor. Then again, she hadn't exactly made the effort to do so. Sometimes it was easier to explain after the fact than before.

"So tell me," Prestwick said after the aperitifs had been served, "What is the reason for this delightful rendezvous?"

She pretended not to understand.

"There has to be a reason?"

"Isn't there always?" He smiled at her blank expression. "Come now, Cecily, we both know that this isn't a purely social visit. You want something from me, and hazarding a wild guess, I'd say it has something to do with either the accident that killed one of your guests, or more likely the death of your maid, does it not?"

She kept her expression of pure innocence. "Why, Kevin, I'm surprised at you. Surely you know me better than that?"

"Indeed, I do." He took a sip of his gin and put down the glass. "Which is why I presume you have an ulterior motive. I'm certainly not vain enough to assume you have invited me here to bask in my considerable charm."

She had to laugh at that. "Oh, very well. What can you tell me about the deaths?"

"Not much that you probably don't already know. Your guest died from injuries received when his motor car went off the cliff. As for the maid, she bled to death from the wound in her throat. Someone slashed her with a kitchen knife, apparently from your kitchen."

"Which would seem to rule out the theory that it's someone from the village, as most people seem to think."

Prestwick's expression sobered. "Well, there is one thing that isn't common knowledge, though I'm not sure I should mention it."

"Well, now that you already have," Cecily said firmly, "you are duty bound to tell me what it is, unless you want me to hound you constantly until you give in."

"Well, if you phrase it in that manner, I suppose I have no choice." His tone had been light, but now he leaned forward and lowered his voice. "I found a pearl lodged in the girl's underclothing. The string must have been broken in the struggle. The constables believe she stole the pearls from your housekeeper and met with someone, most likely from London, in order to sell them."

"Then why was she killed?"

"Perhaps she wanted too much money, or refused to give them up. Thieves fall out all the time, for a number of reasons."

Cecily frowned. "But the kitchen knife?"

"She could have taken it along to defend herself, perhaps anticipating some form of violence from her client. Mind you, he didn't get away unscathed. There was blood under her fingernails. She fought hard."

Cecily shook her head, remembering

Jeanette's vehement protests of innocence when the pearls were first discovered missing. "I still can't believe that young lady was capable of such a deliberate crime."

"Ah, Cecily, you would not do well at Scotland Yard. You are much too reluctant to see the ugly truth about some people."

"I haven't done so badly in the past," she reminded him. "I have solved more than one murder behind these walls."

"More by luck than judgment, I'd venture."

She made a face at him. "You never were able to credit a woman with any grain of intelligence. That could well be the reason that you and Madeline are at such odds lately. Madeline is an extremely intelligent woman, and in my opinion, you are a little afraid she will outsmart you, especially when it comes to medicine."

His smile faded. "If you want our friendship to continue, Cecily, I must ask you to refrain from interfering in matters that don't concern you."

"But they do concern me. Madeline is one of my dearest friends, and it disturbs me to see her in so much pain when I know very well that you both care a very great deal for each other. It is such a dreadful waste. You two could achieve so much together."

Prestwick tapped the white linen tablecloth with his fingertips. His voice sounded casual enough, but his blue eyes mirrored his interest. "Madeline is in pain?"

Cecily crossed her fingers under the table. "Very much so, though she does her best to hide it. She is pining for you, Kevin. Isn't it time you swallowed some of that infernal pride and accepted the fact that Madeline Pengrath is exactly what you need to give your life purpose as well as pleasure?"

He gave her a long, thoughtful stare, then said slowly, "I'll take it under notice."

"Very well." Pleased with herself, she leaned back in her chair.

"Is *that* why you asked me here today?"

"Actually, I asked you here so that you might look in on Ross McBride, Gertie's husband. She's concerned about his health."

Prestwick stared at her a moment longer, then burst out laughing. "Cecily, you are priceless. Your husband is a lucky fellow."

She grinned happily at him. "Be sure to tell him that when you see him next."

For the rest of the meal she chatted with him about mundane matters, though never far from her mind were the questions she couldn't answer. Was Jeanette a thief, and was she killed by an accomplice? If so, where did Peebles's death fit in if, indeed, it was murder and not an accident? To whom did he owe such a large sum of money? Who or what was Cureagambler? And what about Wrotham's death? Was that an accident or yet another murder? There didn't seem any end to the questions, and none of them had answers. It would seem she still had a lot more digging to do.

The pantomime began promptly at eight o'clock that evening. Phoebe had persuaded the ballroom orchestra to provide the music, and the curtains opened to reveal Phoebe's dance troupe, clad in filmy trousers and quite scandalous upper garments that revealed bare arms to the shoulders.

The fact that some of the young ladies had gained a few pounds since their last appearance and were revealing a little more than decorum dictated aroused some horrified responses from the audience as the dancers pranced around the stage.

They were soon forgotten, however, with the appearance of Aladdin. Doris's beautiful voice soaring to the rafters kept the audience entranced, so much so that they generously forgave Raymond, in the guise of the genie, when he tripped over the lamp and sprawled on the floor.

Phoebe's loud hissing from the wings could be heard quite clearly at times, especially when her girls stumbled over each other, threatening to bring down the entire temple that had been hastily and somewhat haphazardly erected by Samuel and his assistants earlier. It didn't help matters when the colonel, resplendent in his guard's uniform, bellowed at Phoebe to "stop that blasted interfering."

The final scene called for Doris and a young maid to mount the lower steps of the temple and sing the final song together with the genie hovering behind them.

Phoebe's dance troupe had built a tableau, balancing precariously on various body parts of their companions. Due to the aforementioned extra weight, the unfortunate girls on the lower end were not able to hold their positions, and the entire human pyramid collapsed, revealing even more human flesh than was proper.

Raymond leapt down from his perch, obviously eager not to miss this golden opportunity to assist half-clothed damsels.

Phoebe ran screeching onto the stage, then backed hastily off again as Doris gamely launched into her song, despite the mayhem going on behind her.

The audience, having recovered from their earlier shock, politely struggled to hold their mirth until Doris had finished her song and the curtains drew to a close. Then, as one, they surged to their feet, the men whistling and cheering while their wives demurely applauded.

Relieved that everyone had survived the ordeal without serious injury, Cecily went backstage with Baxter to congratulate everybody. She was intrigued to note that Kevin Prestwick had also wandered backstage and was engaged in an earnest conversation with Madeline. It would seem that her little chat with him had done some good.

Now she could only hope that the two of them could mend their differences and take this opportunity to work together, perhaps with an eye to a permanent relationship in the future. She couldn't ask for more for her friend.

"I suppose we should thank our lucky stars that it wasn't a total disaster," Baxter commented as they made their way back to the still crowded ballroom.

Several of the staff were hurriedly moving the chairs closer to the walls, so that the orchestra could take the stage and the room would be clear for an hour or two of dancing.

Cecily caught sight of Fitzhammer and his wife taking to the floor for a lively waltz, just as Baxter exclaimed, "Isn't that the Gilroys over there? His wife appears to be hurt."

Cecily followed his gaze. It was, indeed, the Gilroys, and they were almost at the door, proceeding slowly as Lady Lucille leaned on a cane while her husband supported her with an arm beneath her elbow.

"I heard that she sprained her ankle," Cecily said, quickening her pace. "I really should have a word with her." She caught up with the couple, followed closely by Baxter, who seemed reluctant to converse with the pair.

Lady Lucille appeared ill at ease, her fingers plucking at her husband's sleeve as if urging him to cut short the conversation.

As usual she wore no hat, and her hair, draped in a rather unique style covering most of her forehead and down her cheeks, was adorned with tiny silk violets.

She looked utterly divine in an exquisite pale violet ball gown, artfully tucked at the bodice in figured net over silk. Even the gold-topped cane could not deter from her sophisticated elegance.

"Lady Lucille," Cecily said breathlessly, having sped a little faster than she was accustomed. "I heard that you had injured your ankle. I do hope it isn't giving you too much trouble. I happen to have a doctor visiting us tonight. Would you like him to examine it for you? I'm quite sure he won't mind a bit."

Lucille glanced at Sir John, whose attention seemed to be caught by someone in the crowd of dancers. "Thank you, *madame*," she murmured, "but there is no cause to disturb the good doctor. It is merely a sprain and will soon mend."

"Very well." Cecily sought for a way to continue the conversation. "I must compliment you on your hair," she said, a little desperately. "It is such a charming style."

"Merci, madame." Lucille tugged on her husband's sleeve. "It is the very latest fashion from Paris."

"Ah, I thought it must be." Cecily paused for a second, then added, "We are all deeply saddened by the death of Mr. Peebles. It must have been such a dreadful shock for all of you."

This time it was Sir John who answered.

"Please excuse us, Mrs. Baxter. My wife is tired and needs to rest." Without giving Lucille a chance to say more, he hurried her through the door and down the hallway, apparently oblivious to the way she hobbled painfully to keep up.

"Well, that was a bit abrupt," Baxter said, staring after the couple. "I wonder what's biting him?"

"I don't know," Cecily said thoughtfully, "but I have the impression that he didn't want to talk about Peebles."

"Probably still in shock," Baxter observed as he held the door open for his wife to pass through. "After all, by all accounts they were pretty close friends."

"Unless," Cecily murmured, "something happened to destroy that friendship. Now wouldn't *that* be interesting."

Chapter
18

The following morning Cecily waited until the morning rush was over, then went in search of Moira. Mrs. Chubb greeted her as she entered the kitchen, which was surprisingly quiet, thanks in part to the absence of Michel, who was taking a short respite from his busy schedule.

"I hear the pantomime went very well, madam," Mrs. Chubb said, her hands wrist deep in a large slab of bread dough. "Everyone said that Doris did a wonderful job. I wish we could have been part of it, but then again, I'd just as soon be right back here in my kitchen again. I'd quite forgotten how good it feels."

Cecily smiled. "I can't tell you how good it feels to have you here." She looked around. "Is Moira here?"

"Oh, she's taking a tray up to Lady Lucille. The lady didn't come down for breakfast. Coming down with a nasty cold by all accounts. Seems to be doing the rounds, it does. Hope we don't all get it or this will be a poor Christmas, that's for sure."

"How are things working out with Gertie and the twins?" Cecily sat down on the nearest chair. "Is Daisy managing them? I imagine taking care of them can be hard work."

"Daisy is used to hard work." The housekeeper pounded the dough with her fist. "She loves those little scamps, that she does. She's so good with children, she should get a real job as a nanny. Be right up her alley, it would."

The door swung open and Moira rushed in with an empty tray. "Lady Lucille said to thank you for your kindness and —" She stopped short when she saw Cecily and dropped an awkward curtsey. "Good morning, m'm."

Cecily rose to her feet. "Moira, just the person I wanted to see. I'd like a quick word with you if you can spare the time?"

Moira glanced at Mrs. Chubb who, without looking up, answered for her. "She's got time."

"I won't keep her long," Cecily promised. She looked at Moira, whose face was creased with apprehension. "Perhaps we should step out into the hallway for a moment."

"Yes, m'm." Moira followed her out into the corridor, her fingers twisting the folds of her apron.

Cecily led her a few feet away, out of earshot of the kitchen. "I know you want to protect your friend," she said quietly, "but in order to know what happened to Jeanette, I need to know the truth. Everyone thinks she stole Miss Bunkle's pearls, especially since one was found hidden in Jeanette's clothing."

Moira gasped, her eyes wide above the hand she pressed to her mouth.

"You wouldn't want her to go to her grave with everyone believing she's a thief, now would you?"

Moira shook her head.

"I need to know, Moira," Cecily said gently. "Did Jeanette steal those pearls or not? If she did, then we'll say no more about it. After all, the girl is dead and can't be in any more trouble now. On the other hand, if she didn't steal them, I'm quite sure Jeanette would want everyone to know that. I know I would."

Moira lowered her hand, gulped, and looked down at her shoes. "I think I'd better show you something, m'm. It's down here in me room."

Cecily followed her down the hall to the

tiny room Moira had shared with the dead girl. She watched the young girl dig her hand under the mattress on Jeanette's bed and withdraw a package, which she handed to Cecily with downcast eyes.

Carefully Cecily unwrapped the package and poured the contents into her hand. The lamplight glinted on the perfectly matched pearls, and Cecily caught her breath. "So she did steal them."

"No, m'm." Moira's voice rose a notch. "She didn't really steal them, m'm. She was only going to borrow them. She was going into Wellercombe with her boyfriend, Wally, and she wanted to dress up for him. Only they had a big row over that Mr. Peebles, like I told you, and somehow the string got broke."

"I see," Cecily said slowly. "And she was afraid to tell Miss Bunkle what she'd done."

"Yes, m'm. She picked up all the pearls and hid 'em. She didn't have enough money to get them mended right away, so she was keeping them until she could get enough money. She was hoping to put them back before Miss Bunkle noticed they was missing, but then Miss Bunkle said they was stolen and Jeanette had to find the money in a hurry."

"I see." Cecily smoothed out the paper to wrap the pearls up again. As she did so, she noticed the printed heading at the top of the paper. It was a strange, yet familiar word. *Cureagambler.* The page had obviously been torn from the same notepad as Roger Peebles's IOU.

Baxter stared at the crinkled paper lying in front of him on his desk, his brows drawn together in a frown. "What *is* this?" he demanded. "Cureagambler? I've never heard of it."

"Neither had I until yesterday." Quickly Cecily explained about the IOU while Baxter's frown grew darker by the second. After delivering his usual lecture on the risk of invading the privacy of their guests, and the ramifications if she had been discovered, he calmed down enough to ask, "So what does it mean, this Cureagambler?"

"I'm not sure." She reached for a sheet of embossed notepaper, dipped Baxter's pen into the inkwell, shook the excess drops from it, then scrawled the name out on the paper. "Look, does this make more sense?"

"Cure a gambler," Baxter read out loud. "No, not really."

"I have a theory, if you'd like to hear it."

He gave her a look of pure irony. "Do I have a choice?"

She grinned. "Not really."

With a sigh he leaned back in his chair. "Oh, very well. Let's have it."

She paused for a moment to get her thoughts in order, then said, "Suppose that Cureagambler is an organization that helps cure people of a gambling habit. Suppose that Roger Peebles had a serious gambling habit, which judging by the IOU seems feasible. Now, Peebles was an important and respected Master of the Bench. If word got out that he had gambling problems, that surely wouldn't bode well for his career."

"I suppose not," Baxter said slowly, "but I don't see —"

"Wait." Cecily held up her hand. "I'm not finished yet."

"Pardon. One always lives in hope."

Ignoring his sarcasm, she went on, "Now, Jeanette also had a sheet of paper with the heading of this organization. Let us suppose that she discovered Peebles had a gambling problem. She could have found the sheet of paper earlier while cleaning his suite and reached the same conclusion we did. Then, when the string of pearls is broken, she needs money to have them restrung . . ."

"So she blackmails Peebles for the money."

She beamed, delighted that he had followed her train of thought so well. "Peebles already owes two thousand pounds that he can't afford to pay, since he has to issue an IOU. He certainly can't afford to pay a blackmailer."

"So he has to get rid of her instead."

"Precisely." She watched anxiously as Baxter thought it over.

"Well," he said at last. "If Peebles killed Jeanette, then his death must have been an accident. Just like Wrotham's."

Cecily sighed. "None of this really makes sense, does it. I still feel certain that someone tampered with Peebles's car, and I can't convince myself that Barry Wrotham fell into that well all by himself. It's all too close to be a coincidence. Yet there's absolutely nothing to connect them. So where do we go from here?"

"Nowhere," Baxter said firmly. "All of this is pure conjecture. Except for the theft of the pearls. Whether or not Jeanette planned to return them, she did steal them. In the eyes of the law, anyway. We shall have to report this to Northcott and see that these are returned to Miss Bunkle."

Cecily frowned. "I suppose we must. I just can't accept the fact that we'll never know what really happened."

"You might as well. The best thing we can do now is put this all behind us." Baxter replaced the pearls in their package, opened the drawer of his desk, and tucked them inside. "After all, if your theory is right and Peebles did kill Jeanette, he got his just reward."

Cecily scrawled aimlessly on the notepad, doodling circles around the words she'd scribbled earlier. "I wish I knew what this name really means." She looked up at him. "You have some influential associates in the city. I don't suppose you could ask some of them if they've ever heard of a company named Cureagambler?"

He narrowed his gaze. "I don't suppose you'll let it rest until I do."

She shrugged. "Just out of curiosity, that's all."

He sighed. "All right. I'll see what I can do. In the meantime, I'll give Northcott a ring and tell him to send someone for the pearls."

"Very well." Cecily rose from her chair.

"By the way," Baxter said casually, "I

heard that you entertained a guest for lunch yesterday."

"Oh, you mean Dr. Prestwick." She headed for the door, saying lightly over her shoulder, "I asked him here to look at Ross McBride. Gertie seemed most concerned about his health and I thought the doctor should take a look at him."

"Is that the only reason you invited him without telling me?"

She looked back at him. "No, actually I invited him here in the hopes that he would make up his quarrel with Madeline."

Baxter sighed, though his frown relaxed. "Cecily, when will you cease interfering in people's lives?"

"When everyone is as happy as I am, dear Bax."

To her relief, a smile warmed his face. "Amen."

With that, she left him to his work. There was much to be done before Christmas Eve, and she had neglected her work enough. Even so, the questions surrounding the three deaths still haunted her, and she knew she would not be able to rest until she had all the answers.

It was much later in the afternoon when

Baxter caught up with her again. She was in the laundry room with Mrs. Chubb, trying to decide whether or not to invest in some new tablecloths for the dining room.

"Gertie told me you were here," Baxter said when Mrs. Chubb discreetly withdrew to leave them alone. "I thought you'd like to know that I have some news about Cureagambler."

Cecily dropped the pile of tablecloths onto the counter. "You found out what it is?"

"I did indeed." Baxter looked pleased with himself. "And it's not an organization to cure gambling, as we thought. Quite the opposite, in fact. It's a company, or rather a partnership, that owns two rather notorious gambling houses on the southeast coast. One is in Brighton, the other is in Southampton. Apparently both houses are quite well known among the more affluent citizens of London."

"Oh, my, how very intriguing." Cecily studied his face with interest. "Did you find out anything about them?"

"Only that there have been several brawls and incidents of . . ." He cleared his throat.

Cecily waited for a moment, then asked impatiently, "Incidents of what?"

"Well, it's a rather delicate matter, but the rumors have it that certain young ladies in the establishments are offering their . . . ah . . . services for payment."

Cecily opened her eyes wide. "A brothel?"

"Hush!" Baxter looked wildly around, though they were quite alone in the room. "A lady shouldn't even know the word, much less utter it."

"Oh, come now, Bax. I read the newspaper. Those women have been trading their wares since the beginning of time."

"That doesn't mean that it's a matter for discussion."

She stared at him, her mind busily digesting this latest information. "Roger Peebles must have visited those places, since he had their IOU slips in his pocket."

"Well, if so, I can certainly understand why he wouldn't want that to be common knowledge. From what I hear, the police are constantly raiding the place in an effort to shut them down, but so far the owners have been clever enough to avoid that."

"How interesting." She frowned. "I wonder who else knows about Peebles's indiscretions."

"I can't imagine he publicizes the fact."

"I wonder if this has anything to do with his death."

Baxter sighed. "Peebles's death was an accident. I thought we agreed on that."

"Now why would you think we'd agreed on anything?" She smiled sweetly. "I think, my dear husband, that you should have a word with the rest of the Benchers. Perhaps suggest you have some influential friends who are looking for somewhere out of town to indulge their habit?"

Baxter's pursed his lips. "And why, pray, would I do such a thing?"

"I think it would be most interesting to know who else knows about this Cure-agambler. I have a feeling that it might have something to do with why Peebles died."

"A feeling," Baxter repeated. "You mean one of those infernal notions that invariably land you in trouble."

"And more often than not have led to some very satisfying conclusions."

"Not without hovering on the brink of disaster."

"Perhaps, but when a young girl in our employ is brutally murdered, isn't it our duty to discover why she was killed and by whom? Up until now we have been guessing. I think it's high time we made a concerted effort to solve this puzzle. Once and for all."

For several seconds their gazes clashed, then Baxter muttered, "Oh, very well. It can't do any harm, I suppose. I'll pay a visit to the card room, since the gentlemen in question seem to spend a vast amount of time in there."

"Thank you, Baxter." She laid a hand on his arm. "I don't have to remind you to be careful not to let slip that we know about Cureagambler. After all, three deaths have occurred within a very short time. I'm not anxious to see a fourth. Particularly if it's yours."

"You surely don't suspect one of the Benchers of being involved in murder," Baxter exclaimed.

"I'm considering all possibilities, that's all." She smiled at him. "I know I can trust you to be discreet."

"Something tells me I'm going to regret this." He moved to the door, then paused to look back at her. "If you're free for lunch, perhaps you'd care to join me in the dining room."

"I would adore to have lunch with you."

"I think the staff should see us together, just in case they should have any false impressions about your tryst with

Prestwick yesterday."

She controlled the urge to laugh and instead murmured demurely, "I think that's a very good idea."

Seemingly satisfied, he left.

Cecily turned back to the task of counting tablecloths. Poor Baxter. He couldn't forget that once Kevin Prestwick had pursued her, even though she had never entertained any notions of romantic attachment to him. Then again, it really didn't hurt to remind him every now and then. Just to keep him on his toes, so to speak. Smiling, Cecily started counting tablecloths.

It was an hour or so later before she had completed enough of her schedule to indulge in some free time with her husband. Baxter was waiting for her in his office, and she knew at once by his heavy scowl that something had upset him.

Somewhat alarmed, she hurried to his side. "What happened? Surely there hasn't been another death?"

"No, no." He shook his head. "It's just those blasted Benchers. They were all in the card room, so I approached them and, as delicately as possible, broached the subject of gambling in general."

Cecily sat down, afraid of what she might hear. "So what did they say?"

"Well, the conversation went on and on, mostly rubbish that I didn't understand, about odds and bets and bluffs and a number of terms of which I had no idea of their meaning. I had to pretend interest, of course. I thought I was never going to get away."

Feeling somewhat disappointed, Cecily asked, "But did they mention Cureagambler?"

"Not one word. I mentioned the fact that I knew several wealthy gentlemen in the city who love to gamble, but found our meager card rooms too tame for their adventurous spirits."

"That was extremely clever of you," Cecily said, beaming at him in admiration. "So what reaction did you get to that?"

Baxter shrugged. "Well, Sir John Gilroy's features remained carved in stone. Chatsworth looked interested but didn't say anything."

"And Fitzhammer? If anyone would spill the beans, it would be him."

"Well, he did hint that he might know a place where my gentlemen friends might find enough excitement to satisfy them. He suggested I join them in a few rounds of baccarat this evening, when we might discuss it. Naturally, I had to decline the invitation."

"Baxter!" Cecily sat up straight. "How could you? This is the perfect opportunity for you to find out more about Cureagambler. Especially if Lionel Fitzhammer knows about it, too."

"I didn't say that. I merely said that Fitzhammer knew of a place. He didn't mention it by name."

Ignoring him, Cecily went on blithely, "We'll send in a few complimentary bottles of brandy and they'll be talking in no time. Lady Lucille complained of her husband taking part in something that didn't include her. Perhaps all of these gentlemen are paid members of these houses. If so, they would all have a motive for murder. You have to go to the game. It's the only chance we might have of catching all three of them unawares. You must pay strict attention to everything that is said."

His expression of sheer alarm was almost comical. "Have you forgotten that I know nothing about cards? I seem to remember you volunteering my participation in a poker game, giving my opponents the impression I had played professionally. I was hopelessly inept, and suffered agonies at that table. That was one of the most embarrassing and nerve-racking evenings of my life."

"We found out what we wanted to know, however," Cecily pointed out.

Baxter glared at her. "I *cannot* play baccarat."

"You can learn."

"In one afternoon?"

"Enough to get by. Yes."

"That's what you assured me about the poker game. And this time you won't be able to coach me as we play, since you're not allowed in the card rooms."

"Idiotic rules and regulations," Cecily muttered. "They should be outlawed."

"The rules are what make this a club and not a hotel."

"Exactly. That's my point." She drew a deep breath. "Darling, from what I hear, baccarat is much simpler to play than poker. We have the rules for them right here in your office. I suggest we have a leisurely lunch, then we'll return here and learn the rules of the game. You don't have to play with the Benchers all evening. Just long enough to find out what they know about Cureagambler, and anything else they might say."

"And how will that tell us who killed Jeanette?"

"I don't know," Cecily confessed. "But I can't help feeling it's all connected somehow. What's more, I think the Benchers know more than they are saying."

"Why are you so sure they are involved?"

Before she could answer, he held up his hand. "No, don't tell me. It's just a feeling."

She looked up at him in appeal. "It's a very *strong* feeling."

His sigh told her he'd capitulated. "I know I'm going to regret this, but all right. I'll make an attempt to learn the game. But I have to tell you, if I don't feel I know enough about it by this evening to put on a good show, then I'm calling it off. Agreed?"

Reluctantly, she agreed, though secretly she vowed that, come hell or high water, she'd make sure he learned how to play baccarat before the day was over.

During lunch Cecily deliberately kept the conversation away from the subject of gambling, or indeed, anything to do with the Benchers or their wives. She was half afraid that Baxter would change his mind. She would have felt a great deal better about the whole venture had she been able to join him in the card room. She made up her mind that, at the first opportunity, she would talk to Edward about changing some of the rules that offended her.

As soon as they had finished their meal, Cecily led the way back to Baxter's office, assuring him that their duties could wait until they had mastered the game of baccarat.

The game called for at least three decks of cards, and she had to wait for him to collect them, as well as the rules, before they could begin.

"This looks heinously complicated," Baxter complained after scanning the closely written rules.

"Not for a man of your intelligence," Cecily replied blithely. "Really all you have to do is know how to count to nine. You simply add two cards together, and take the last digit. For instance, if you have an eight and a five, you add them together, which is thirteen, so your count is three. It's simple."

Baxter looked unconvinced. "What's all this about a shoe? And what the devil is *cheval,* or banco?"

"It all depends on how you bet. The punters sit on either side of the banker and you bet on them being able to beat the banker's hand." She studied the rules over his shoulder. "Look, banco means the punter is betting the total value of the banker's funds."

Baxter shook his head. "This is not going to work. Why don't I simply ask them if they've heard of this Cureagambler? It would save a lot of trouble."

"Because no self-respecting barrister as important as the Masters of the Bench is going to admit he knows of a gambling brothel in Brighton."

Baxter winced, but refrained from chiding her for using the forbidden word. "Then what makes you think that playing this dratted game with them is going to open up their mouths?"

"It won't be the game that loosens their tongue," Cecily said smugly. "It's the free brandy they'll be pouring down their throats. Trust me, Bax. This will work. I have —"

"A feeling," he said in unison with her. "Very well, I'll do my best. I can only hope it doesn't turn into the disaster I experienced in the poker game."

"Don't worry, darling," Cecily said with a great deal more confidence than she felt. "You'll manage beautifully and I'm sure you will even enjoy it. Take my word for it."

Chapter
19

"So what did Dr. Prestcott say about Ross?" Mrs. Chubb asked, stirring her cup of tea vigorously with a delicate silver teaspoon.

Seated opposite her at the kitchen table, Gertie uttered a gloomy sigh. "He says he's exhausted. Needs a good rest. I could have told 'im that."

Mrs. Chubb lifted the cup to her lips and sipped cautiously in case it was still too hot. The steaming liquid stung her tongue and she hastily put the cup down again. "Well, he's getting that here, isn't he?"

"I suppose so. He's not very happy with me working, though. Even though I explained I was doing it as a favor for Mrs. Baxter. He said as how everyone would think it terrible for him to let his wife work and he's lying around doing nothing."

"Well, it won't be for long, will it." Mrs. Chubb tasted the tea again and this time managed to get a mouthful down without burning her tongue again. "Whereabouts is Ross now, anyway?"

"He's taking a walk around the grounds to get some fresh air, ain't he."

Mrs. Chubb watched in awe as Gertie chugged down the hot tea without even blinking. That girl had to have a constitution made of iron, that's all she could say.

"He wanted to take the twins with him," Gertie added, dropping her cup on its saucer. "But Daisy's taken them into town to look at the toy shops."

"Well, that's a mistake. Now they'll want everything they see on the shelves."

"Don't I bloomin' know it," Gertie said mournfully. "Course, they won't blinking get it, will they. We'll have to watch the bloody pennies now, that's for sure."

The maid seated next to her sniggered, and Mrs. Chubb gave Gertie a look that she hoped she would interpret as a command to watch her language. Gertie was trying, but she never could get rid of that smutty mouth of hers.

"Better not let Ross hear you say that," she warned. "He won't want to be reminded that he's not bringing home the fatted calf like he was."

"He's not even bringing home a scrawny

chicken." Gertie picked up her empty cup and saucer and got wearily to her feet. "Never mind, that's what I say. He'll find something else to do before long, that I do know. Until then, well, I'm getting paid so that'll help."

Mrs. Chubb watched her carry her cup and saucer to the sink. Poor Gertie. She put on a good face, but it was pretty plain to her that the girl was worried sick. She could only hope that something good would turn up for Ross, or she might be out of a job herself. And that's what frightened her most of all.

That evening Cecily paced around her suite, unable to settle down. She had found a decent copy of Louisa May Alcott's *An Old-fashioned Girl* in the library and had promised herself she would read it at the earliest opportunity.

Knowing that Baxter was at that moment cornered in a card room with the Benchers was a distraction that made reading impossible. Sending him down there to find out what they knew had seemed a good idea at the time. Now that she'd had an hour or two to think about it, however, she was having qualms about the whole thing.

Baxter was right when he'd reminded her that he was no gambler. Without her there to prod or guide him, he could be getting in over his head, not to mention arousing the suspicions of three very influential barristers, all of whom possessed extraordinary intelligence, or they would not be in that particular profession.

They would easily see through Baxter's clumsy attempts to extract information from them, and could very well be extremely offended. On the other hand, if they did have something to hide, and were somehow connected to Peebles's death, the situation could actually be dangerous.

Once more she had acted on impulse, with dubious results. Now all she could do was sit and stew while Baxter dug a hole for himself that just might be too deep for him to climb out.

She was in such a state by the time the door to their suite finally flew open, that she wasn't at all surprised to see the heavy scowl on Baxter's face.

What did unsettle her was the cold fury in his eyes as he stalked across the room, dragged off his evening coat, and flung it on the bed.

Watching him stomp to the window, she tried out several questions in her mind and discarded them all. *How did things go?* was not a good one, since it was quite obvious from his dark expression that things did not go well at all. *What happened?* seemed equally precarious, and at that moment it didn't seem prudent to ask him if he'd found out anything helpful.

In the end, she kept silent, while viewing his stiff back with some trepidation. It wasn't often that Baxter lost his temper, but she'd learned to hold her tongue on the rare occasion he had become this incensed.

It seemed like an eternity before he finally spoke, and when he did, his voice was clipped and chipped with ice. "Well, you have certainly outdone yourself this time, Cecily."

As guilty as she'd felt earlier, she wasn't prepared to take all the blame for whatever disaster had transpired in the card room. Lifting her chin, she said quietly, "Perhaps if you explain what it is I'm supposed to have done, I might be able to understand why you are so angry."

He turned then, and this time the bleak expression on his face frightened her. "I tried to tell you I was no gambler. You wouldn't listen. I knew as soon as I started playing that dratted game that I had no business there, but there didn't seem any way I could withdraw without appearing to be a dishonorable, underhanded cad. So I stayed."

"I'm sorry if you were embarrassed —" she began, but he interrupted her with a roar that startled her half out of her wits.

"*Embarrassed!* Dammit, Cecily, if that were only all of it. I'm afraid there's a great deal more than embarrassment involved here."

She sat down, afraid of what she might hear next. "What happened? Did you find out more about Cureagambler?"

"No, I did not." He came toward her, his fists clenched at his sides. "I didn't find out a blasted thing. It was all for nothing, Cecily. All of it."

He stopped short, closed his eyes, and slapped a hand to his forehead in a way that at any other time would have seemed melodramatic.

At the moment, however, she recognized his anguish, and rose quickly to her feet. "You are frightening me, Hugh. Please, tell me, what is it? What's wrong?"

He lowered his hand and gazed at her with such sorrow her heart began pounding with fear. "It's all gone, Cecily. Everything we have. It happened so fast I found it hard to believe. I kept betting more and more, hoping to recoup at least some of the loss, but it just kept mounting up and . . ."

His voice broke, and she stepped toward him, her arms outstretched to comfort him.

To her shock and alarm, he turned his back to her. Regaining control of his voice, he said harshly, "We shall have to sell the house in London in order to pay the debt."

She uttered a cry of dismay. "No, it can't be that bad. Surely there is a way —"

"There is no way. This is your doing, Cecily. I hope you are satisfied." With an abrupt movement he strode to the door and dragged it open.

She started after him. "Where are you going?"

"I don't know. I need to be alone. Go to bed. There is nothing you can do that you haven't already done."

The door closed behind him, and she sank onto her chair, utterly at a loss. Stunned with disbelief, she tried to make sense of what he'd told her. Sell the house? No, surely not. And what of his business? How would that fare if the house had to be sold? His office, all his associates, all the work he'd ever done was tied up in that house. To sell it now would surely mean ruin.

Now she was truly frightened. She couldn't wait for him to return, so that he could calm her fears and tell her he was simply overreacting to a distressing situation. Even Baxter, in all his ineptitude for gambling, couldn't have possibly lost that much money. No matter how humiliating the circumstances.

No, he was trying to frighten her so that she would never put him in that position again. In that, he had succeeded. She had already vowed to herself that very thing, even before he'd returned in such a temper.

Now all she could do was wait for his return and beg his forgiveness. Promise him anything he wanted as long as he did not look at her with that terrible coldness in his eyes.

She waited all night, but he did not return. And in the grayness of the next morning, as the snow began to fall once more, she faced the fact that this time she had gone too far. She could only hope that it wasn't too late for forgiveness, and that she hadn't lost the love and respect of the man she so greatly adored.

It was much later that morning when

Baxter finally returned to the suite. He changed his clothes and went down to his office without saying a word to Cecily about where he had been. Her brief attempt to open a conversation was met with a stony stare and a chilly silence and she withdrew, knowing it would take time before she could approach him.

After picking at a solitary breakfast in her sitting room, she approached her desk with the idea of working on a shopping list for Christmas gifts. The prospect of Christmas with Baxter ignoring her was too dismal to contemplate, and she pushed the list aside. She reached instead for a pencil and started doodling aimlessly on the blotting paper. She wished now she'd simply asked the Benchers about the IOU she'd found in Peebles's wardrobe. Or at least questioned Mrs. Peebles.

Then again, it would be difficult to explain how she had come about it, or what her interest in it might be, and since the other notepaper with the name of Cureagambler on it had been wrapped around stolen pearls, that, too, would have been a little awkward to explain.

She should have done as Baxter had suggested and left well alone. She was no closer to solving the puzzle, and now she had possibly lost her home. Though now that she'd had time to think about it, she failed to see why she should take all the blame. After all, Baxter had been foolish to the extreme, risking everything they had to salvage his pride. This was every bit as much his fault as hers. And she would point that out to him. Just as soon as he got over his snit. If he ever got over it.

More dispirited than ever, she stared at the word she'd written down. Cureagambler. It did seem odd that a company that apparently made a fortune from gamblers would form a name suggesting a cure for gamblers. That didn't make sense at all. The name must mean something else.

Her heart still ached so badly it hurt, and she did her best to keep her mind off her problems by rearranging the letters of the word that had caused so much trouble. Forward and backward, in and out. Nothing made sense. She began to play one of her favorite games, seeing how many words she could think of using the letters of Cureagambler. *Game, crab, blur, bar, luck* . . . no, there was no *k*. She crossed off the last letter, then stared at what she'd written. She started scribbling again, becoming more excited as she wrote. Then, with a small cry of triumph, she wrote rapidly on a piece of notepaper, then headed for the door. Angry at her or not, Baxter had to see this.

A few minutes later he answered her light tap with a curt, "Come in, come in then!"

When she put her head around the door, her heart sank at his forbidding expression. "I'm busy at the moment," he said shortly. "Whatever it is will have to wait."

She tightened her lips, but ignored his attempt to be rid of her and advanced into the room. After sitting herself down firmly on her chair, she slid the notepaper across the desk toward him.

For a moment she thought he would simply pretend it wasn't there, but evidently his curiosity got the better of him and he picked it up. "What the devil is this?"

Delighted to have drawn even that curt communication from him, she said quickly, "I broke the word *Cureagambler* down into four parts."

He made a sound of disgust and threw the paper at her across the desk. "You simply do not have the sense to know when you have gone too far," he snapped. "Enough of this. I refuse to listen to any more wild conjecture about this company.

No matter what it is. What these people do is none of our business, and quite frankly, the very thought of gambling right now is like waving a red rag at a bull. Please give me the courtesy of eliminating the subject from your mind, unless you want to conduct the rest of our lives together in silence."

All notions of attempting to placate him vanished in the face of this onslaught. Her own voice trembled with outrage when she answered him. "You are being most unfair. It wasn't I who gambled away our home which, in case you are under some misapprehension, is every bit as important to me as it is to you. Had you been more vigilant and less concerned with your insufferable pride, you would not have allowed the situation to arrive at such a disastrous conclusion. I suggested you attend the game, yes. I certainly did not sit there prodding you in the back while you recklessly threw away our entire assets. That is entirely on your shoulders, not on mine."

His chilling gaze was formidable, but she held her own without flinching. After a moment he said quietly, "This is not the time to discuss this matter."

"Perhaps not, but the very least you can do is listen to what I have to say. What I have discovered is of the utmost importance, and could very well shed a light on the reason why Roger Peebles died. Perhaps Jeanette, too. And be good enough to spare me the black looks until you have heard the entire story."

His mouth tightened, but he held out his hand for the paper she thrust at him. Taking it from her, he scanned it, then said brusquely, "I still do not understand what you are trying to show me."

"Look at the four names written there. Lucille, Gretchen, Amelia, and Barbara. Take the first three letters of each name, rearrange them, and you end up with . . ."

"Cureagambler." He stared at the paper. "My God. The partnership that owns those two gambling houses . . ."

"Unless it is an extraordinary coincidence, it would seem the partnership consists of the Benchers of Lincoln's Inn. I can think of no other reason for such an odd name."

"If this got out, the scandal could cost them their careers."

"Not could, but certainly would. According to Percy Chatsworth, the Masters of the Bench are prohibited from owning or being engaged in outside businesses. They would be instantly disbarred for life."

After another long moment, Baxter handed her back the paper. "Well, I see what you mean. This would certainly be a good reason to silence someone."

"Particularly if he or she threatened to disclose this interesting fact to the authorities."

"So you're saying that Roger Peebles discovered his fellow Benchers owned not only a business, but a disreputable one at that, and threatened to expose them? But why would he do that? What would he have to gain?"

"Professional jealousy, perhaps. After all, one must suppose that they are in competition with each other for influential clients."

"From what I understand," Baxter said dryly, "there are more than enough clients to keep them all busy. But what would this have to do with the death of our maid?"

"I have no idea at this point. Moira seemed to think that Jeanette and Peebles were personally involved, since she saw them together. On the other hand, perhaps Jeanette knew about the partnership somehow, and threatened Peebles. Perhaps he killed Jeanette to silence her."

"Then one of the partners killed Peebles? That doesn't make sense at all."

"Nothing makes sense until we see the

reasons behind it. In any case, I'm not really sure what I'm saying at this point. I haven't had time to think about it." She rose from her chair. "I've taken up enough of your time. I wanted your opinion in the hopes that you would help confirm my suspicions. Now I need to ponder on it all and try to remember what it is I keep forgetting."

He looked as if he would say something, then shook his head. "I can't think about this now. I have some serious work to do if I'm to salvage anything from the fiasco of last night."

Aware of the barrier still between them, she took her leave, her heart heavy with anxiety. If this catastrophe caused a permanent rift between them, she would never forgive herself. Or him. She could only hope that his coldness was a temporary condition that would soon be remedied. If not, this Christmas Season would be a depressing affair indeed.

Although Baxter shared her bed that night, he did not turn to her as he normally would, but instead presented her with his back and in a very short while was snoring heavily. She eventually fell asleep, but awoke sometime in the night, feeling decidedly chilly without the warmth of

Baxter's body to comfort her.

He lay on the very edge of the bed, and although she was tempted to move closer, she refrained for fear she would tip him off onto the floor. He surely would not appreciate such a rude awakening in his present mood.

Instead, she lay on her back, staring at the shadows on the ceiling, and thought about the new development in the puzzle of Peebles's death. It was a risky venture indeed for the Benchers. The partnership must be extremely lucrative for them to take such a chance, though one would suppose it would not be difficult for barristers to keep such an enterprise a secret. After all, it was merely by chance that she had come upon it.

She tried to imagine the Benchers engaged in such a dubious association. It was difficult to imagine Sir John Gilroy in that role, or even Percy Chatsworth, who was so quick to advise her that Benchers were not allowed to own outside interests.

As for Roger Peebles and Lionel Fitzhammer, if Peebles killed Jeanette and Fitzhammer found out about it. . . . She sat bolt upright in bed, dragging the eiderdown from Baxter's shoulders. His snoring ended in a snort. He grunted, and tugged the warm covering back under his chin.

Cecily opened her mouth, then snapped it shut again. He would not appreciate being woken up in the middle of the night to listen to yet another of her rash theories. This would have to wait until the morning.

Excited now, she lay back down and reviewed the whole sequence in her mind. The thing she had buried in her memory had suddenly resurfaced, so clearly she couldn't imagine how she could have forgotten it in the first place.

It was when she'd offered her condolences to Chatsworth and Fitzhammer after the news of Peebles's death. Fitzhammer declared that Peebles was careless and most likely hadn't bothered to get his brakes examined before he left London. But she was quite sure that Samuel had told no one that the brakes had failed, and she had told no one but Baxter. She could safely assume that he had not passed on the information, in which case, the only way Fitzhammer could have known was if he had something to do with it.

The memory of Samuel's soft voice came back clearly to her. *I'd say someone helped them along a bit. Not likely they'd both go at the same time without a bit of nudging.*

It would seem she finally had her killer.

Chapter 20

Unable to sleep now, Cecily wrestled with her thoughts. If Fitzhammer had killed Peebles, it was entirely likely that he had killed Jeanette, too. Perhaps even Barry Wrotham as well. The big question was, of course, if he had indeed killed three people, why had he found it necessary to take such drastic steps? If she thought about it long enough, perhaps she could determine the reason.

She frowned in the darkness. If only she could talk the whole thing through with Baxter. Curses on the entire gambling scene. Once she had been tolerant of the practice, particularly when it had been an integral source of income for the Pennyfoot, albeit illegal. But now she had nothing but disgust for gambling and the men who perpetuated it. Too many lives had been ruined by the habit. And many more would certainly follow suit. Even murder.

She was convinced that the three deaths

had something to do with the gambling houses. What if Wrotham were a gambler also, and had frequented the gambling houses, somehow discovering the identity of the owners. If he had suffered a loss comparable with Baxter's devastating misfortune, he might have hoped to recoup his money by blackmailing the partners. Or one partner such as Lionel Fitzhammer.

Wrotham would then have to be silenced. Jeanette might have found out about the murder and confided in Peebles, with whom she was apparently enamored, in which case Peebles might have confronted Fitzhammer, who then had to silence them both.

It was a possible solution, and pleased with herself, Cecily uttered a small sigh of satisfaction. That certainly made more sense than all her other scenarios, and would justify her conviction that none of the deaths was an accident.

Now the problem was, how to verify her suspicions, much less prove them. Inspector Cranshaw was hardly going to pay any attention to her vague theories, unless she had something substantial to provoke his interest.

Something else occurred to her. Something that disturbed her a great deal. If her suspicions were correct, then Fitzhammer was a very dangerous man. He apparently had no reservations about killing a close associate, not to mention an innocent young girl. It was entirely possible he had killed Wrotham because of what he knew. If Lady Lucille had been close to Barry Wrotham, then her life could very well be in danger, too. If Fitzhammer should decide that Lucille might suspect him and was a threat to him, he would have no hesitation in killing her as well.

No matter how vague her suspicions might still be, it was her duty to warn Lady Lucille, and Sir John Gilroy as well, that they could very well be keeping company with a mass murderer. Of course, that would mean she'd have to reveal what she knew about the Cureagambler partnership, but it couldn't be helped. It was up to her to see that another murder did not take place.

Having come to that conclusion, she finally allowed herself to fall asleep.

The next morning Baxter was still acting cold toward her, though he did answer her comments with a grunt or a nod. Somewhat encouraged by this first sign of thawing, she approached him as he was about to shave his chin.

One of the maids had brought a jug of hot water to their suite, and he was using the last of it in the wash-basin. At the moment he was peering into the mirror at his lathered face.

As he brandished the long blade of his razor, about to stroke it down his cheek, Cecily said tentatively, "I've remembered what it was I'd forgotten yesterday."

She took his grunt for consent to continue and quickly told him about her conversation with Fitzhammer and the brakes on Peebles's car. When she received no response to that, she launched into her speculation of what might have happened, and why Fitzhammer might have seen fit to kill three people.

Baxter appeared to be listening as he scraped his chin and throat with the razor, though he kept his gaze squarely on the mirror in front of him.

"I think I should warn Sir John and Lady Lucille," she said as she came to the end of her story. "If I'm right, then Lionel Fitzhammer is a very dangerous man. I think they should be aware that he could be a threat to them, especially Lady Lucille."

"*If* you are right," Baxter said pointedly. "If you are mistaken, as you so often are, you could be exposing yourself to a great deal of embarrassment. You will also offend some very influential members of this club, whose loss your cousin Edward would surely resent. Not that I expect you to heed my advice, Cecily, but if I were you, I would think long and deeply before you embark on such a dubious mission."

"Then what do you suggest I do?"

His glance at her was heavy with scorn. "Since when did you take notice of what I might advise? I see no point in offering my opinion, since you no doubt have already made up your mind and, in spite of what I might think, will indubitably take matters into your own hands. All I can ask is that you consider the consequences of your actions. And now, if you will excuse me, I have work to do."

"You are not taking breakfast with me?"

"I'll have something sent to the office."

Miserably she watched him head for the door. "Is there any word on the state of our finances?"

He paused and without looking at her muttered, "Contrary to what you might think, miracles are not performed every day, even at Christmastime. Nothing has changed. The house will be sold to cover the debt. I am . . . . sorry." The door closed behind him with a snap.

She twisted her lips in a wry grimace. At least he expressed some regret. It was a start in the right direction. Patience, that's what it would take. A good deal of patience on her part. She could only hope he wouldn't keep her waiting too long. She couldn't bear the thought of spending Christmas at odds with him.

She was about to follow him out when a tap on the door announced the arrival of Gertie, whose engaging grin went a long way to lifting Cecily's spirits.

"Just wanted to let you know, m'm, there's a gentleman waiting to speak to you on the telephone. I think he's ringing all the way from a foreign country, 'cos I heard the operator speaking to someone with a funny accent."

"I wonder if it's Michael, or Andrew." She hadn't heard from her sons in so long. The thought of talking to one of them right now was like a candle lighting up the dark.

"I don't think so, m'm. The operator said it were that Mr. Sandringham what bought the Pennyfoot."

"Edward? Oh, dear." For a moment Cecily was tempted to have Gertie tell Edward that she had gone out for the day.

Things were bound to be awkward. She didn't want to worry him with the news that three deaths had occurred in as many weeks, but on the other hand, he should be told. Perhaps Baxter . . .

Shaking her head, she said briskly, "I'll come down right away, Gertie, thank you."

She hurried out the door and closed it behind her. "How are you all managing in the kitchen?" she asked as she followed Gertie to the head of the stairs.

"Very well, m'm, thank you. Mrs. Chubb has got everyone running around like a bloody blue-ass fly, but she's getting things done on time, which is what counts." Gertie hesitated at the top of the stairs. "I know this isn't the time, m'm, but when you have a moment, I'd like a word with you if I may?"

"Of course, Gertie. I'll come down to the kitchen just as soon as I'm free."

"Thank you, m'm." The maid sped down the stairs ahead of her and disappeared around the turning.

Cecily frowned after her, wondering what was coming next. No doubt Gertie had seen enough of kitchen work. She was more than likely about to ask to be released from her duties. Not that she could blame her, Cecily thought desolately, but her absence would leave a huge gap. What's more, without Gertie's strong arms and brazen confidence to help things along, Mrs. Chubb might well decide to desert her post as well.

Cecily's stomach was tied up in knots by the time she arrived in the foyer to answer the telephone. Edward was bound to ask how they were faring. She could hardly blurt out to him that three people had died and the housekeeper had walked out on them, leaving them to the mercy of good friends who were now reaching the limit of their goodwill.

Her hand actually shook as she took the receiver and placed it to her ear. After speaking to the operator, who appeared to be in conversation with another faraway operator, there followed a series of buzzes, whistles, and shrieks, then a faint echo of Edward's voice crackled on the line. "Cecily? Cecily? Drat this interference. Is that you, Cecily? This is Edward."

"Edward, hello! It's good to hear from you."

She pressed the receiver closer to her ear as Edward spoke again through all the crackling and buzzing. "Can't hear you too well, so I'll make this brief. I'm off to Bermuda . . . probably be there for a while. I need to . . ." His voice disappeared beneath a barrage of buzzing and whistling.

She waited for an anxious moment or two, then shouted, "Edward? Hello? Hello!"

The buzzing quieted for a moment and once more Edward's voice could be faintly heard. "Cecily? Need you to find a new manager. All right? I'll ring you again after Christmas. Hope you have . . ."

This time the crackling went on even longer, then finally cut off. The operator's voice sounded so loud in her ear Cecily almost dropped the telephone. "I'm sorry, madam," she said, "but we have lost the connection."

"That's all right," Cecily said quickly. "Thank you, operator." She replaced the receiver and smiled at the desk clerk, who had been doing his best to look as if he couldn't hear a word she'd said.

Weak with relief, she made her way back to the stairs. She'd been saved the embarrassment of having to explain to Edward, in front of anyone who happened to be passing by, the events that had been taking place since she had arrived. Not that the deaths, or Miss Bunkle's defection for that matter, were much of a secret. Still, they weren't things she wanted to shout about.

She could have talked to Edward in

Baxter's office, of course. It would have been more private. But frankly, the thought of facing that formidable stony face again that morning was more than she could tolerate.

She supposed she should let him know about Edward's request to find a new manager. Then again, this probably wasn't a good time to give him that news. Better to wait until he had recovered his good nature.

She forced herself to stop thinking about her angry husband and concentrated instead on the beautiful work Madeline had put into the decorations. The stair bannisters had been swathed in fir and holly, and smelled divine. Huge red ribbons clung to the holly boughs, matching the firm red berries nestled among the shiny green leaves. Tiny sprigs of mistletoe peeked out at intervals, which would no doubt arouse Phoebe's contempt when she saw them.

Which reminded her, she hadn't seen the tree in the library since Madeline had decorated it. She would do that just as soon as she'd spoken to Sir John and had that word with Gertie that she'd promised. If Madeline had taken as much trouble with the tree as she had everywhere else, it would be quite a sight to see.

She missed her friends, Cecily realized as she climbed the stairs to the first floor. As soon as she had spoken to Sir John, she would send messages inviting both Madeline and Phoebe to tea that afternoon in her suite. They could sit and relax, gossip a little, and perhaps for a short while she could forget her troubles.

Feeling more cheered than she had in quite a while, she reached the top of the landing and headed down toward Sir John Gilroy's suite.

Her light tap on the door was answered by Lady Lucille, who seemed a little put out upon greeting her. Her eyes were watery and her red nose looked painfully raw from an overuse of a handkerchief.

In spite of her malady she still managed to look elegant, though her hair still draped her face in that peculiar style, which really wasn't suitable for day wear, Cecily thought uncharitably. "I trust your cold is improving?" she inquired.

"It is a little better, *merci, madame.*"

"I'm happy to hear that. If there's anything you need, please let us know." She glanced into the room. "I'd like a word with Sir John," she added. "Is he here?"

"No, *Madame* Baxter, he is not here. He

is in the card room, as always, with Mr. Chatsworth and Mr. Fitzhammer. Even the death of his very good friend does not prevent him from spending his time with those card games. *C'est si tragique.*"

Cecily stared at her. Until that moment she had forgotten that part of her conversation with Lucille earlier. She had been too engrossed with the woman's confession that Wrotham had been her lover. But now she remembered something else Lucille had mentioned. *I do not understand why he needs all this extra work and demands. I tell him over and over again, I wish the others would leave him alone.* Of course. Now she understood. The thing that kept him so busy was his partnership in Cureagambler.

Fitzhammer had already killed one of the partners. Could he possibly be planning on killing the others, in order to gain sole ownership of Cureagambler? It was something she hadn't thought of before, but now it seemed a distinct possibility.

"Lady Lucille," she said, advancing uninvited into the room. "I must speak with Sir John as soon as possible. It is a matter of great urgency. His life might very well be in danger."

Lucille's eyes opened wide, and she

374

clutched her throat. "Whatever do you mean?"

"The accident that took the life of Roger Peebles." Cecily drew a deep breath. "I have reason to believe that it was not an accident. I must warn you to be on your guard. Your husband, too. It is imperative that I speak with him about this. Do you have any idea how long he plans to be in the card room?"

Lucille's face looked white and drawn. She shook her head, and her lips trembled when she whispered, "About an hour, *madame*. No longer, I should think. He plans to dine with me in the dining room." She gestured at her ankle. "I am not feeling well, and I still cannot walk far on my own. In any case, my husband prefers to accompany me when I am in public."

"In that case, perhaps you would be good enough to ask him to meet me. I have to pay a visit to the kitchen, but I shall be in the library after a while. I shall wait there until Sir John can join me."

"I will be happy to pass on your message." Lady Lucille limped to the door and held it open. "Thank you for your concern, Mrs. Baxter. I pray that you are mistaken in your fears. I cannot imagine anyone wishing to hurt my husband, or Mr.

Peebles for that matter."

"Or Jeanette and Barry Wrotham, either. Nevertheless, someone did."

Lucille's lips were colorless. "Barry, too? No, I cannot believe . . ."

She swayed on her feet and Cecily looked at her in alarm. "Lady Lucille, if you are feeling faint, I can send for some salts . . ."

"No, *madame,* thank you." Her voice was stronger now. "It was momentary, that is all." She turned her head as a sneeze interrupted her, then added a little thickly, "I am quite well. Please, do not concern yourself."

"Very well." Reluctantly, Cecily moved to the door. She couldn't help feeling that she was making a mistake leaving this vulnerable woman alone, yet she could not spare the time to sit with her until Sir John returned. "If you should need assistance," she told her, "please don't hesitate to summon one of the maids. They'll be only too happy to oblige."

"*Merci, madame,*" Lucille murmured. "You are too kind."

Still feeling uneasy, Cecily made for the stairs and descended them swiftly. Her urge to confide in Baxter was strong, but she decided to delay it until she had spoken to Sir John. She intended only to warn him, since she could not accuse Fitzhammer of murder without more proof. But she also nursed a hope that the conversation might reveal something more tangible on which to hang her suspicions.

At that moment she would welcome anything that would make her case stronger when she presented it to Baxter later. If only she could convince him that her actions were justified, and that she was doing her utmost to apprehend a genuine murderer, he might find it easier to forgive her for pushing him into the situation that had cost them both so much.

For the time being, however, she had to take advantage of the morning lull to speak with Gertie, which could very well add yet another burden to their mounting concerns. Holding on to the hope that Gertie and Mrs. Chubb would at least see them through Christmas, Cecily headed for the kitchen.

The maids were seated around the main table, chatting among themselves as they shared creamy coffee and huge slices of Dundee cake. Mrs. Chubb and Gertie sat apart from them, their chairs drawn up in front of the stove. The doors were open, and emitted a fierce heat as the flames roared and rattled up the wide chimney pipe.

Cecily was surprised to see Samuel seated with them. She gave him a delighted smile as he leapt to his feet. "I thought you would be in the George and Dragon, Samuel," she told him. "It's past opening time already."

Samuel shrugged. "Gertie told me you was having a word with her this morning, m'm. I wanted to be in on it."

Worried now, Cecily took the empty chair closest to the stove. "Well, this sounds serious. You had better tell me what this is all about."

Samuel and Gertie looked at Mrs. Chubb.

"Don't look at me," she said sharply. "You go first, Gertie. Seeing as how you're the one who started all this."

Gertie's cheeks were flushed, though Cecily couldn't tell if it was from nervousness or the heat from the stove, which was already beginning to toast her own knees through the thick folds of her skirt.

"Well, m'm," Gertie began, "it's like this." She wound an apron string around her finger, then unwound it again.

"Go *on,* Gertie!" Mrs. Chubb said irritably. "Get on with it. We haven't got all day."

Gertie sent her a quick glance, then blurted out, "It's Ross, m'm. He's been walking around the grounds, you see, and well, now that he's sold the business and everything —"

Cecily uttered a muffled exclamation. "Of course. He must be upset. I'm so sorry."

"Oh, it's all right, m'm, really. It were getting too flipping much for him anyway. Riding around them streets in the snow on his bicycle. Couldn't keep up with it anymore, that's the trouble. Anyway, since he don't have no bleeding —"

"Gertie, you promised!"

She sent Mrs. Chubb a lethal glare. "I'm doing me flipping best."

"Just tell me," Cecily said quickly. "What's wrong with Ross?"

"Oh, nothing's wrong, m'm." Gertie's smile was lovely to see. "Well, he's tired, of course. Exhausted, the doctor said. Nothing what a bloody rest won't do him good."

Mrs. Chubb opened her mouth to speak, then shut it again when Gertie said hurriedly, "All right, I'm bleeding getting there, ain't I." She took a deep breath. "My Ross needs a job, m'm. He was wondering if you'd take him on as gardener.

He's been looking around, like I said, and he can see what needs to be done. Bloody lot of work, so he says. He's really good at his job, he is, m'm. Mrs. Chubb will tell you. He does marvelous things —"

Cecily interrupted her. "Gertie, I would simply love to hire Ross as a gardener. I'm sure Edward would be overjoyed to have such an expert in his employ, but what about your home in Scotland? You can't live there without your husband."

Gertie shrugged. "Never did like it there, did I. I only stayed there because of Ross. I'd rather be living in Badgers End than anywhere else on earth, and that's the truth. Besides, me babies are bloody English, aren't they. They don't belong in Scotland. Different bleeding lot they are up there, m'm. Don't even talk English, half of 'em."

Cecily shook her head, bewildered by this turn of events. "Well, I'll be happy to talk to Ross, of course, and if this is what he really wants, I'm quite sure we can work something out."

"Well, that's not all, m'm." Gertie chewed on her bottom lip, then mumbled in a rush, "Me and Mrs. Chubb want to work here again, too, m'm. We missed it, we really did. Ross says as how he'd be all right with it as long as he worked here, too. And Daisy said she'd stay here as well, and look after the twins for me. With both Ross and me working, I could afford to pay her a proper wage. So I s'pose it's the three of us what want a job."

"Four," Samuel said, surprising them all.

Gertie looked at him in amazement. "Go on! You, too? What about your job in London? What about Doris?"

Samuel shrugged. "Doris don't care about me. She never did, really. She just needed a friend." He sent a worried glance at Cecily. "I'm not supposed to say nothing yet, but Raymond's thinking about going back to London with her. Doris reckons he can get a job with the theater. That'll leave you without a stable manager, m'm, and since I know about motor cars, well, I thought . . ." His voice trailed off, leaving them all sitting in silence.

Cecily did her best to gather her thoughts. She tried to speak, but the tightness in her throat prevented her for several seconds. Finally, she cleared her throat. "I think I need to remind you that Baxter and I won't be here for much longer —" She stopped short as a stupendous idea occurred to her.

"Oh, that's all right, madam," Mrs

381

Chubb said quickly. "We know that. We'll all miss you dreadfully, of course, when you go back to London, but you can come and visit us sometimes, and although it won't be the same without you, we'll still be here at the Pennyfoot."

"Yeah," Samuel said with a grin. He held up his cup as if offering a toast. "Just like old times."

Chapter
21

Overwhelmed by Gertie's surprising announcement, Cecily had some trouble finding words to say. She would have to keep her marvelous idea to herself for the time being, at least until she'd had time to discuss it with Baxter. The thought of everyone coming back to the Pennyfoot, however, was too wonderful to believe.

"I . . . can't tell you how happy this makes me," she said at last. "I shall have to address the issue with Baxter, of course, and we must have the final word from Mr. Sandringham, but in view of the difficulty in finding good people, I really can't see how either one of them could possibly refuse. I'm sure they will both be delighted to welcome all of you back to the Pennyfoot Hotel. I mean Country Club."

Gertie jumped to her feet with a yelp of joy. "I just knew this was going to be a bleeding great Christmas. What'd I tell you!" She nudged Mrs. Chubb's arm in her excitement. Unfortunately, the house-keeper was holding a cup of coffee in that hand, and the hot liquid spilled all over her lap.

Cecily used the ruckus that followed to quietly make her escape. Excited herself now, she rushed up the steps, across the foyer, and down the hallway to Baxter's office.

Without bothering to knock, she flung open the door and marched inside. Eager to share her idea with him, she'd forgotten all about his foul mood.

He looked up, one hand holding his pen poised above an open ledger. "What the devil — ?" Dropping the pen, he surged to his feet.

"I have so much to tell you." She ignored his scowl, and plopped down on her chair. "So much I don't know where to begin."

"Don't tell me," he said dryly. "The entire male population of this club have been brutally murdered, and you have deduced that Father Christmas is responsible." He sat down and reached for his pen again.

Her smile faded. "I should think you would have more sensitivity than to jest about such matters."

He sighed. "You are quite right. My

apologies. So what is it this time?"

Quickly, she informed him that Gertie, Mrs. Chubb, and Samuel had applied for permanent employment at the club.

He seemed pleased about it, though all he said was, "We will have to notify Edward, of course. He will have the final say. I'll send him a telegram."

"Well, that's the other part of it." She leaned forward, her hands clasped together. "Edward rang me on the telephone this morning."

He looked astounded. "From South Africa?"

"Well, I'm not really certain where he was ringing from, though it sounded more like France. I swear the operator on his end was French."

"Well, what did Edward want?"

"Oh, yes!" She beamed hopefully at him. "Well, he said he was being sent to Bermuda and he would be there for quite a while and he wanted us to hire a new manager."

Baxter frowned. "That might take a while."

"Exactly what I was thinking." In her eagerness she rose to her feet, forcing him to do the same. "Baxter, this could be the solution to our problems. Why can't we be the managers? It worked well for us before, and you know how I adore being here and you love being in a position of authority. We would have a place to stay while we get our finances in order — it would be too, too perfect."

The expression in his eyes worried her. "Please sit down, Cecily."

She sat, waiting anxiously for him to seat himself. For a long moment he said nothing, but sat tapping his pen on the paper. At last he sat back in his chair and smoothed a hand over his hair, a sign that Cecily recognized well. She braced herself.

"I'm going to give you the benefit of the doubt," he began, "and dismiss the possibility that you engineered this entire situation."

She stared at him in disbelief. "How can you possibly say that? I was not responsible for Barry Wrotham's death, nor Jeanette's. Certainly not Roger Peebles's death, either. How can you accuse me of manipulating everything?"

He shrugged. "You have to admit, it has all fallen rather nicely into your lap. You have never been truly happy away from the Pennyfoot, and it seems you have found a way to remedy that. I would be uncommonly suspicious of everything that has happened, were it not for the fact that I have to believe even you would be incapable of trickery on such a grand scale."

Relieved, she tried her best to smile. "You give me far too much credit, my dear husband."

"Nevertheless, I can't help feeling you had a hand in this somewhere."

"It is pure providence, I assure you." She watched his face, hopeful that she had won him over. "So you agree?"

"To what?"

"That taking over the management of the Pennyfoot would be the perfect solution to our troubles."

"No, I do not agree." He laid down his pen. "The perfect solution would be that none of this had happened, and that I still had a house and a business of my own. I do not relish the thought of working for Edward, managing a country club, at the beck and call of every pesky guest who feels it his right to make trivial complaints and waste my time. No, Cecily, it is not my idea of a solution."

She took a deep breath. "Well, then, let *me* do the managing. I can hire an accountant to keep the books, and I can manage everything else."

"And what am I supposed to do in the

meantime? Sit and twiddle my thumbs?"

"No, of course not. I would certainly not expect you to while away your life unoccupied."

"Then what do you suggest?"

"There is no reason why you cannot conduct your business from here. You can use the bedroom in our suite for an office. It's certainly large enough. We would have a telephone put in there and you can be in contact with your associates just as you were in London. You might have to travel to the city now and then, but think how much your clients would adore spending a night at the seashore to conduct their business. You could start a whole new trend in business travel."

She had caught his interest — she could see it in his eyes. For a moment hope leapt like the flames up a chimney, then he said brusquely, "It's out of the question, Cecily. How the devil do you concoct such harebrained schemes?"

Dismayed, she rose to her feet. "But Bax, darling —"

His roar startled her. "Don't 'Bax, darling' me! I will not allow my wife to work, even if you are the cause of our financial ruin. Now, leave me! I have to finish these infernal accounts. Just leave me in peace."

Angry herself now, she placed both palms on the desk and leaned into him, nose to nose. "You had better watch that sharp tongue of yours, Hugh Baxter, *and* that insufferable attitude, or I might just be tempted to leave you altogether." With that, she spun around and headed for the door.

Unfortunately, her heel caught in the hem of her skirt, tripping her. Her outstretched hand slammed into the door, causing her to gasp in pain. Incensed now, she tugged the offending door open, ignoring Baxter's quick query of concern. To blazes with him. If she had broken her hand, she would not give him the satisfaction of knowing it.

More upset at ruining her exit than of any damage to her fingers, she stomped down the hallway to the library. Perhaps a few minutes admiring the magnificence of a Christmas tree would calm her.

Carefully she pushed open the door to the library and peeked inside. To her relief, the room was empty. She really wasn't in any mood for polite conversation. All she wanted was to have a few moments to herself, where she could cool her temper and collect her thoughts.

She wasn't about to give up on the idea

of taking the manager's position. She was well qualified, having owned the Pennyfoot at one time, and even though Baxter would be attending to his business, he would be there to advise and guide her, should she need it. In any case, there had been a long period, when he had left her employ and moved to London, when she had managed the hotel quite well without him. Thanks to an incompetent replacement manager.

As for his objection to her working, that was adding insult to injury. He knew very well how she felt about such matters. Her association with the Women's Movement had been a bone of contention with him, but he had never openly opposed her opinions and beliefs in that respect.

Women were entitled to do what they wished, and if working for a living appealed to them, no one had a right to prevent them from doing so. Not even their husbands. Especially not their husbands. She had given up all thoughts of working upon marrying him because it was her choice. Even though she had allowed him to think it was his decision.

But now the decision was up to her, and the more he opposed her, the more determined she would become. Sooner or later he would see things her way. At least, she very much hoped he would.

Her heart aching, she wandered over to the tree. She needed the solace of gazing at its lush branches, now laden with delicate ornaments and pretty velvet bows.

As she came closer, however, she could smell something other than the fragrant pine she had enjoyed earlier. A smell of burning? Surely . . . ?

She advanced around the side of the tree to where the back was hidden against the wall. In disbelief she stared at the tiny flames licking along the branches. Someone, it seemed, had lit the candles on the back of the tree. Not only that, but several of them were tipped over, so that the wicks lay on the dry needles. Who on earth . . . ?

Startled, she watched the flames suddenly leap to the branch above. Thoroughly alarmed now, she attempted to blow out the candles, but it was too late. Even as she gathered a deep breath, a loud pop sounded above her head, and the entire top of the tree became engulfed in flames.

Black oily smoke poured from the melting ornaments, and glass popped and shattered at her feet. She backed away, aware that there was nothing she could do except summon help as quickly as possible.

She looked around for the bellpull, but it had been removed for some reason. No doubt Edward had thought it less troublesome for the kitchen staff if they were not constantly summoned to the library. She would have to go back to Baxter for help.

The smoke was already stinging her throat as she hurried across the room to the door. Grasping the handle, she turned it and tugged. To her amazement, the door refused to budge. In disbelief, she rattled the handle and tugged harder. There was no doubt about it, someone had locked the door.

Cecily frowned. The library was never locked as far as she knew. It certainly hadn't been when the Pennyfoot was a hotel. The key to it was on the set of master keys behind the reception desk, and presumably a copy on the set that was kept in the manager's suite. Someone must have used one of the keys to lock the library door behind her.

Turning back, she stared at the burning tree, now completely enveloped in the greedy flames. Whoever had lit the candles had to be the same person who had locked the door.

For a moment she thought it might be Lionel Fitzhammer, but then, in a burst of enlightenment, she realized who it was who wanted her dead. Of course. How stupid of her. She'd had all the clues right in front of her and hadn't put them together. Until now. Now that it could very well be too late.

Fearful for her life, she lifted her skirts and ran for the French windows. As she'd expected, they were jammed shut. A walking stick had been thrust through the handles. The smoke was choking her, burning her lungs. Heat from the burning tree made her feel faint.

Coughing uncontrollably, her eyes streaming with tears, she reached for her shoe. Her only hope lay in breaking the window and removing the cane. Even as she raised her hand with the heel of her shoe poised to strike, the strength sapped out of her knees and she sank to the floor.

As the darkness whirled around her, she heard the tree crash to the floor. She thought she heard Baxter's beloved voice calling her name. "Forgive me, my darling," she whispered, and knew no more.

Baxter took the kitchen stairs two at a time and strode swiftly across the foyer.

He'd been looking for Cecily for the last several minutes. No one seemed to have any knowledge of her whereabouts. He'd sat for a while after she'd left his office earlier, fighting his own dratted pride. His anger had faded the moment she'd smashed her hand into the door, his concern for her easily outweighing his temper.

She'd left without a backward glance, and he'd nursed his hurt feelings awhile longer before surging to his feet. Enough was enough. It was time to make amends with his wife and put an end to this ridiculous squabbling.

If he were honest, he'd have to admit that her solution to their current difficulties held some merit. He hated the thought of losing his business, after working so long and hard to build it up. He was just beginning to make a name for himself in the city, and this time away had already cost him some transactions. He was itching to get back to it, and with Cecily managing the club, with his limited help, he could easily pursue his profession from Badgers End.

On his way to the suite, he'd faced the fact that no matter how he felt about his wife being employed, he was unlikely to prevent Cecily from doing what she wanted to do. As long as her work didn't interfere with their marriage, he could tolerate it. At least they would still be together under one roof, which was all he really could ask.

Disappointed at finding the suite empty, he had proceeded to the dining room. Moira had told him she'd seen Cecily go into the kitchen, so he'd gone straight there, only to be told that she'd left a few minutes earlier.

There was only one place where she could be now, and that was the library. As he hurried down the hallway, he was aware of a strange sense of urgency, and he quickened his pace.

He saw the smoke wreathing from beneath the closed door when he was still a few strides away. Raymond was coming toward him from the opposite direction, and Baxter shouted out to him. "Get everybody down here with buckets of water. We have a fire in the library. Now!"

After one startled glance at him, Raymond raced for the foyer, yelling at the top of his voice.

Thankfully Baxter heard him tell the clerk to ring for the Fire Brigade, though he knew it would be some time before they would arrive. His heart pounded hard in his chest when he thought what this could mean. If the fire took hold, the Pennyfoot could burn to the ground.

He turned the door handle, and was stunned when he realized it was locked. Apparently alerted by Samuel, two of the footmen were rushing toward him, and he yelled at them. "Help me break this down. All together, with your shoulders. Now!"

Within seconds the door burst open, sending all three of them stumbling into the room. One horrified glance told him the story. The room was filled with smoke. The tree had overturned and was lying across the fireplace. Fortunately, a good deal of the smoke was drifting up the gaping chimney, and the marble hearth had prevented most of the flames from reaching the floorboards.

He saw one corner of the carpet smoldering, and rushed to stamp it out. It was then that he saw her. His wife, lying on her side, her eyes closed and her dear face heavily smudged with smoke.

With an agonized cry, he leapt to her side and gathered her into his arms. Weak with relief, he saw she was still breathing, and he scooped her up in his arms.

He barely had time to register that a walking stick had been thrust through the handles of the French windows, before he lifted his foot and smashed it against the doors. They flew open, breaking the stick in two. With a muttered curse, he stepped through them and carried her into the life-giving fresh air.

Behind him in the library he heard people shouting to each other, while across the rose garden several men ran toward him with buckets filled with water, presumably from the fish pond.

In the distance, he could hear the faint clanging of the fire bell. They must have harnessed the horses in record time. Then he forgot about everything except for the white, lifeless look on the face of his beloved wife.

She was cold. So cold. Which was odd, because the last thing she remembered was the heat of the flaming tree. The fire! She had to escape!

She opened her eyes, and blinked. Instead of the burning room she'd expected to see, she saw instead the wide expanse of a gray sky. A snowflake drifted down and landed on her nose. She barely felt it. She was too engrossed in looking at her husband's face.

She was lying on the ground and he was

huddled over her, chafing her cold hands in his warm ones, with tears clearly visible in his wonderful gray eyes.

"Thank God," he kept whispering over and over again.

She was aware of several people standing around, murmuring expressions of relief. . . . and then they had disappeared and only Baxter remained.

Her throat hurt like the devil, but she managed to speak. "The last time we did this," she said unsteadily, "I seem to remember you proposing."

His smile warmed her heart. "Did you accept?"

"I think so." Her voice sounded odd, and she cleared her throat, then winced when the effort stung. She caught her breath. "The fire?"

"The fire brigade is here. They have saved the hotel, but I'm afraid the library and the suite above it will have to be renovated. The hallway, too, will need some attention, but we were lucky. The fireplace saved quite a lot of damage."

He reached for her suddenly, gathering her into his arms. "Oh, Cecily, what a fool I've been. What a stubborn, selfish fool. My pride would not allow me to take the blame for losing our home, and so I blamed you. Then, when I thought . . . all I could think about was how would I possibly survive without you?"

Vastly appreciating the warmth of his body, Cecily murmured, "You would survive quite well without my reckless behavior to impede you."

He sighed, resting his chin on her head. "Ah, but it is reckless behavior such as yours that brightens my world, and fills it with the spirit of adventure. Were it not for you, my love, I should be a lonely, miserable recluse, poring over my accounts like Ebenezer Scrooge."

She managed a hoarse laugh. "I shall remind you of this moment the next time you howl at me for landing you in trouble." She sobered, lifting her head to look at him. "I am truly sorry, Bax, for all the trouble I've caused. I am devastated that we have to sell the house, and I quite understand if you do not wish to stay here at the Pennyfoot. After all, it will serve as a reminder of everything we have lost."

"Perhaps, but then again, the Pennyfoot owes us a debt. This would be a good way to collect it."

She stared at him. "Are you saying you will stay on here as manager?"

"No." He smiled at her. "I'm saying that

you will manage the Pennyfoot, as you so ably have done in the past . . ."

"With your help."

"And without it if I recall."

"And you will continue with your business?"

"Precisely."

"That is wonderful news." Now she really felt better. "There's just one thing I have left to do now."

He looked concerned. "I don't think you should be attempting to do anything just yet. You have just been through a traumatic experience. You need to rest."

"I will," Cecily told him. "Just as soon as we have taken care of one small task."

He shook his head. "What is so important that it cannot wait until tomorrow?"

She sat up, then waited for her head to clear before allowing him to help her to her feet. She felt a little weak, and none too steady, but she was determined to see this through. "First of all," she said more firmly, "you must ring the police station and ask Inspector Cranshaw to get here just as soon as he possibly can."

Baxter frowned. "The inspector?"

"Yes." Cecily lifted the hem of her skirt and stepped gingerly across the porch to peek in the shattered French windows. The scorched walls and burned curtains made her feel like weeping. Then she noticed the shattered stick at her feet. She had been extremely fortunate. She could well have died in there.

"Come," Baxter said, taking her arm. "We'll go around through the front door. And you can tell me why it is so urgent to send for the inspector."

"Because," she said as they walked briskly through the rose garden, "we are on our way to confront a particularly devious murderer."

Chapter
22

Cecily refused to answer Baxter's questions as he followed her up the stairs. She didn't want to argue with him again, as she knew he surely would do if she told him of her suspicions.

The smell of smoke clung to everything, overwhelming the fragrance of the pine that had pleased her so much. "We must open every window in the entire place," she told him as they reached the first landing. "Just as soon as possible. I want to smell Christmas again."

"I'll see to it," he promised her. "But right now I need to know where —" He broke off as she paused in front of the Gilroys' suite. "Sir John? Surely you don't suspect him of murder? This is ridiculous . . ."

"Shh!" She put a finger over his lips. "Just listen and observe. I promise you, everything will be very clear in just a few moments." Without giving him time to argue further, she tapped on the door.

At first there was no answer to her summons, and she rapped again, louder this time.

"He is most likely in the card room —" Baxter began, but then the door opened a mere crack.

Lady Lucille's voice sounded muffled when she said, "Who is it?"

Cecily unceremoniously pushed the door open. "It is I, Lady Lucille."

The other woman fell back, her hand covering her mouth. Her eyes were wide with shock and disbelief, giving Cecily a grim sense of satisfaction.

"Mon Dieu!" Lucille muttered. "You are alive. I thought . . . I was told . . ." She recovered quickly. "I am so happy to see you are unhurt, *madame*. I heard about the fire. My husband . . . he came to me and demanded that we leave, but by the time we reached the ground floor, the fire had been put out. Such a shame to spoil the Christmas, *non?*"

Without answering her, Cecily barged into the room.

Lucille took several steps backward. "My husband is not here, *madame*. As you can see. He went back to the card room to finish his game."

Baxter hovered anxiously in the doorway. "Well, as long as he's not here, Cecily?"

"I'm not here to see Sir John." Cecily advanced on the cowering woman. "I believe Lady Lucille knows quite well why I am here."

Lucille violently shook her head. *"Non, non, je ne sais pas!"*

"Then I shall enlighten you." Cecily gestured at Baxter. "Perhaps it would be better if you came inside and closed the door."

Obviously reluctant, he did what she asked. "Cecily, if you are mistaken —"

"I am not mistaken, I promise you." Cecily faced Lucille again. "You lit the candles on the Christmas tree, knowing I went there to meet your husband. You were afraid of what I might tell him. You took the key from the reception desk and locked the library door behind me, then you jammed the French windows with your cane."

"I certainly did not, *madame*. How dare you accuse me —"

"You killed Jeanette, did you not?"

Again the violent shake of the head. *"Non, non, madame*. You are mistaken. I know not what you mean."

"I think you do." With a swift movement, Cecily reached out and dragged back a portion of Lucille's hair to reveal a deep scratch gouged into the woman's forehead. "An unusual style, Lady Lucille, but most assuredly not from Paris. I remember seeing an article in a magazine just a few days ago. The French have been cutting their hair quite short all year. You combed your hair in that peculiar style to hide the scratch that Jeanette gave you when you fought with her."

"I did no such thing! I —"

"You took the knife from the kitchen and went to meet her in the equipment shed, where you cut her throat."

Lucille whimpered, and drew back. "I do not understand why you are saying these dreadful things to me," she whispered.

"Yes, you do." Cecily advanced on her, heedless of Baxter's muttered warning.

"*S'il vous plaît, madame,*" Lucille pleaded, her hand at her throat. "I did not —"

"That's how you caught Jeanette's cold," Cecily went on ruthlessly. "And it's my guess that you didn't turn your ankle on the stairs, but that your ankle was injured when you struggled with Jeanette. I also believe that you pushed Barry Wrotham down the well. He was going to tell your husband about your association with him."

"Non!"

"As for Roger Peebles, he must have found out about Barry Wrotham. Did he threaten to tell Sir John, too? Is that why you killed him?"

"I did not kill him!" Lucille whirled on her. "It was Lionel. He did something to the brakes, I don't know what . . ."

Cecily withdrew the hand she'd kept hidden behind her back until now. "This is part of your cane, Lady Lucille. I recognized it. I'm giving it to the inspector when he arrives, which should be any minute now. You will go to prison for the murder of Jeanette and Barry Wrotham."

"Ah, Barry. *Mon amour.*" Lucille sank onto a chair, weeping profusely.

After a moment's hesitation, Baxter stepped forward and offered her his handkerchief.

She took it, and blew her nose. Then, between sobs, she said brokenly, "I never meant to hurt Barry. I loved him. He made me feel like a beautiful woman again. I was devastated when he died."

Cecily sat down opposite her and said, more gently now, "Tell me what happened."

Lucille gulped. "I knew it would only be

406

a matter of time before someone found out. It matters not, for nothing has been the same since Barry died. I care not if I go to prison, or if they hang me. I am dead inside without my Barry."

Cecily could almost feel sorry for her. "Then why did you kill him?"

Lucille sniffed, blew her nose again, then said softly, "It was an accident. We spent some wonderful afternoons in the farmhouse. It was all so cozy, so romantic. We had champagne, and sometimes I felt a little foolish, *oui?* Perhaps a little sorry for myself. One afternoon I told Barry that John spends all his time with his gambling houses, and never has time for me. I told him how he cares more for his partners than he does for his wife." She shook her head. "It was stupid, I know. It was supposed to always remain a secret. But I never imagined for a moment that Barry would use what I said against John."

"So Barry threatened to disclose Sir John's business dealings with Cureagambler."

Her eyebrows arched in surprise. "How did you know that name? How did you find out?"

"Never mind," Cecily said brusquely. "Go on with the story."

"Ah well, a few days after I told him, he said he had the money to start a new life. He wanted to buy a farm in Cornwall. He wanted me to run away with him. I could not do that. I loved him, *oui,* but I could not possibly live in a farmhouse cleaning the pigsty and cooking the meals. I told him I wanted everything to stay the same, but then he became angry. He left me alone, saying he was going to ruin my husband, so that John would not have the money to keep me in fine things. I ran after him. I begged him not to do it. He would not listen. I became angry myself. In my temper, I pushed him. So!" She lifted her palms and pushed them out in front of her. "He fell back against the well, he stumbled . . . and fell in . . ."

She began weeping again, and Cecily waited for her to control herself before saying, "And Jeanette found out what happened?"

Lucille shook her head. "No, she did not find out. She thought it was Roger who killed Barry."

Cecily frowned. "Why did she think that?"

Lucille dabbed at her eyes and blew her nose again. "After I told Barry about the gambling houses, he looked for . . . how

408

you say? Ah, yes . . . evidence . . . to prove that John and the others had the gambling houses. He searched Roger's room and found papers, but Roger surprised him and caught him. Roger said he would call the police, but Barry told him he will tell everyone about the gambling houses and all of them would lose their seats on the Bench. He asked for money to keep quiet. Lots of money. So he could buy the farmhouse."

"I see," Cecily said slowly. "Then Barry was blackmailing Roger Peebles."

"That is what you call it, *oui*. But Jeanette, she must have been in the next room, listening. Because when Barry died, Jeanette went to Roger and said she would tell the police all about Cureagambler, and that he was giving Barry money to keep it quiet. She said she knew he had killed Barry and he would be arrested for murder unless he gave her the money."

"She wanted the money to have the pearls restrung," Cecily murmured.

Lucille looked puzzled. *"Pardon?"*

Cecily shook her head. "Never mind. But that doesn't explain why you had to kill Jeanette."

Lucille sat silent for a long moment, then in a voice heavy with weariness, she said, "Roger came to our suite. He was looking for John. He said he wanted to borrow money to keep Jeanette quiet about the gambling houses. He told me everything that happened. I was afraid. If he talked to John, he would find out about my rendezvous with Barry and I could not allow it." She held her hands up in appeal. "What was I to do? If John knew I betrayed him, he would desert me. I would have nothing."

"So you killed Jeanette."

Lucille worried at her lip with her small, even teeth. "Roger made the appointment to meet Jeanette in the shed. I told him not to worry. I would talk to John and he would take care of everything." Tears started spilling down her cheeks. "I took the knife when no one was looking . . . I just wanted to frighten the girl, that is all. But she fought with me. I was afraid she would kill me . . . I had . . . to stop her. I raised the knife and . . ."

Cecily waited for her sobs to subside, then said gently, "That's why Roger Peebles had to die."

Lucille gulped and nodded. "It is wintertime. I did not think anyone would go into the shed until the spring. By then no one would know what happened or who killed her. But when she was found, Roger came to me. He was very upset. He thought John killed the maid and he told me he was going to see the constables that afternoon and tell them everything. I warned him he would lose everything as well, but he would not listen. He kept saying he would not be a part of murder."

"So you persuaded Lionel Fitzhammer to sabotage the brakes of his car," Cecily said, understanding at last.

Lucille nodded. She sent a quick, embarrassed glance at Baxter, then said in a low voice, "Lionel . . . he wanted . . . favors from me for a very long time. I told him Roger, he killed Jeanette and he deserved to die. I made him see we could not tell the constables, because everyone would know about Cureagambler. I promised him . . . just one night . . . in return. He was so besotted he agreed." She shuddered. "Thank heavens I have not yet had to fulfill that promise."

Baxter cleared his throat, and Cecily got to her feet. "It appears very likely you never will," she said. "I must ask you to remain here until the inspector arrives. Mr. Baxter will stand guard outside, just in case you should decide to leave without permission."

Lucille's misery was plain on her face when she looked up. "I am going nowhere, Mrs. Baxter. My life, it was over when Barry fell down the well. I knew it from that moment. I just did not want to believe it."

"I'm so sorry." Cecily nodded at Baxter, who opened the door for her, then followed her into the hallway. "It is better that you stay here," she told him. "Just in case, though I don't think she's going anywhere."

"You sounded genuine when you said you were sorry."

She sighed. "I do feel sorry for her. Everything that happened was because she made the mistake of falling in love with the wrong man. And even *that* wouldn't have happened if Sir John had paid less attention to his business interests and more to his wife."

Baxter caught her hand. "You could have died in that library. I swear to you, Cecily, I will never neglect you for my business. Never."

She smiled sweetly at him. "Of course you won't, my dear Hugh. Because, quite simply, I won't allow it." She sailed off, preventing him from delivering the retort that was obviously hovering on his lips.

She had barely descended the stairs before P.C. Northcott arrived. He marched into the foyer, helmet slightly askew, notebook under his arm, and his chest puffed out with assumed importance.

"Mrs. Baxter," he announced the moment he caught sight of her. "I h'understand you 'ave h'apprehended one of your guests on suspicion of murder, is that right?"

"Not on suspicion, Sam," Cecily murmured. "I have a full confession. I trust the inspector is on his way?"

"Inspector Cranshaw has informed me he will arrive here within the hour. He asked me to keep an eye on things until he arrives."

"Well, the lady in question is confined to her suite." Cecily glanced at the grandfather clock. "As of now, her husband is unaware that she is being apprehended. I think perhaps you should inform him. You will find him in the card room."

Northcott seemed put out. "Well, as long as you have things under control so to speak, Mrs. B., I wonder if you might inform the gentleman. Ladies always do a better job of such delicate matters, that's what I always say."

Cecily sighed. "Very well. I left Baxter

outside Lady Lucille's room to keep an eye on her. I'd be obliged if you would take his place and release him to get back to work. In the meantime I must hire someone to make repairs to the damaged rooms."

"Yes, I heard about the fire." Northcott rubbed his nose with the back of his fingers. "Nasty business that. Glad to see you're all right, Mrs. Baxter. So, it were one of them toffs, eh? And a lady, too. Would never have guessed that one. Not in a hundred years. You did it again, Mrs. B. The inspector will be pleased the case is solved." He leaned forward and added in a loud whisper, "I'd be much obliged if you'd put in a good word for me when you talk to him. Maybe tell him I gave you the idea, like?"

"I'll put in a good word for you," Cecily said, "if you promise never to call me Mrs. B. again."

"Right you are. Sorry, m'm." He touched the rim of his helmet with his fingers. "Better get on with it, then. I'm hoping I'll have time for a quick visit to the kitchen. Got me mouth all ready for one of them mince pies, I have. I haven't had me elevenses yet, and I'm feeling a bit peckish, if you know what I mean."

"Well, I suppose Baxter can wait another

minute or two." She started to move away, then added, "But I warn you, my husband has a nasty temper that is sure to explode if he's kept waiting too long."

"Gotcha, Mrs. B. . . . er . . . Baxter. Won't be more than a minute or two, I swear."

She watched him sprint for the kitchen steps, wondering what he'd say when he discovered Mrs. Chubb and Gertie back at their posts. She felt a little lift of her spirits when she envisioned telling them her good news. Perhaps, once this was all over, it would be a good Christmas after all.

At Cecily's request, the entire staff assembled in the ballroom late that afternoon. Having forgotten her invitation to Phoebe and Madeline, Cecily spent a few minutes recounting to them everything that had happened, then invited both her friends to join her for her official announcement.

Although Phoebe pestered her with questions, Cecily refused to tell either her or Madeline what the announcement would be, and they had to be content with joining the anxious group in the crowded ballroom.

Cecily was pleased to see a Christmas

tree had been placed in two of the corners, which Madeline promised would be decorated in time for Christmas Eve. She had suggested leaving off the candles this time, but Cecily insisted that the tradition be followed as usual. Except the ceremony would now be held in the ballroom instead of her beloved library.

As she and Baxter took the stage, the chattering spectators fell silent. Cecily stepped to the center, and looked down on the sea of faces in front of her. She spoke briefly about Jeanette, announcing that her murderer had been apprehended, and asking everyone to remember the young maid this Christmas and pray for her soul.

Then she called upon Mrs. Chubb, Gertie, and Samuel to join her on the stage. She introduced them, explaining to the rest of the staff, amid a great deal of cheering and clapping, that the three new members were permanent.

Gertie left the stage grinning from ear to ear, while Samuel gave the crowd a jaunty wave. As for Mrs. Chubb, she marched off with her head held high, as befitting her esteemed position as housekeeper of the Pennyfoot Country Club.

When everyone had quietened down, Cecily turned to her husband. "Do you want to tell them, or shall I?"

"No, my love," he said with a smile. "This was your idea and you deserve the entire stage. Enjoy this moment." He walked off and left her alone.

She faced the crowd, who once again waited in silent expectation. "I have one more announcement to make," she said, smiling down at them. "In view of the fact that Mr. Sandringham will not be returning for a while, I have accepted the position of manager of this establishment, until such time other arrangements are made. With the help of my husband, and you, my wonderful staff, I hope to make the Pennyfoot Country Club the most favored resort on the southeast coast. I look forward to working with you all, and I wish every one of you a very happy Christmas."

Cheers rang out again, and Cecily smiled when she saw Mrs. Chubb and Gertie hug each other in delight. Things had all worked out rather nicely after all, she thought as she walked off the stage to join her husband. It was going to be a good Christmas.

Later, as she and Baxter stood in the warm kitchen accepting the congratulations of an excited Gertie and Mrs. Chubb, she really felt as if they had come home again.

After answering their questions as best they could, leaving out the fact that Baxter had gambled away their house, they joined everyone in a glass of hot cider punch, celebrating the return of the Pennyfoot staff.

"I never would have thought that Lady Lucille would have killed poor Jeanette," Mrs. Chubb said, her cheeks glowing from the effects of the cider. "She looked like such a delicate creature. As if one sneeze would knock her off her feet."

"Just goes to show," Gertie said, smacking her lips in enjoyment. "You never can tell with them toffs." She glanced at Cecily. "What's going to happen to them all?"

Cecily dabbed her mouth with a serviette. "According to the inspector, Lionel Fitzhammer and Lady Lucille will be charged with murder. Sir John will have to stand witness, I'm afraid. It will be hard on him. I imagine both he and Percy Chatsworth will lose their seats on the Bench."

"It's the bloody wives I feel sorry for." Gertie wiped her mouth on her sleeve. "That Mrs. Peebles lost her husband, Mrs. Fitzhammer's old man will be in jail, and Mrs. Chatsworth's will be out of a job. Not a very good Christmas for any of the buggers, is it."

"Well, by this afternoon they will all have

left." Cecily put down her glass and stood up. "I must talk to the men who are working on the library. They have promised to have most of the mess cleared up by Christmas Eve, though I'm afraid it will be a while before we can use the library again."

"We're just glad you got out of there alive," Mrs. Chubb said with feeling. "Thank Gawd Mr. Baxter went looking for you."

In a rare public show of affection, Baxter placed an arm about her shoulders and pulled her close. She looked up at him, warmed by the love glowing in his eyes. For a while she had thought she might lose that devotion, and the prospect had terrified her. One never knew how much one had until one was in danger of losing it.

"Here, here." Samuel lifted his glass. "Right now I'd like to make a toast. To the staff of the Pennyfoot, and our new manager."

"Yeah," Gertie said, raising her glass. "It'll be just like old times!"

Everyone raised their glasses at once and chorused, "Just like old times!"

Cecily blinked back tears. "It is, indeed, like old times. I'm so happy we are all together again. Happy Christmas, everyone. And God bless you all."

We hope you have enjoyed this Large Print book. Other Thorndike, Wheeler or Chivers Press Large Print books are available at your library or directly from the publishers.

For more information about current and up-coming titles, please call or write, without obligation, to:

Publisher
Thorndike Press
295 Kennedy Memorial Drive
Waterville, ME   04901
Tel. (800) 223-1244

Or visit our Web site at:
www.gale.com/thorndike
www.gale.com/wheeler

OR

Chivers Large Print
published by BBC Audiobooks Ltd
St James House, The Square
Lower Bristol Road
Bath BA2 3BH
England
Tel. +44(0) 800 136919
email: bbcaudiobooks@bbc.co.uk
www.bbcaudiobooks.co.uk

All our Large Print titles are designed for easy reading, and all our books are made to last.

R